SOMETHING

CLOSE

TO MAGIC

EMMA MILLS

Something Close to Magic

atheneum

NEW YORK LONDON TORONTO
SYDNEY NEW DELHI

An imprint of Simon & Schuster Children's Publishing Division

1230 Avenue of the Americas, New York, New York 10020

Text © 2023 by Emma Mills

Jacket illustration © 2023 by Kate Forrester

Jacket design © 2023 by Simon & Schuster, Inc.

For information about special discounts for bulk purchases, please contact Simon & Schuster Special Sales at 1-866-506-1949 or business@simonandschuster.com.

The Simon & Schuster Speakers Bureau can bring authors to your live event. For more information or to book an event, contact the Simon & Schuster Speakers Bureau at 1-866-248-3049 or visit our website at www.simonspeakers.com.

The text for this book was set in ITC New Baskerville Std.

Manufactured in the United States of America

First Edition

2 4 6 8 10 9 7 5 3 1

CIP data for this book is available from the Library of Congress.

ISBN 978-1-6659-2691-1

ISBN 978-1-6659-2693-5 (ebook)

to Mama

PART ONE

In Which an Adventure Occurs

One

I t was midmorning when a stranger pushed through the door of Basil's Bakery.

The baker's apprentice, Aurelie, was in the midst of a conversation with a man who was seeking assurance that the cinnamon loaf contained quite enough—but not too much—cinnamon. "Excess cinnamon," he said gravely, as if it were some fatal error, "irreparably unbalances the gustatory experience."

It was a snort that drew Aurelie's attention to the stranger, who was now standing nearby.

Over the course of her three years as an apprentice, Aurelie had grown familiar with the faces of many of the people in the village where Basil's lay, just north of the Underwood. But she had never seen this particular girl before.

The stranger was dark eyed, raven haired, and beautiful, certainly, but there was sharpness to it—a beauty with *teeth*. She wore a traveling coat of black velvet with a matching black dress underneath, a small motif of leaves stitched in gold thread all across it. Even her gloves matched, embroidered in the same fashion. It gave Aurelie pause to see someone in the village dressed so fine, but maybe she was the daughter of a merchant or a particularly prosperous tradesman. *The New Rich*, Mrs. Basil liked to say. *Some people think more of them than they do of the nobility, you know.*

And why is that? Aurelie was duty bound to respond.

Mrs. Basil looked at her squarely. *They've* earned *their wealth*, she replied, and failed to see the irony in it.

The stranger smiled, and even her smile had an edge to it. "Pardon me," she said. "I was just thinking that I would much more readily trust a baker to handle my *gustatory experience* than a"—she assessed the man for a moment—"moderately successful apothecary. Though not nearly as successful as he boasts."

"Why, I—"

"Would like the cinnamon loaf? An excellent choice. Here, Baker." The stranger moved forward and handed Aurelie several coins. Aurelie hurriedly packaged the cinnamon loaf, and the stranger handed it to the man.

"The impertinence—" he blustered.

"Is astounding, yes." She fixed the man with an unwavering stare. "Goodbye."

With a huff and a muttered curse, the man left.

Aurelie was bewildered and awed in equal measure.

The stranger cast her a glance. "I'm sorry, were you hoping to continue that conversation?" Before Aurelie could reply, she went on. "I thought not. Three morning buns, please."

Aurelie went to fetch the buns. She got the curious feeling that the stranger was watching her, but when she snuck a quick look back, the girl's eyes were fixed on the case filled with cakes and patisserie.

When Aurelie returned, the stranger rested one arm on the counter and leaned toward her almost as if they were friends, in on some secret together.

"Do you think you could assist me further?"

"Of course, miss. What else will you have?"

"I need something that's not in the case."

"We can take a special order, but it may be several days, depending on—"

"I need your help in finding someone."

"Pardon?"

"I know there are ways. Ones that most Commonfolk aren't privy to."

Aurelie paused for just a moment before wrapping the buns in paper and passing them across the counter. "I'm sorry, I don't know what you mean."

The stranger extended one gloved hand. Aurelie reached out, expecting payment for the buns, but instead, five smooth, round stones fell into her palm.

Seeking stones.

"Something tells me you know just what to do with these," said the stranger.

The stones felt warm in Aurelie's hand. She couldn't be sure if it was heat transferred from the stranger's grasp or from the hum of magic flaring inside Aurelie, surging up to meet them.

Aurelie swallowed, and her voice sounded strange to her own ears, oddly far away. "How do you know that?"

The stranger's eyes shone. "I know everything."

Two

The stranger was remarkably bothersome.

Aurelie sent her away that morning. With no small feeling of regret, she dropped the stones back into the stranger's hand and said, "I'm sorry, I think you must be mistaken. I can't help you."

The stranger observed her for a moment—there was something a little unnerving about her gaze, something of a challenge in it—and then inclined her head. "Very well."

Aurelie thought that would be the end of it. The notion of seeking again, of casting the stones . . . It was far more tempting than she wanted to admit. She couldn't help but wonder what it would feel like after so long. But there was no use in wondering. Magic wasn't part of her path forward.

In truth, magic wasn't considered to be of much value to anyone anymore. People hardly ever used it, because it wasn't worth using. Magic made work. Magic *took*. The first-year girls at Aurelie's old school used to sing a nursery rhyme about it while jumping rope:

Spell it warm, to double cold.
Spell it clean, to double grime.
Spell the food, to double hunger.
Spell the clock, to double time.

The prevailing theory of magic—not that many people took the time to generate new theories these days—was that all magic came with a consequence. The children's rhyme put it simply: that eating food prepared with magic would later increase your hunger twofold. That speeding up your work with magic in any way would lead to twice as much work in the end, because anything accomplished magically would later fall apart.

It was Aurelie's former teacher, Miss Ember, who told her that the notion was so old and so thoroughly ingrained that it was hard to tell whether it was the actual truth to begin with or if people avoided magic simply because they *thought* it was true. And whether that in turn had influenced magic itself—that the belief, the repetition of it, was enough to make it so.

Aurelie certainly understood that repetition was one way to convince yourself that something was true. She did just that following the stranger's visit to the bakery.

As she packaged loaves of bread for a large order later that morning: *I made the right choice.*

As she swept the storefront during a lull that afternoon: *I made the right choice.*

As she wolfed down a quick supper: *I made the right choice.*

And then, late that evening, there was a knock at the bakery's back door.

Aurelie was in the kitchen, cleaning pans. No deliveries

were expected. The only other employee at Basil's, a journeyman named Jonas, had left for the evening in high spirits. Aurelie suspected that he had plans to visit Chapdelaine's, the rival bakery across town. Mrs. Basil occasionally sent him there at the end of the day to surreptitiously take note of their remaining stock. Jonas significantly preferred to take note of one of the Chapdelaine's bakers, Katriane. Aurelie strongly suspected that Katriane liked to take note of him as well. Jonas was broad-shouldered and thin, a bit like a scarecrow, but one with cheekbones and kind eyes and dark wavy hair that never quite committed to lying flat. He didn't smile often, but when he chose to, it was rather powerful.

When the knock sounded, Aurelie crossed over to the back door, wondering if Jonas had forgotten something. She opened the door slightly, and there was the stranger peering back at her.

Her fine dress and traveling coat had been replaced with a battered-looking greatcoat, trousers tucked into hard-worn boots, and a billowy shirt. Her hair was far shorter than Aurelie expected, free of hat and pins as it was, and it fell back from the stranger's face in a smooth black wave. She very nearly could've been a different person entirely. But the glint in her eyes was the same, the beauty was the same, albeit packaged differently.

"I thought this might be more effective," she said without preamble. "And certainly more comfortable for me. May I? Thank you," and she pushed past Aurelie and into the kitchen.

"What are—you can't be back here!"

"And yet I am. How remarkable. Shall we get down to it?"

"To what?"

"Clearly you weren't swayed by my fashionable 'lady about town' tack earlier today. Which makes me like you all the better, to be fair. So here I am again. To put it plainly, you can seek, and I can't—it's really very big of me to admit that; it's quite against my nature, you know—and there's a person I absolutely need to find. None of my usual methods are working. So humbly, I ask you, Baker—"

"Aurelie."

"Iliana," the stranger replied. "Charmed. And humble, mind you, as I entreat: Will you help me?"

It felt like a second chance. Or a test of Aurelie's resolve. *I made the right choice.* "I told you. I can't."

"I'll pay you, of course," Iliana said. "Ten percent."

"Of what?"

Iliana smiled then, a bit in surprise, a bit in delight. "The bounty, of course."

Aurelie blinked. "You're a finder."

Finders were called "bounty hunters" once, though after a certain point, the title was deemed too mercenary.

"I am," Iliana replied. "And you're a former student from the Mercier School for Girls, dropped out three years ago, talented in seeking, currently wasting those talents at this very poorly managed but well-stocked bakery. Correct?"

Aurelie couldn't speak.

"I told you. I know everything. And I'll pay you, which is more than I can say for your mentor. Am I correct again?"

She was indeed correct. Most apprenticeships came with low pay, but with Mrs. Basil, it was no pay—just a small room off the back of the bakery's kitchen to sleep, one meal a day, and occasionally—exceedingly rarely—Mrs. Basil claimed to send a copper or bronze piece to Aurelie's parents. Aurelie wasn't sure why Mrs. Basil specified copper or bronze when she could just as easily have said she sent a silver or gold piece. No coins were being sent at all anyway.

"I can't just . . . leave my apprenticeship," Aurelie said. It was all she had—the only option presented to her upon her dismissal from school. *You're incredibly fortunate, child*, Headmistress had said. *My old friend Basil is in urgent need of an apprentice.*

"Good heavens, I'm not asking you to *leave your apprenticeship*. We don't even need to leave the room. All I want is for you to cast the stones and tell me something useful."

Aurelie wavered.

"Fifteen percent," Iliana said.

"Twenty."

Iliana smiled.

Privately, Aurelie worried that she had forgotten how to seek. She still practiced magic when no one could see—Mrs. Basil forbade it, lest the bakery get a bad reputation. (*"They split these with magic—you'll be double hungry within the hour!"*) So when Aurelie brought light forth in her fingers or heated water for washing, it was only in absolute privacy. Occasionally, when she spread flour across the counter to roll out dough, she would quickly sketch out the seeking symbols, just to make sure she hadn't forgotten them. But she couldn't practice seeking without a set of stones.

As she sat on the floor of her small room, the straw mattress pushed up against the wall to make space for both her and Iliana, the circle drawn with a piece of chalk that Iliana had produced from a coat pocket, Aurelie wondered if she would see anything at all. If she even *could* anymore.

It's easiest to find those who are known to you, Miss Ember had told Aurelie during one of their private lessons. Although magic wasn't part of the official curriculum at the Mercier School for Girls, Miss Ember had taken responsibility for Aurelie's education in it. *But you can seek those unknown. You'll need a personal belonging or a picture. At the very least, you'll need a name.*

But it can be done? Aurelie had asked. *With just a name?*

Miss Ember nodded. *It can. Though the less you know about the subject, the harder it will be.*

"Here." Iliana pulled something else from one of her coat pockets. "I think we should do a bit of a test, to start."

"A test?"

"Just to make sure you're up to snuff. I'm not one for wasting time, so if you don't have what it takes—"

"I can do it," Aurelie interrupted, taking the object from Iliana's hand.

It was a glove made of soft leather. Pale yellow, with pearls embroidered in a delicate design across the back. It was undoubtedly the most expensive glove Aurelie had ever encountered.

"Name?" Aurelie asked.

"Camille." Something flickered across Iliana's face. "Lady Pith," she amended.

So this Camille was of the nobility. Aurelie met Iliana's eyes for a moment. Iliana looked away first.

Aurelie took a deep breath. She gathered the stones into the palm of her hand and for a moment just allowed herself to feel the weight of them.

Lady Pith, she thought, holding the glove in her other hand, soft and grounding. *Camille.*

Then she closed her eyes and cast the stones into the circle.

It was a sound that came first. It startled Aurelie, but she managed to keep her eyes closed as it grew louder. Music. A single violin, drawing out a sweet refrain.

Aurelie clutched the glove. She saw fingers curving around the neck of the violin, delicate and purposeful.

The musician was a young woman—maybe not much older than Aurelie. She wore an exquisite gown, and her long dark hair was piled in curls on top of her head.

"She's playing the violin," Aurelie murmured.

Iliana's voice was oddly measured. "What piece?"

It was hard for Aurelie not to break her concentration again, if simply to roll her eyes. "I'm sorry. Somehow, in my many trips to the symphony, I managed to miss this one."

Iliana didn't acknowledge that. "What color is the carpet?"

"Blue. There are white curtains. And a music stand, in dark wood . . ." Aurelie paused. Another figure joined the scene—a young man—and approached the violinist.

"A man has entered." The music cut off as Lady Pith turned and regarded him, a small smile of recognition blooming across her face.

"He's wearing a scarlet jacket . . . and a gold ring. He's holding his hand out to her—"

"That's enough," Iliana said abruptly, and Aurelie's eyes sprang open as Iliana pulled the glove from her hand. "Quite enough, thank you. That was . . . adequate."

"Adequate?"

"Yes, quite. On to the main event." Iliana hurriedly shoved

the glove back into one of her coat pockets and handed Aurelie a folded square of paper. "His name is Elias Allred."

Aurelie smoothed the paper out. A sketch of a man looked back at her. He had a small, neat beard and hair that curled around his ears. His eyes were drawn in a way that managed to make them look light, though the rendering was done in dark ink.

"Do you have something of his?"

"No. Let's see what you can do without."

Aurelie closed her eyes. She cast the stones again.

She saw . . . nothing.

She pushed further, pulled more magic up.

Still nothing.

Eventually, Iliana spoke.

"If you don't mind my asking, how long does this sort of thing usually take?"

"I . . ." Aurelie opened her eyes, flustered. "I haven't done it in a while."

"You just found Pith in an instant."

"Is she someone special to you?"

Iliana frowned. "I don't see how that's relevant."

"It is. If the object is treasured. If the target is . . . beloved, I could sort of . . . *channel* the search through you and—"

"I'd appreciate you not doing anything *through* me without my permission."

"I didn't mean to! I'm just saying, it may have . . . made it easier."

"Well, unfortunately, I don't harbor any tender feelings for Elias Allred."

Aurelie's eyebrows shot up. "But you do for Lady Pith?"

"Completely beside the point." Something like embarrassment flashed across Iliana's face. "I mean, no. She's an acquaintance."

"Are you acquainted with many of the nobility?"

"You're surprisingly nosy," Iliana said. "I'm starting to regret this."

"Let me look again," Aurelie replied. "Let me try to seek someone I know."

Iliana reached for the stones. "I'm not here just so you can drop in on anyone you please."

Aurelie reached out to stop her. "Just for practice. Please. Then I'll know better what I'm seeing of Elias Allred." *Or not seeing,* Aurelie thought, though she didn't voice that part aloud.

Iliana paused for a moment and then relented. "Fine."

Aurelie gathered up the stones again, closed her eyes, and let her mind fill with thoughts of a person she had dearly wanted to see these last three years.

It was the light she recognized first—the small green glass lamp on Miss Ember's desk cast a soft glow against the bookshelves lining her office. The desk itself emerged next—dark wood, smooth and worn down in some places. Several large books were open atop it. A silhouette stood in front of the window, looking out—

Miss Ember.

She was there. In her office, like always. Just as Aurelie had imagined she would be—or tried to keep herself from imagining, as the case may be.

Why haven't you written? Aurelie suddenly wanted to yell. Aurelie rarely received letters from her parents, but that was nothing new. Miss Ember, however—Aurelie swallowed past a hard lump in her throat. Miss Ember might have written if she had wanted. She could've checked in on Aurelie. But she hadn't.

The image of the office dispersed before her eyes, like a reflection in water broken by a falling stone.

"Baker?"

Aurelie felt the telltale prickle of tears. Luckily, she was skilled at banishing them. Most people thought the trick was to blink rapidly or scrunch your eyes shut, but really, if you held them open, air would drive the moisture back. Or else you could say it was the dust, but Aurelie never let herself get to the stage of having to blame the dust. She knew that the single easiest way to banish tears was to simply not allow yourself to have them in the first place.

So Aurelie opened her eyes carefully and held them open as she collected the stones, refusing to meet Iliana's gaze.

"Seems to be in order," she said. "I'll try again."

Aurelie focused once more on the drawing of Elias Allred. The sweep of his hair, the curious light eyes. She chanted his name in her mind. She and Miss Ember had practiced this sort of thing before Aurelie left school, but Aurelie wished—certainly not for the first time—that she had learned more.

She cast the stones again. Reached out. And again, felt nothing. Saw nothing.

"I'm sorry," she told Iliana eventually.

Iliana nodded curtly and swept up the stones, depositing them back in the pouch and getting to her feet. "I'll return with something of his."

"When?"

"Whenever is most convenient for me."

"What about payment?"

"No bounty, no payment."

With that, Iliana was gone.

Aurelie slumped back against the wall.

Iliana did return, about a week later. Another late evening, another knock at the back door of the bakery.

This time she produced a pocket watch from her coat. It had initials etched onto the front of it in a curling script—*EA*.

"It was a gift from his father," Iliana said.

Aurelie tried to seek again. And again. But nothing came.

When Aurelie opened her eyes at last, Iliana looked rather grave-faced. "Tell me, Baker. Must a subject . . . still be living in order for you to find them?"

"Yes," Aurelie answered, though she didn't truly know.

Iliana nodded and retrieved the stones. She left without another word.

Aurelie thought that was the end of it. Days passed and then weeks. The chill of winter gradually receded, and the first signs of spring began to show in the village.

And then one day Iliana returned, this time with a new request. A new name, a new sketch, a new object. That was how it came to be between them—whenever Aurelie could scrape together a moment of free time, Iliana would come to the bakery with the seeking stones and Aurelie would do her best to discern whoever it was that she wanted found. *A man with a red beard; here is his pipe. A person with three gold teeth who is missing an eye.*

Aurelie was shocked the first time Iliana slid a packet across the counter and she opened it to find six silver coins inside. "What's this?"

"Your fee," replied Iliana. "I'm honoring our agreement of twenty percent. I assume that's still amenable?"

It was more than amenable.

The thing was, Aurelie knew she couldn't keep all the money for herself. The coins Mrs. Basil posted home to Aurelie's family were imaginary, after all, and Aurelie felt duty bound to help her parents. They had sent her to school when they had little means to do so. She couldn't help but feel indebted to them even after everything. Even though money passed through their hands like water. Even if it would be more expedient to throw it directly onto the trash heap.

So four out of every five coins that came from helping Iliana went to Aurelie's parents. The rest she saved for herself. Mrs. Basil would have found the coins, no doubt, but Jonas offered to help—Katriane's brother was a clerk at a bank, and Jonas took the coins there and had them exchanged for bills, which Aurelie sewed into the lining of her apron.

Aurelie pressed one of the bills into Jonas's hand the first time he brought them back for her. "For helping me," she said.

He refused it. "Keep your money. I'm happy to help. I know how difficult it is to be an apprentice."

"One day I'll be a journeyman, and then I'll get paid too. I won't need to work outside the bakery anymore."

"That doesn't mean you should have to give it up if you don't want to."

"Why?"

Jonas shrugged. "You seem to enjoy it."

Aurelie did. She enjoyed it a great deal. She and Iliana weren't friends—not exactly. But it was still gratifying whenever Iliana's gaze would sharpen at some detail Aurelie mentioned. *White flagstones, you say? What shape? New or worn?* Miss Ember said seeking was useless without the knowledge to interpret the data. Iliana had the knowledge—an impressive font of it.

Iliana was a funny sort. Even over months of acquaintance, the things that Aurelie learned about her were few: that she traveled often but took lodgings at the Marquis flats, that of everything on offer at Basil's Bakery, she liked the morning buns best and that she preferred them with a glass of milk, if possible, or weak tea, if not.

And she knew that Iliana wasn't from the village or even from the Northern Realm. (Her accent told the tale—it was too clipped.) Iliana never spoke of her upbringing, but every now and then she broke out with some curious notion, like an unwavering assertion that *the best sporting horses come from Ardent Fields, and you need at least six of them to truly compete.* Or a suggestion to *take up orchid keeping for your nerves, Baker, it's meant to be remarkably soothing.* There was something about the way Iliana carried herself that inclined Aurelie to think that wherever she came from must have been grand. Maybe it had a fountain or a folly. Half a dozen sporting horses, at the very least.

If Iliana did the same thing—collected the same sorts of observations about Aurelie—she may have noted someone who allowed herself to lick the knife after icing a batch of cinnamon rolls, but only if she'd done a particularly good job and only if there was no way for Mrs. Basil to find out. Someone who was still deeply, pathetically grateful for Mrs. Basil's patronage, despite any bit of hardship that came with it.

Maybe she saw someone in need of an adventure. Or someone to pity. Aurelie didn't know.

When Jonas spoke again, pulling Aurelie from her thoughts, there was a gentle note to his voice. "We can't live and die by mastery alone, you know. There's more to life than that."

A corresponding softness in his eyes made Aurelie look away. She didn't really know what to do with softness.

"I know it's not easy," he continued. "But don't forget to . . . to take joy in things too. When you can. Do something that makes you happy, whether it's working with your finder friend or just . . . taking a walk in the park with someone you love."

Aurelie couldn't help but smile a little. "Is that something you've been doing lately?"

Jonas deliberately avoided Aurelie's gaze, looking a bit bashful. "Maybe."

It was late summer when Mrs. Basil was called to the Capital for a meeting of the baking masters. She was bringing Jonas along, as he hoped to finally sit for mastery.

When someone advanced from apprentice to journeyman and was deemed ready to sit for mastery, they presented their goods or skills to the Court to be judged. It was the same for any medium—cooking or blacksmithing or weaving, sewing or architecture. Even the students from the ateliers, studying art or design, came to have their work assessed by members of the nobility.

Jonas would have to prepare a number of bakes and submit them for judgment. No doubt he would pass—of course he would. He was a brilliant baker, a genius with flavor and technique. Jonas didn't just follow recipes—he improved them, or invented his own. Aurelie had never really thought of baked goods as an art form, but Jonas was an artist, undeniably.

As for what would happen after he achieved mastery, Aurelie wasn't sure. How long would Jonas be content to work for Mrs. Basil after reaching mastery himself?

Aurelie didn't want to ponder it.

"Of course, the bakery will be closed in my absence," Mrs. Basil told Aurelie, the evening before she and Jonas were to depart. It was a three-day trip to the Capital. All that time alone in a carriage with Mrs. Basil—Aurelie didn't envy Jonas one bit. "I expect you can find your own lodgings."

"I can't stay here while you're gone?"

Mrs. Basil looked as if Aurelie had suggested something completely outlandish. "Of course not. Without me? Who knows what you might get up to?"

"I'd just . . . need a place to sleep," Aurelie said.

"Surely you can return to your parents."

Aurelie's family home was quite a bit farther north, and buying passage there would carve into her hard-earned savings. And anyway, the idea of returning to her parents wasn't something she relished. She'd rather have her little room in the bakery and the guarantee of solitude.

"For all my generosity," Mrs. Basil continued, "it's the very *least* they can do, to take back the burden of boarding you for so trivial a time. I'll be losing money while I'm away, so paying to keep a fire burning here is simply out of the question."

"It's high summer," Aurelie said. "I wouldn't need a fire—"

"*Out* of the question."

Jonas, having observed the conversation, stepped forward. "Mrs. Basil, surely you can't mean to just leave Aurelie out in the cold—"

"I should hardly say so. We've just affirmed it's high summer."

"But she'll need a place to stay."

Mrs. Basil was unmoved. "I've offered reasonable suggestions, have I not?"

"But—"

"Do you wish to say I'm being *unreasonable*?"

"That's not what I—"

"I should think not. I'm very generous, as I'm sure you'll agree. *Unusually* generous, for someone of my station, that's what I've always heard. A great deal of mentors would do a great deal less for those beneath them."

Jonas's face was flushed. Normally he was unflappable. This was the most *flapped* Aurelie had ever seen him.

"It's all right," Aurelie told him quietly.

"But, Mrs. Basil—"

"The matter is settled," Mrs. Basil said with an air of finality, and then swept out of the kitchen.

Jonas let out a breath.

"Really, it's fine," Aurelie said.

"It's not." He turned suddenly to Aurelie. "You should stay with Katriane." He smiled a little then, frustration ebbing away. "You should stay with my wife."

Aurelie's eyes widened. "You got married?"

He nodded. He suddenly looked happier than Aurelie had ever seen him. "It was—we didn't tell anyone, really, but it was . . . We decided . . ." He shook his head. "This is it,

Aurelie. I'm going to sit for mastery, and then things will be different. I'll be independent. So we figured, why not now? Why shouldn't we?"

"Congratulations. That's wonderful," Aurelie said, and she truly meant it.

The following morning, she watched as Mrs. Basil and Jonas set out, Jonas weighed down with Mrs. Basil's luggage.

"Go to Katriane's," he told Aurelie before parting. "We haven't found a place together yet, but she rents at the Belmont with three others from Chapdelaine's. She said they'll make room for you. It's no burden at all."

As the carriage retreated in the distance, Aurelie turned back to look at the bakery, its doors locked against her. She rarely ever came in through the front of the shop, but it did look charming from out here—the blue door, the clapboard siding, the window boxes that Mrs. Basil paid the milliner's youngest son a copper every week to tend to. The sign was painted with angular letters, black on a white background: BASIL'S BAKERY.

Aurelie felt a bit . . . hollow. It was selfish. She was happy for Jonas—sincerely happy—but she couldn't imagine Basil's without him. She couldn't imagine withstanding it.

And she knew, as the midmorning light glinted off the bakery's front window, that she couldn't impose on Katriane. Jonas was right—things would be different once he achieved mastery. He would go off and make his own way, free from Mrs. Basil. Free from any obligation to Aurelie. Not that he even had any obligation to her now. He was just kind.

Aurelie knew she shouldn't rely on kindness. She would have to make her own way too.

"Are you planning an oil painting?" someone said.

Aurelie turned. It was Iliana, leaning against the wall outside the alleyway between Basil's and the adjoining shop.

"Or were you memorizing the look of it in order to perform some sort of curse or dark ritual?" she continued. "I wouldn't blame you, of course."

Aurelie looked away. It was just like Iliana to show up at a moment like this. A moment that Aurelie would rather keep to herself—shut out of her own place of work, her own *home*, really, with nowhere to go.

"What do you need?" Aurelie asked. Iliana wasn't often troubled with *How are you?* or *Some weather we're having, isn't it?* or any other such lines of inquiry.

"I've got to leave town."

Aurelie made a show of checking their surroundings. "Funny, I don't see any pitchfork-wielding hordes around."

One corner of Iliana's mouth lifted. Aurelie hated to admit it, but it was a tiny bit gratifying.

"I need to travel south," Iliana said. "Would you consider accompanying me?"

"Why?"

"I may need some help, and it'll be too much trouble to travel back and forth, considering how far I need to go. If you're with me, you can seek on-site—it'll make everything easier."

"How long will you be gone?"

Iliana eyed her. "A week or so."

Aurelie hesitated, though she wasn't quite sure why. She really did have nowhere to go. And this sounded suspiciously like an adventure, and she had never had one before (unless the journey from school to Basil's several years ago counted as one, but that was doubtful—they hadn't even stopped to eat).

Maybe Aurelie was worried that if she saw a bit of the world, she wouldn't be content to come back. And she knew she had to come back—her apprenticeship was her only way forward.

She spoke tentatively: "I have to return before Mrs. Basil does."

"Of course."

"You're not even going to bother asking where she's gone?"

"Because I already know. What sort of finder would I be if I couldn't even track the movements of the people around me?"

Aurelie raised an eyebrow. "Do you track me?"

"You're the easiest one of all—you never go anywhere." Iliana smiled. "So what do you say?"

Three

W hat about your things?" Iliana cast a look over at Aurelie before they set out.

Aurelie frowned. "What things?"

"Don't you want to pack a bag?"

Aurelie didn't have a bag. She had very few possessions in the first place. Not to mention, Mrs. Basil had already locked the bakery.

She wasn't sure which was the least embarrassing of these points to admit. So she said nothing and headed around to the back of the bakery instead. To her chagrin, Iliana followed closely.

Aurelie tried the knob to the back door, but as expected, it was locked too.

She cast a quick glance at Iliana and then put her palm over the keyhole.

It wasn't a spell—not exactly. It was the sort of thing Aurelie figured you just had to think around the edges of. If you thought about it too hard—the intent, the *process*, if you stared it in the face, it was sure to unravel.

The lock clicked open. Aurelie turned the knob.

When she glanced back, Iliana was looking at her with interest.

"That's quite handy."

"It's nothing."

Iliana turned the knob experimentally as Aurelie headed into the bakery's kitchen.

"What happens to it? Will it jam later? Twice as hard to open?"

"I don't know." Aurelie went into her room and quickly gathered up her only change of clothes.

"Surely it must take something."

"I suppose I haven't done it often enough to notice," Aurelie called. "I try not to make a habit of breaking into places."

When she returned to the kitchen, Iliana had a curiously intent look in her eyes.

"What does seeking take?"

"Sorry?"

"*All magic has consequences*, et cetera, et cetera. What are the consequences of seeking?"

"It's different." Aurelie cast a look around and spotted an empty flour sack. She crossed over and picked it up, giving it a few shakes before shoving her clothes inside. "It takes, I suppose, but only from within. Everything takes energy, though. Working toward mastery takes energy. Getting out of bed takes energy sometimes. So why not magic?"

"Why not indeed," Iliana murmured, and then her expression cleared. "Shall we?"

"Where are we going?"

Aurelie glanced back at the village as she and Iliana walked the road out of town. Every time she checked on it, it was smaller than before.

"I told you," Iliana replied. "South."

"To do what?"

"Important business."

Aurelie knew there was no point in pressing further, so she set about tearing two holes in the flour sack so she could wear it over her shoulder.

Iliana conspicuously lacked any sort of luggage. She was outfitted as she normally was during their consultations— dark trousers, tall boots, a buttoned shirt, hair smoothed back, and despite the warmth of summer, the long black greatcoat. She looked like she could run the length of a field or scale any tree she wanted. She was like a coiled spring— all potential energy—but at the same time, appeared completely at ease. Totally at her leisure.

Aurelie was certain there was still flour somewhere on her own clothes. (That was so often the case.) She was wearing what she always wore, consultation or no—a white blouse tucked into pants of a coarse brown linen that were voluminous enough to give the appearance of wearing a skirt (Mrs. Basil insisted, for "propriety's sake") but were significantly more utile. She wore her apron as well, which was pale blue and featured her own pathetic attempt at embroidery across the pockets.

They had been walking for some time—the village had all but disappeared in the distance—when Aurelie realized they were approaching the Underwood.

Not just approaching it—approaching it with *intent*.

She slowed to a stop. "Where *exactly* are we going?"

Iliana paused a few steps ahead and turned back. "Why do you insist on wearing that apron?" she said, instead of answering the question. "You're literally wearing handles. Anyone could grab you at any moment."

"It has pockets," Aurelie replied, and Iliana scoffed, quite hypocritically—she had no fewer than a dozen pockets combined across her ensemble. "Why do you insist on that coat? It's full summer."

"It has pockets," Iliana said mockingly.

"Aren't you hot? Constantly?"

"So I've heard."

"Iliana."

"If you must know, it's enchanted. It maintains a comfortable temperature for the wearer, regardless of the season."

"That's not possible."

"It is if you know the right people."

"If you knew the right people, you wouldn't need me. Which brings me back to the question at hand—what are we doing?"

"Having a bit of banter, I thought," Iliana replied with a grin. It was irrepressible. Aurelie hated it.

"Tell me or I'm leaving."

"We have to cut through the woods," Iliana said.

"Through the Underwood."

"That is what these woods are called, yes."

"You want us to go *into* the Underwood."

The Underwood was the biggest forest in the Kingdom. Few people strayed beyond its outer edges. There were long-held notions about the sort of creatures that inhabited the vast stretch of woods, rumors about the properties of the trees and plants that grew there. Everyone had a cousin's neighbor's husband's sister who owned a chair carved from Underwood timber that one day became sentient and took its vengeance. Or a teacher's nephew's friend who stole a snowdrop or some interesting-looking rock from deep within the forest and went through life from then on out seeing pink stripes on everything.

And there was always talk of folks who went into the forest and simply never returned—*Mrs. Hasting's stepgrandson? Never seen or heard from again! Perished in those woods, he did! Lost and never found!*

Everyone in these parts agreed—it was best to leave the forest well enough alone. And Aurelie wasn't without a bit of that superstition as well.

Of course Iliana would propose a waltz through the Underwood like it was a casual stroll through the park, never caring that one foul move might mean the difference between life as they knew it and life that was pink-striped.

"It's the fastest route," Iliana said. "It's days out of our way to go around."

Aurelie didn't speak.

Iliana backtracked and threw an arm around Aurelie's shoulders, guiding her forward. "It's fine, Baker. Ignore whatever country gossip you've heard at your shop. Plenty of people have entered these woods and lived to tell the tale."

They continued forward, though Aurelie shrugged off Iliana's arm. Iliana didn't even pause or break stride as they reached the tall line of trees, passed through it, and entered the woods.

Aurelie wouldn't break stride either, then. She could be fearless too (or so she told herself).

A dense canopy hung overhead, dappling the light that managed to break through. The distance between the trees narrowed as they progressed. Some of the trunks were so thick, Aurelie's arms wouldn't reach around even half their circumference. Some trees were heavy with moss, hanging from notches that dotted their trunks.

"Cation trees," Iliana told her as they squeezed through two particularly large ones. "They're native to this stretch of the forest. Same as the marybells." She gestured to the small, deep purple flowers that bloomed in patches here and there.

They walked in silence for a while, with just the crunch of twigs and leaves underfoot. (*Step on one wrong leaf, and you'll be turned into a tree frog. Heaven forbid you step on a tree frog itself—your life will be forfeit!*)

Eventually, Iliana stopped near a copse of thin trees with peeling white bark. She reached into a coat pocket and pulled out the small leather pouch that held the seeking stones. "How about a search?"

"Here? Now?"

"No time like the present." Iliana extended the pouch toward Aurelie, along with a folded square of parchment. "Are these trees sufficiently . . . mystical?"

Birchwood was thought to amplify magic. Aurelie hesitated for a moment—surely doing magic in the Underwood was ill-advised—but she took the stones and the parchment nonetheless and entered the circle of trees.

"I'll be over here if you need me," Iliana called, settling down on top of a nearby log. Aurelie snorted. Iliana would certainly be no help in seeking. Before a consultation of particular importance some months ago, she had described herself to Aurelie as *about as magical as a twig.*

"That could be quite magical, you know," Aurelie had replied, "depending on the properties of the wood—"

"As magical as a bag of beans, then," Iliana amended.

"Again, that could depend on the beans. I've heard there are farmers in the south who can—"

"Good gracious, I have nothing of it in me, is that clear enough? I don't know a whit about illusions or enchantments or *magic rocks* or what have you, so let's just leave it be. Wave your little stones around, hum something, feel the vibrations or whatever it is you do, and just tell me what I need to know to get this done."

Aurelie had promptly sent Iliana away.

Iliana had returned to the bakery the next day uncharacteristically quiet, bought six morning buns, and then, standing awkwardly at the end of the counter, had mumbled, "I know it's not just . . . waving rocks around and whatever else."

"What's that?" Aurelie was occupied in restocking the shelves, taking even more care with it than she usually would.

"I appreciate that it's difficult, and I . . ." *Mumble, mumble.*

"Come again?"

"I *need you,*" Iliana replied, louder. "I need your help. All right? Will you wave the stones around now?"

Aurelie's answering expression had made Iliana go shame-faced.

"Will you perform your *complex ritual* and provide me with *much-appreciated assistance*?" She grasped the box of buns. "Darling. Please."

The endearment was what did it. Iliana was all humor and sharp edges. Sincerity wore uncomfortably on her. But it was sincere all the same.

Aurelie had led her to the back of the shop and set up the seeking circle.

Now Aurelie surveyed the circle of trees and found a bare patch of earth near the center. She knelt and opened the parchment.

A familiar face looked out at her.

"Him again?" Aurelie called. It had been months since she first searched for Elias Allred. "But you came to me about him ages ago."

"Yes, Baker. Historically, missing people remain missing until they're found."

Aurelie chose to ignore that. "Do you still have the pocket watch?"

"Not anymore."

"Of course not," Aurelie muttered to herself. She opened the pouch of stones nonetheless. Maybe the birchwood really would help.

Repeated handling imbued seeking stones with magic. The set Aurelie had worked with at school would give off a subtle glow when she held them. Iliana's set wasn't quite the same, but Aurelie had used it enough that the stones felt familiar; they responded to her. She never asked where or how Iliana had gotten them. They were exceedingly rare these days, with seeking having fallen out of fashion years ago.

Aurelie drew the symbols and then gathered the stones together in one hand. She shut her eyes, letting the magic hum. Then she cast the stones into the circle.

Elias Allred, she thought. *Elias. Elias. Elias.*

For several long moments, Aurelie thought it would be the same as before, that she would see nothing. But then, slowly, it began to materialize—a hand, clutching a set of reins. The sound of carriage wheels crunching over uneven terrain and the slow progress of horses. Dappled light from a heavy canopy of trees.

A familiar canopy.

"Could he be . . . here?" Aurelie called. "In the Underwood? Is that possible?"

Iliana's voice was charged. "You can see him?"

Aurelie stretched her mind. She pulled up more magic. She sensed further.

The hand on the reins—the knuckles were wrinkled, the skin on the back weathered. It was not a young man's hand.

She tried for more, but sometimes pushing too far, too hard, broke the connection, and that was what happened now. The image dashed in front of her eyes and melted away.

"It's not . . . It doesn't make sense."

When Aurelie looked over, Iliana was no longer lounging on the log. She was on her feet, her gaze intent.

"What is it? What did you see?"

"A carriage, passing through the woods. *These* woods, I think. And a man, but it couldn't be—he was too old—"

"How did you know it was the Underwood?"

"The cation trees. You said—"

"They're nearby." Iliana pulled a pair of gloves out of one of her pockets and put them on hurriedly. "Did you see anything else that would—never mind, I'll track them myself." And then she headed swiftly off in the opposite direction.

"Wait—" Aurelie turned back to the circle to grab the stones.

But the circle was empty. The stones were gone.

The ground wasn't entirely bare to begin with. There was some patchy underbrush, some stray leaves. Aurelie reached out to quickly comb through them—could the magic have kicked up debris?—but her fingers suddenly pushed into the earth with no resistance. In an instant, she was elbow-deep in the ground, the cool, damp dirt surrounding her arms. And then there was something much worse—the feeling of a hand, under the earth, grasping hers.

She must have cried out—she heard the pounding of footsteps, and then Iliana was at her side, a dagger drawn.

"Stay back!" Aurelie warned. The ground beneath her knees was still stable, but everything that lay before her was potentially dangerous. The last thing they needed was Iliana slipping through too.

The hand held fast, its grip hard and cold.

"What do I do?" Iliana said. *Who do I stab?*

"I can't—" Aurelie tried to pull out of its grasp, but the hand pulled back, one powerful tug forcing Aurelie's arm deeper into the ground, past the elbow, up to the shoulder.

Iliana discarded the dagger and grabbed Aurelie around the waist, trying to pull her up.

"Don't—" Aurelie barely choked out, before her face was pulled under as well.

There was hardly time to close her eyes. She was completely submerged, the damp earth pressing in on her from all sides. The bottom half of her body was still aboveground—she could feel Iliana's grip, hear her muffled grunts.

Rather than something useful, something survival oriented, the absurd thought that popped into Aurelie's head was this: *Maybe the ladies of the village were right. Maybe this was how Mrs. Hasting's stepgrandson met his end.*

With every tug she or Iliana attempted, the hand pulled back harder, so Aurelie let her arm slacken, frantically thinking that maybe its grip would loosen when met with no resistance. But she couldn't convey that message to Iliana, and Iliana just pulled harder on her. The hand gave another sharp tug in response.

Aurelie felt herself growing light-headed from lack of air, her heart pounding ever faster in fear, and still the hand clung on. A sort of buzzing filled her ears like a swarm of bees, growing closer and louder and more erratic until suddenly it coalesced into a voice.

When the time comes, it said, *speak his true name.*

Let me go, Aurelie thought back, but the hand gripped impossibly tighter.

When the time comes, speak his—

Let me go, let me go, let me go!

When the time comes—

I will! Aurelie thought desperately.

Speak his true name.

By this point Aurelie would have agreed to dance a jig in the central square wearing a saucepan on her head. *Yes! Now let me go!*

Tell no one, the voice said.

I won't tell!

Swear it.

I swear!

Two things happened at the same time: first, there was a great pulse of magic from above. Aurelie felt it ripple through her. And second, the hand let go. With a jolt, Aurelie was yanked out of the earth and thrown onto her back.

She spat out some dirt and took a great gulping breath, and then another.

"Easy." When Aurelie shook a cascade of dirt free from her face and opened her eyes, she saw that Iliana was kneeling at her side.

"The stones," Aurelie gasped. "They've still got the stones."

"I'll handle it," someone who was very much not Iliana replied. Instead of Iliana's smoky voice, this one was high and a bit reedy.

"Aurelie, this is Quad," Iliana said, as Aurelie took in the sight of the stranger. "She's got an impressive knack for timing."

Quad inclined her head.

She was dressed in the Common fashion, but she was undoubtedly one of the Uncommonfolk found in rare corners of the Kingdom. To be certain, Commonfolk couldn't do the sort of magic that had just occurred.

Quad was a fair bit shorter than Iliana and quite broad. Her eyes, as they caught the light, looked like sunlight glinting off a pond. There was something about her that made Aurelie feel strangely . . . calm, just by looking at her. It was like resting your eyes on a beautiful vista.

"You must be the baker," Quad said evenly. "Gone and gotten yourself entangled, did you?"

Aurelie shook another shower of dirt from her hair. "How do we get the stones back?"

"Give me a moment. Best leave the trees, both of you. You'll be safer on the outside."

"What the devil was that?" Iliana asked, guiding Aurelie through the circle of trees.

"It had a *hand*," Aurelie said. "A hand! With fingers!"

"How many?"

"Shockingly, I didn't have time to count as it was *pulling me into the earth.*"

"Here." Iliana led her to a fallen log to sit.

"We need the stones back."

"You could've died," Iliana said. "Take a moment to collect yourself." She handed Aurelie a handkerchief. "Go on, you look frightful."

"Yes, that should be our primary concern at the moment," Aurelie snapped, her heart still beating uncomfortably fast, but she took the handkerchief nonetheless and set about trying to get some of the dirt off her face.

Before Iliana could respond, Quad emerged from the circle.

"Did you get them?"

Quad looked into her hand. "Pink, blue, red, green, and yellow. Yes?"

"Yes." Aurelie took the stones with relief and held them tight. "Thank you."

Quad shrugged. "It was nothing. They owed me a favor."

"You knew that . . . person?"

"Person. Plant. Something in between. An earth-dweller. A sort of . . . tree demon, I suppose."

"Demon?"

She shrugged. "It's reductive. Your sort would call it a demon."

"Why did it have a hand?"

"Why do you have a hand? Why do any of us?"

Aurelie couldn't for the life of her think of an answer. Though she wasn't sure whether Quad really expected one, as Quad simply stood there placidly, as if she had centuries to contemplate the gentle breeze moving the cation moss above them.

"How did you come upon us?" Aurelie asked instead.

"I was looking for you," Quad said.

"Quad is an associate of mine," Iliana clarified, and then bristled at Aurelie's answering expression. "Don't give me that look. I have associates. You should know—you're one of them."

"We're associates?"

"Colleagues, if you prefer. I asked Quad to help us pursue Elias Allred, though now we may not have to journey nearly as far as I'd thought. However, that does involve us finding that carriage as quickly as possible, so if you're quite recovered, shall we be on our way?"

They started off together in the direction Iliana indicated. She led the way single file, with Aurelie in the middle and Quad bringing up the rear.

"In case you fall into the ground again," Quad told Aurelie. "Why would you cast magic in a sacred circle anyway?"

"I didn't know it was sacred."

"Well, it was. And the earth-dweller wanted me to tell you so. Not the first time they've been disturbed, they said."

"I'm very sorry. *Someone* neglected to mention it was a possibility." Aurelie glared at Iliana's back.

"My sincerest apologies," Iliana replied. "I would've endeavored to avoid your interment, if possible."

As they journeyed through the woods, Aurelie learned that Quad was indeed Uncommon—a troll, to be specific. She and Iliana had met sometime during their travels. (That was as precise as Quad got.) Quad was not her given name, but one that she had chosen after consultation with Iliana. She refused to reveal what her true name was.

"You can't comprehend it."

"Sorry?"

Quad regarded Aurelie with luminous eyes. "Can you mimic the sound of light on water? The rustle of an autumn breeze through the leaves of an ancient oak?"

"No . . ."

"Then you can't even *begin* to comprehend my name. Moreover, you don't deserve to hear it in the first place."

"Brutal," Iliana said from the front. "I love it."

Quad had chosen her nickname based on the quadrille, which Iliana claimed was a popular dance. Aurelie didn't know much about dancing beyond what she had learned in school during Miss Fletcher's second-year deportment lessons, where she had been primarily occupied with trying not to get stepped on.

"It's the perfect name," Iliana said. "Quad's elegant, nimble, light on her feet—it just fits."

Quad was nothing like the trolls Aurelie had read about in stories. "Living under bridges! Demanding tolls!" Quad said with indignation as the three of them maneuvered through a particularly dense patch of trees. "Do you know why you'd find me under a bridge? To avoid the likes of you. But mortals have gotten it into their heads that we live that way. That we just *hunker* under there, charging passersby *fees* for crossing! As if we've established some sort of bridge-based infrastructure, relying on something as petty and mortal as *income*! Please know, sincerely: it's not the case. Stop being terrible, and we won't need to go under bridges to avoid you."

"Are Commonfolk truly that terrible?" Aurelie asked, concerned.

"In general, yes, you're a bit terrible," Quad replied. "No regard for nature. No regard for magic. Assuming that this Kingdom is yours for the shaping, when in fact we have been and will be here long after all of you are gone. You know, the king himself is trying to cut down part of these woods, when there are leaves on these trees with more years than he has."

"Why would the king want to cut down the Underwood?" Aurelie asked. She didn't keep up much with news from the Capital—only what filtered in through customers at the bakery.

"Not the whole thing," Iliana said. "Just a piece of it."

"Oh, that's much better," Quad said with sarcasm. "How about I cut off *just a piece* of you?"

"I'm not in favor of it. I'm just explaining for Baker, who's woefully uninformed."

"Hey!"

"The king wants a proper road," Iliana continued. "Safe passage between the Capital and the Scholar's City. It'll never proceed without the Court's approval though, and the Court will never approve. No one wants to risk upsetting the forest."

"They have no right to touch the woods," Quad said adamantly.

"Believe me," Iliana replied. "I don't want to make any enemies in the Underwood." Her lips twitched. "I've got enough of them outside the woods as it is."

They stopped eventually so that Iliana could evaluate their direction. This consisted of standing atop a fallen tree with her hands on her hips, peering one way and then the other. The trees grew so close together that it was impossible to see very far in any direction, but Iliana seemed to glean something from it nonetheless.

"By the way, were you able to get everything?" she asked Quad before jumping down from the fallen tree.

"Mostly."

Iliana raised an eyebrow. "Copperend?"

"No." Quad reached into her pack and pulled out a bundle of cloth. She laid it out on the tree trunk and began to uncover a series of objects. "But everything else." Her fingers brushed over each object in turn as she spoke—"Lester," a blue enamel hand mirror; "Elridge," a cloudy silver watch fob; "Price," a nub of a charcoal pencil, almost spent.

"Good," Iliana murmured, and then she crouched down and touched the ground, seemingly evaluating the dirt.

"Are you a finder too?" Aurelie asked, watching as Quad rolled the objects back up and stuck them in her pack.

"More or less."

"What does that mean?"

"These days, I focus more on the acquisition of items."

Aurelie frowned. "So, you're a thief."

"Hardly." Quad looked offended. "Some people give freely. And if they don't, I return the item." She tilted her head from one side to the other. "Usually."

"Why work at all? I thought you didn't rely on something as *petty and mortal* as income."

"I don't rely on it. But I won't say no to it either."

"You should be thankful to Quad," Iliana said. "If it weren't for her acquisitions, you'd have hardly as many useful items to seek with."

"That's how you get the objects for seeking?"

"Of course," Iliana said. "I'm not nearly as good at it. I can't go invisible like Quad can."

"I can't go invisible either," Quad said. "I just know how to blend in."

Iliana got to her feet. "Obviously there's no formal road through the wood, or the king wouldn't be so hell-bent on making one. But there is somewhat of a path nearby—I believe the only path that would be wide enough to fit a carriage. If Elias Allred's carriage has passed through already, I'll know. If it hasn't, we'll wait and try to intercept him."

"What do you do when you've found the person you're looking for?" Aurelie asked.

"It depends on the bounty," Iliana said. "Sometimes laying eyes on the person is enough. But sometimes the person needs to be . . ." She looked up, as if searching for the word, before settling on "retrieved."

"What if they don't want to be retrieved?"

"We retrieve them anyway," Quad said. "We're quite good at it."

"What about Elias?" Aurelie said, as Iliana evaluated one direction and then another, several degrees to the left.

"We don't need to retrieve him," Iliana said. "We just need to find him." Her gaze narrowed, and then she pointed definitively in the more leftward direction. "It's this way."

They started off in that direction, but suddenly Quad stopped in her tracks. A strange expression crossed her face.

Aurelie stopped too, and Iliana got only a few steps farther before turning back.

"What is it?" Iliana asked.

"Nothing," replied Quad after a moment, though her expression still looked somewhat uneasy. "It just . . . feels as though someone might die."

"Someone here?" Aurelie said, alarmed. "Someone as in one of us?"

"Someone nearby," Quad said, and then shrugged. "It's probably nothing."

Aurelie looked at Iliana with wide eyes. Iliana just shrugged too.

"You heard her. It's probably nothing."

"But—"

"Come along, Baker! We're losing daylight!"

Four

At the very same moment, Prince Hapless—second in line to the throne, peer of the Scholar's City, and self-declared ruler of the best portion of the Royal Gardens—was thinking of something other than his untimely demise.

He was in fact reflecting that a journey by carriage through the Underwood was undoubtedly a foolish idea. It wasn't the prince's idea, but it was exactly the kind of thing that he would be credited with—*oh, but of course, another one of the prince's follies!*

Hapless had follies, certainly—that wasn't by any means inaccurate. He discovered a new favorite color or fashion almost by the month and insisted on refreshing his wardrobe each time. (Right now he favored midnight blue and a voluminous sleeve.) When Hapless was younger, he had seen a particularly moving production of *The Pauper's Play* and insisted that he be allowed to star in a staging of it, only to change his mind upon learning how many lines he'd have to memorize. (The actors had already been assembled, much to his steward's chagrin. Though to Hapless's credit, it was no great hardship for Steward to substitute for him; truth be told, the production was all the better for it. The man had hidden depths. Never had Bastian Sinclair been played with such a passion.)

When Hapless was very young, and had wandered into the kitchen to plunder some of Cook's jam-filled butter cookies and observed the kitchen staff peeling and boiling potatoes, he had cried and insisted that the palace stop serving them. (Potatoes had eyes, after all, which certainly meant that they must have feelings too, which in turn meant that they could definitely, undoubtedly feel pain. *Imagine being tossed in a giant pot that way! Imagine being mashed!* he had sobbed to his mother, and bless her, she had indulged him.)

Hapless's sister, Honoria, had no less than six yapping dogs—small and white with curly tails and floppy ears—and no one called that a folly, how she doted on each one and named them absurd things like Baron Twinkle and Lord Cheeks. Hapless's brother, Gallant, though respected and peerless and worthy of having his face on coinage, et cetera, did once at the age of eleven insist on dressing the dogs in costume for a midsummer festival, and no one called that a folly either.

Sometimes Hapless felt like the only one who had to be indulged. Everyone else was allowed their eccentricities, allowed to say or do something somewhat outside the bounds of the done thing, and it was still considered respectable. But for Hapless, it was just . . . foolish, and frivolous; it was what you expected of him.

Nonetheless, the carriage, the woods, the journey in general—none of it had been his idea. There was something of a rudimentary path through this portion of the Underwood, but every so often the guards had to dismount to clear fallen branches away. It was slow going. Tedious. Completely unnecessary.

Steward had insisted that Hapless stay in the carriage: *You must be exhausted, Your Highness. You should rest. It would be too much riding alongside, far too much.*

It begged the question of just how delicate Steward thought Hapless's sensibilities were. Then again, when Steward looked at him, maybe he still saw the small, jam-covered child crying over potatoes.

However, Hapless was a child no more. He was studying to become a scholar, after all. Heaven forbid a scholar ride alongside the carriage. Perish the thought that he might enjoy it.

But even returning to his studies was fraught, wrapped up in another of Hapless's *follies*. The quest. Or rather, the failed quest.

Hapless had wanted nothing more than to undertake a quest before the start of the fall semester. Quests were old-fashioned, of course, but that was part of what he liked about the idea. Just the notion of going out and searching, doing something and doing it *purposefully*, appealed in a way that he couldn't quite convey to his family.

Honoria had despaired, her brows drawn together in an expression that was part concern and part scorn. "Hapless, no one's consulted the Sworn Scrolls in a hundred years."

Hapless hadn't let it dampen his enthusiasm. "I know!

Time to blow the dust off them, don't you think? Give them a good once-over?"

The Sworn Scrolls were a collection of prophecies. Some of them were incomprehensible—*on the fifty-third moment east of iron, a great act of bravery shall there flow o'er.* But some of them mentioned specific tasks or magical relics, and those were the ones that interested Hapless the most. Particularly the entry about the Sun Stone. It was prophesized to cast an eternal light, and what could be better than that? A candle that needed no flame, a lamp that needed no oil. And who didn't love a bit of mood lighting? When Hapless read about it, he knew that was it for him—quest sorted. He had to go find it. Or at least, he had to try.

"Dearest, please," Honoria had said. "The Sun Stone's not even thought to have magical properties."

"Not true!" Hapless insisted. "It glows!"

"We've got plenty of lighting here. You don't have to *wander* the Kingdom for it."

Gallant had turned to their father. "You'd really allow this?"

Hapless's father shrugged in that world-weary way of his. "Hapless is of age. Let him seek his fortune before he returns to school."

"It's not a fortune though, is it?" replied Gallant. "It's a glorified paperweight."

Amusement had shone in their father's eyes. "And it will weight the papers of the Kingdom in fine fashion."

So Hapless had studied the Scrolls, copying out the relevant passages. People back then used the strangest language, the most convoluted riddle sort of writing (*Mythic mists divide the stones, e're the white walls sway,* that sort of thing). But there was enough information to give him at least a bit of a notion—he was to head north and to the east and seek a ruin of stone adjacent to a field of purple. There could only be so many ruins near so many fields, just as there were only so many types of purple flowers and even fewer capable of growing in the northern climate—it was narrowing itself down already!

But when the time came for Hapless to leave for his quest, Gallant wouldn't allow it. "I thought we settled against that."

"But what about—"

"Hapless. You can't truly be serious."

"Father said I could go."

Gallant raised an eyebrow.

They both knew that their father was not the utmost authority over any of them, or anyone really. The king-father had never been prone to the royal life—the fourth son of a baron, he had barely qualified as peerage himself before meeting and wedding their mother, the crown princess. Honoria loved to hear the story of it, insisting on its retelling often when they were young: how their mother was meant to marry a duke, but after seeing their father at a wintergarden—poorly dressed for the cold, attempting to calm a fearful horse—she had fallen in love.

At the time of their mother's passing, Gallant was just old enough to inherit the throne, and so he had. Their father, meanwhile, retreated further and further into his own pursuits—falconry, gardening, collecting rare books. He retreated further into himself, as well, though he had always been prone to deep contemplation and faraway looks.

Gallant was more of a disciplinarian to Hapless than their father had ever been. It made Gallant's approval matter a little more to Hapless. It also made Gallant all the more annoying at times like this.

"You were king when you were my age," Hapless said.

"Your point being?"

"You were deemed fit to rule an *entire Kingdom*, but I can't go on *one* little quest?"

"That's different."

Hapless tried to make a joke of it. "How? Is the correlation between birth order and general competency really that significant?"

"Hapless, you know how you are sometimes."

It no longer felt lighthearted. "How am I sometimes?"

Hapless could see it on Gallant's face—those *follies* of his, reflected back at him.

But Gallant surprised him. After a long moment, he let out a sigh. "You'll have to take a full party."

Hapless brightened. "Certainly."

"At least two sets of guards and a coachman. And Steward, of course."

"Of course," Hapless replied, already elated.

It was all fine and good when they first set out—there were people to tend to the horses and to worry about things like provisions and luggage, lighting campfires, et cetera. But they rather did cramp one's style at certain moments. Hapless wanted to discover a secret cave or explore an abandoned village. He wanted to climb hills and look out over beautiful vistas, and to do so alone, a greatcoat billowing out behind him. He wanted to be dignified in his solitude, stolid and alone, to *think great thoughts*. There was something about Steward following behind him and making sure he'd buttoned his jacket properly that made him feel as if he wasn't truly adventuring. As if it wasn't so much a quest as it was a glorified day trip.

And inevitably, it was Steward who informed him that the time for questing had ended—that Hapless was soon due to the Scholar's City to prepare for the start of the school year.

Hence the present journey through the Underwood.

Hapless let out a sigh, leaning his head back against the plush seat of the carriage. Was it really a quest if you didn't achieve your objective? Was it a quest if you didn't accomplish much of anything at all, beyond traveling in the direction that you needed to travel anyway in order to get to school? Part of him felt as if he had been tricked. That Gallant had simply been pacifying him and counting on Hapless being too dim or too self-absorbed to notice.

The carriage slowed to a stop. Another obstacle in the road, then.

Hapless reached for the door and had only begun to open it when Steward appeared in the gap.

"Your Highness? Is there any way I may assist you?"

Steward was terribly old-fashioned. He could have ridden in the carriage—at least then Hapless would have someone to talk to—but he insisted on sitting out front with the coachman, to preserve the prince's privacy. (What was it he thought Hapless would be getting up to in there? Or was his company really so burdensome?)

"We've stopped?" Hapless asked.

"Several fallen branches. The guards will make quick work."

"Could I step out for a moment? A bit of fresh air."

Steward's mouth flattened. "I'm dreadfully sorry, Your Highness. The woods, as you know, may be treacherous, and we received strict instructions to only stop at the designated outposts—"

"We're stopped now, though."

"No *extended* stops," Steward clarified, "at undesignated outposts."

"Well, perhaps we could just . . . designate this . . . to be one of them." Hapless pushed the door open farther. The carriage felt too hot all of a sudden, too dark with the shades drawn, too closed off. "Surely I have the authority to designate, do I not? I'm nearly certain I do."

"But, Your Highness—"

"One feels so cooped up, after an extended ride—"

"We really must adhere to our schedule—"

"Just one little breath of fresh air is all I need. Or two or three. Five at most!" He nudged the door open wide enough to angle his body out, and Steward had no choice but to move aside.

Hapless had only just set both feet on the ground, had only just stepped past Steward, when there was the sharp whiz of something shooting by him, followed by a loud *twang*.

He looked to his left and saw an arrow driven directly into the side of the carriage, just a hand's width from his head. It was still vibrating with the force of its entry.

For a moment everything else was still.

Then Hapless grabbed Steward and pushed him into the carriage, just as Steward reached for him, likely with the same intent. Hapless slammed the door shut. Steward wasn't infirm by any means, but he did have several very young grandchildren and Hapless knew that he doted on them, knew that they would hate for their papa to leave this earthly plane because he felt duty bound to protect some idiot second spare with his life.

Hapless ducked behind the carriage. One of the guard's horses reared back as more arrows whizzed past. The other guards circled in.

"The trees!" someone called.

Hapless kept low. How many bowmen were there? Would they pick his entire party off from above? If he ran, would the attackers follow? Would that spare the guards? Too many thoughts were running through his mind at once, when suddenly a group of people emerged from the woods on foot. For a second Hapless's heart grew light—they wore white and blue and burnished gold, the colors of the Kingdom— until they began clashing with his guards.

The young guard nearest to him had dismounted. "Your Highness," he said, with surprising command, "get in the carriage."

"But I—"

"Don't be foolhardy. I've no wish to die today, and certainly not on your account."

Before Hapless could respond, he was shoved to the ground, just as an ax flew his way.

Five

The ax buried itself into the trunk of a tree, directly behind where a young man had just stood.

Aurelie's breath came fast and painful. She, Quad, and Iliana had sprinted the last bit of distance between themselves and the party, coming upon an ambush well in progress.

The horsemen had dismounted, the horses run off with the sounds of fighting. Everywhere was the clash of metal on metal, the scrabbling of feet in the underbrush. Everyone wore the same white and gold livery, the same blue capes and metal helmets with plumes of white.

Nearest to them, two people fought with swords. One guard forced the other back toward the trees surrounding the clearing.

Iliana's eyes narrowed, weapons already drawn. *How do you fight when you don't know who to fight?* Aurelie wanted to ask, but Iliana charged into the fray nonetheless, shoulder-checking one guard to the ground and approaching his pursuer with two daggers.

"Get the prince!" she called to Aurelie.

Iliana couldn't mean anyone but the tall, extravagantly dressed young man currently pulling himself to his feet. Aurelie had never seen a member of the royal family in person. Her mother had seen Queen Noble once when the queen's carriage rode through a festival in the Capital.

She had a glow about her, Aurelie's mother recalled, before clucking her tongue and shaking her head. *A tragic loss, that was*. (Aurelie's mother always preferred to ruminate on the tragic.)

There was no time to consider the prince's glow at this moment, with arrows flying through the air and swords clashing left and right. Aurelie rather hoped to prevent another tragic loss instead. She threw herself in the prince's direction, pushing him up against a tree as a knife flung past and struck the ground behind them.

He looked at her, eyes wide. "What—"

Quad angled past them then with a measured "Hold your breath," as she pulled something from her belt and crushed it in her hand. Without a second thought, Aurelie clapped a hand over the prince's mouth and another over his nose for good measure as Quad moved to the center of the clearing and blew the *something* into the air—it looked a bit like the dust from dried leaves, a cloud of dark green and brown. It expanded, billowing up large and spreading through the clearing.

In an instant, the guards—all of them—crumpled to the ground and lay motionless. What had been a rush of movement and sound just seconds before was now eerily still.

Aurelie felt a puff of air as the prince exhaled through

his mouth. She dropped her hands immediately and stepped back.

"Beg your pardon," she said, though it seemed wildly insufficient. "I was . . . That was . . . just in case you didn't hear."

The prince nodded, looking slightly dazed. Maybe some of Quad's *something* had hit him nonetheless. "Better safe than sorry is what I always say."

"You've never said that in your life," Iliana said, reholstering her daggers and stepping over a guard to join them.

"Untrue. I said it just now."

Iliana smiled. "Prince."

A broad grin broke the prince's face in return. "Iliana."

Aurelie's eyebrows shot skyward. "You know each other?"

"We do," the prince said. "Iliana's reputation is unparalleled."

"As a finder, you mean," Iliana said.

The prince's eyes shone. "That too."

Amusement played across Iliana's face as she inclined her head toward him. (Aurelie would hazard a guess Iliana had probably never deigned to curtsy in her life.) She then gestured to Aurelie and Quad. "This is Aurelie, the baker, and Quad, a fellow finder, both of the Northern Realm."

Aurelie couldn't keep from dropping into a curtsy herself, with a "Your Highness" thrown in for good measure, since that was what propriety dictated. Though propriety had probably gone out the window the moment she had clapped her hands over the prince's face.

The prince didn't seem at all bothered, bowing to each of them in turn, even though they were undeniably nobodies, and he was second in line to rule the Kingdom. He then stood before them with a smile, looking like he could just as well be any one of the bright and sunny young clerks from the bank on High Street who stopped by the bakery now and then to order sweets before work. Albeit one wearing much flouncier sleeves and a significantly tighter waistcoat than Aurelie had ever seen on a banker. Or, frankly, anyone at all.

"Prince Hapless," he said. "Or just Hapless, if you prefer it, and I hope you do. Delighted to make your acquaintance." He then turned and surveyed the guardsmen, his expression falling a bit. "Though I do regret the circumstances."

"What did you do to them?" Aurelie asked Quad. "What was that . . . dust?"

"A charm," Quad replied. "Rendering them asleep."

"It was . . . very effective."

"I'd hope so. You don't just come across those every day. I'd been saving it for a special occasion."

"Well, thank you for using it on my account," Hapless said, and then moved toward the closest guard. "But I don't under-stand . . . Surely they couldn't have come from the palace?"

No one replied. Iliana moved over and kicked the sole of one of the guards' boots. The guard didn't move. "Asleep, you say?"

"A deep sleep," Quad clarified.

Iliana looked up at the prince. "Well, Highness, which ones are yours? Show us friend from foe."

Hapless walked them through the group, pointing out four guards, a coachman, and at the open door to the car-riage, his steward.

"Bless poor Steward, he should've stayed inside," he mur-mured, gazing upon the man, who looked to be in his fifties, with graying hair and strong dark brows. He was on the ground, leaning against the door as if he had collapsed in the process of exiting the carriage. "He does his level best to look after me."

Aurelie glanced over at Iliana, who was looking at the steward intently.

"What is it?"

Iliana didn't reply, instead crouching down beside the steward and pushing one side of his jacket back. Hanging from his waistcoat was a delicate gold watch chain. Iliana lifted the chain, pulling a watch from his pocket. It was engraved with initials: *EA*.

"That's the watch from before," Aurelie said without thinking. Elias Allred's watch.

"It is."

"But he's not—"

"No. He isn't." Iliana tucked the watch back into the steward's waistcoat pocket and stood.

"What's this?" Hapless asked.

"Nothing of your concern," Iliana replied, and Aurelie's eyes widened. Didn't the prince have a right to any kind of information he wanted? Could you even speak to a member of the royal family that way?

Apparently you could, because Iliana had. And Hapless didn't balk or demand Iliana's arrest or do anything other than cast a look of concern in the steward's direction.

"He'll be all right, won't he?"

"Of course," Quad said.

Iliana turned to regard the prince, her expression still intent. "What exactly happened here?"

"We stopped to clear a path. I asked to get out of the

carriage for some air, and when I opened the door—" He gestured to the carriage, a black-plumed arrow sticking out of the side. "They just attacked. Arrows first. Then the rest of them appeared."

"Why would they shoot first and then continue in on foot?" Aurelie asked. "Why not stay in the trees?"

"Perhaps to capture the prince alive?" Quad asked.

"I wouldn't be so certain," Hapless said. "That first arrow shot . . . rather close to me."

"Not to mention the ax and the knife," Aurelie said, watching as Iliana crossed over to inspect the arrow.

When Iliana looked back at the group, her expression was grave. "Whatever was intended, it's clear you're not safe here. I'd strongly recommend you leave your party behind."

"And how should I get by without them?" It wasn't an uncivil question—it seemed the prince was genuinely asking, as if Iliana were going to direct him to the nearest stables conveniently situated in the northeastern Underwood. "I'm due back to the Scholar's City for the start of classes."

Iliana looked deep in thought, as if she was performing a series of calculations before speaking the solution aloud: "We'll escort you."

Hapless brightened. "Truly?"

"I don't see why not." Iliana turned to Aurelie. "Baker, will the change of plans suit you?"

"I wasn't too clear on what the plan was in the first place."

"Delightful," Iliana said. "Quad?"

Quad shrugged. "Some leaves fall regardless of the change in season."

"Pardon?"

"Makes no difference to me."

"You've got your party then, Prince."

Hapless looked delighted. "Excellent! I'll just grab some essentials, shall I?"

He crossed over to the carriage, and Aurelie took the opportunity to pull Iliana aside.

"Something wrong?" Iliana asked.

"Why does the prince's steward have Elias Allred's watch?"

Iliana sketched a quick glance in the direction of the carriage. "Because Elias is his youngest son," she replied quietly. "Steward's been employed by the royal family for years. He's very dear to them. Therefore, finding his missing son is . . . a priority."

"I've never mistaken anyone like that before," Aurelie said. "Seeking someone and finding a relative instead."

"I guess there's a first time for everything?"

Aurelie contemplated this, her gaze landing on the prince, who was attempting to take a trunk down from the top of the carriage. Quad stood watching him, her hands on her hips, her expression skeptical.

"Maybe you could do some sort of spell or some such, if you wouldn't mind terribly?" Hapless called to Quad. "Just . . . zip the trunks down?"

"I don't *zip*," she said.

"If we phrased it as 'levitating' rather than 'zipping,' could you do that?"

"I could," replied Quad. "I choose not to."

Hapless grinned. "Fair enough."

"How do you even know the prince?" Aurelie asked, looking back at Iliana.

Iliana waved a hand. "I have a vast and varied acquaintance."

"And what am I supposed to do around a member of the royal family? How am I meant to act?"

"Honestly, Baker, nearly five years at that school of yours and they didn't teach you a lick of deportment?"

"They didn't prepare us to *receive royalty*."

"Act like a normal human being. And treat him like one as well. Royals are no different from us."

"Oh really? I don't remember ever being gifted a dukedom for my birthday."

"Well, I'd say a dukedom is more suitable as a solstice gift," Iliana said, and then broke into a grin. "You know, sometimes you get this very specific expression that looks as if you're trying to immolate me through sheer will."

"Believe me, if that were something I was capable of, I would've done it by now."

When Aurelie and Iliana rejoined Hapless and Quad, the prince had succeeded in bringing down one of the smaller trunks. *How much does he need to travel with, anyway?* Aurelie wondered. What sorts of things did a royal carry with them? A dozen embroidered waistcoats, by the look of the trunk's contents.

Hapless held up a pair of boots toward Quad, as if in consultation, and Quad shook her head.

"Not with that jacket."

"But I think the piping rather complements—"

Quad gave a skeptical, "Hm," and Hapless sighed and plunked the boots back in the trunk. He didn't look like someone who had just had an ax thrown at his head. He didn't look like someone nearly concerned enough about just having had an ax thrown at his head, either.

"I thought you were grabbing essentials," Iliana said. "What are you even looking for?"

"Well, I've just had a lovely set of shirts made—"

"Goodness, Prince, heaven knows we won't judge you for your sartorial choices."

"*I'll* judge me," he said, pulling out a different pair of leather boots. "Besides, I need something that lends itself more to walking."

"We'll have to disguise you anyway when we leave the woods."

"Ah." The prince looked down at his clothes. "Maybe I should change into something a bit more *rustic*—"

"You're fine as you are for now," Iliana said. "Shall we proceed?"

Prince Hapless dutifully shut the trunk nearest him. "Could you wake up my people?" he asked Quad. "Or will the counter-charm wake everyone?"

"I can be selective," Quad replied.

She revived the members of Hapless's party one by one. The prince's steward seemed truly shaken upon waking. He moved as if to grasp at Hapless, but then pulled back and sketched a bow instead.

"Your Highness. I'm relieved to see that you're all right."

Hapless clapped a hand on his shoulder. "Nothing to fear, Steward. My friends stepped in, and all is well."

Unsurprisingly, the steward was not pleased with Hapless's plan to leave the party.

"But surely, Highness, you will be in safer hands with—"

A slight movement from Quad caught Aurelie's eye as the steward spoke. Quad had reached into the pouch at her side and retrieved what looked like a small dried plant. Aurelie watched as she crushed it in her palm and then stepped up to the steward, blowing it quickly into his face.

He stepped back, coughed, stammered—"Well, I say—" and then his eyes met Quad's.

"You should take the attackers back to the Capital," she said. "The charm will hold until you reach there. Leave us."

The steward's brow smoothed, and suddenly he straightened and nodded decisively. "I'll leave you," he said. "Take the attackers back to the Capital."

"The prince will make his own way," Quad continued.

"Make your own way," the steward agreed. "You must." He bowed again to the prince and then set about directing the guards to load the attackers into the carriage and repack Hapless's strewn-about luggage.

Aurelie, Iliana, Hapless, and Quad watched as the steward finally climbed into the seat next to the coachmen and the carriage pulled away, Hapless's guards following on foot.

"What did you use on him?" Iliana asked, when the party had all but disappeared through the trees. "And can I have ten of them?"

"Certainly not," Quad said. "Burned two good charms today already. An alarming rate." After a pause, she added: "I didn't trust him."

Hapless frowned. "Steward? Really?"

"Him. Any of them."

"You'll be safe with us," Iliana told Hapless, and Aurelie snorted. "Problem, Baker?"

"Sorry, but I'd feel a lot more certain of that if I hadn't just been sucked into the earth earlier."

Hapless looked alarmed. "Pardon?"

Iliana spoke before Aurelie could. "We should continue west through the woods and then head north from the river."

"That's a bit out of the way, isn't it?" Quad said.

"I'm sure the university would rather the prince arrive alive than in a timely fashion."

"Could we not strive for both?" asked Hapless.

"Impossible," Quad said. "Mortals may be either alive or on time. They cannot be both."

Hapless grinned.

Six

"Well, I for one am happy to be on foot," Hapless said, and it was the truth. "If we must go through the woods, we must! Though . . . what of provisions? Food and such?" He considered the fact that they had just sent a carriage stocked with both food *and* such on its merry way. Perhaps that wasn't the wisest decision in the moment? Not that it had been much of a decision—more of a thing that just happened. Hapless was principally skilled in those things, the kind that sort of just happen.

(*"Dearest,* how *did you manage to spill grapefruit juice all over Duchess Pious?"*

"Hapless, how could anyone have destroyed the portrait of Great-Uncle Sprightly so irreparably?"

"Son, kindly explain to me how one accidentally *sets a dressing gown aflame."*

It just sort of happened—that was how.)

Iliana walked in front. "We'll manage," she said decisively, and Hapless was then certain that they would. Nearly everything about Iliana was decisive, and Hapless admired that immensely. He could barely choose what to have for breakfast each morning. He couldn't even commit to a favorite color.

(He was secretly thankful that the current color was midnight blue, for dirt would wear poorly on his previous color à la mode aquamarine. As it was, he'd left his jacket behind in the carriage already, and he would probably lose the waistcoat too before the afternoon was out, leaving him only in shirtsleeves. A multiday journey on foot would probably not do his clothing well. He wasn't sure how Iliana managed to look so jaunty all the time, adventuring as she did.)

"When we reach the river, we'll follow it up and then cut to the nearest village beyond the woods. We should be able to find transport there."

"Oh, so we're just going to package the prince up in a hackney coach?" Aurelie asked, incredulous.

"Don't be silly," Iliana replied. "We'll be packaging ourselves up as well."

Hapless didn't hate the idea. He'd never been in a hackney coach. Only the palace carriages, which were obviously well appointed (he couldn't complain), but there was too much of the familiar about them. He was willing to trade comfort for novelty, no question about it.

He felt an undeniable excitement. Four disparate adventurers, making their way through an enchanted forest. This had the feeling of a genuine quest about it.

"Tell me," Hapless said, as they wove through the trees in a line—Iliana in front, then Quad, then Hapless, then Aurelie. "How did you all come upon us? I didn't think people often took jaunts through the Underwood."

"We were on our way to a birthday party for Quad's second cousin," Iliana said from the front.

"Truly?"

She glanced back, her eyes dancing. "I wish."

"Do you celebrate birthdays, Quad?" Hapless asked. He didn't know much about Uncommon traditions. Uncommon-folk had an affinity with nature, his father had once told him. They were attuned to the earth in a way that mortals couldn't grasp. It affected everything about them, from their magic to their physiology.

"Hardly," Quad replied.

"Let me guess," Iliana said, and then she and Quad both spoke together—

"Mortal invention."

"Quad has a fascination with mortal invention," Iliana added.

"There are many interesting and unusual mortal inventions," Quad said. "Carriages. Overcoats. Government. Misery."

"Oh, surely trolls know misery," Iliana said.

"Mortal invention," Quad insisted. "And anyway, why would you wish us misery?" After a moment, she answered herself: "I know why. Ill will."

"A mortal invention as well?"

"Certainly not our handiwork."

Hapless broke in. "If you don't have birthdays, then how do you keep track of your age?"

"I just know how old I am."

"And how old is that?" Hapless said, and then dipped his head. "If it's all right to ask."

"Older than many trees," Quad replied. "Older than some rocks."

"What does that mean?"

"It means what it means."

Hapless couldn't argue with that. "So . . . how did you come upon us, then?" he asked as they navigated through the trees.

"I was passing through on business," Iliana replied. "I collected Baker, who led us in your direction, and then Quad collected us, and then we collected you. Fortunate, wasn't it?"

Fortunate indeed. Hapless would still be in the carriage, stuck with his own thoughts, or worse—he'd have an ax through his head. Worse by a fair margin, he supposed.

"Iliana, your cunning and foresight know no bounds. I'll have you knighted for this."

"You'll do nothing of the sort. See that big oak up there? We'll veer right."

"Just a tiny knighthood," Hapless said, climbing over a particularly large fallen branch. "A cheeky little honorary."

He turned and held a hand out to help Aurelie, but she just gave a small smile and clambered over the branch herself.

"Yes, a cheeky knighthood!" Quad said, and Hapless caught a flicker of amusement crossing Aurelie's face before he faced forward again.

"I'd rather perish," Iliana replied flatly.

"Lady Iliana," said Aurelie. "I like it. Though you'd need a proper Court name."

"Lady Danger," Hapless suggested, and glancing back, he could see Aurelie smile a little bigger. It was a gratifying thing somehow.

"I thought those names were meant to be aspirational," she said.

"Iliana aspires to danger, doubtless."

"How about Lady Doubtless?"

"Is that better or worse than Lady Danger?"

"I hate both," Iliana interjected, "and if we continue in this vein, I'll do something violent."

"Danger it is," Hapless said, and Aurelie snorted. Definitely gratifying.

They walked in silence for a bit.

"I'm older than those trees," Quad said eventually. "Just so you know."

"Are you?"

"Yes. And that rock. These rocks too."

"This rock?" said Hapless, pointing to one as they passed.

"Not that one."

Hapless stole another glance at Aurelie. She was smiling for real now, full out.

He looked away, and though he couldn't articulate quite why, he was secretly pleased.

Seven

Eventually—and somewhat to Aurelie's alarm—they stopped for the evening to set up camp.

"We're going to sleep here? In the Underwood?"

"No, I figured we'd just hover somewhere above it," Iliana replied.

Aurelie opened her mouth to say something that probably wouldn't have been particularly dignified, but Quad interrupted.

"It's quite safe," she said, and then cast a look around. "At the moment."

"I'm sure we'll be just fine!" Hapless said heartily. "It's a much more pleasant wood than I imagined."

"Pleasant, yes," Aurelie muttered, and tried to put the thought of the earth-dweller's grip tight on her hand out of her mind.

She had contemplated telling Iliana what the earth-dweller had said, but they had specifically told her not to. Had made her *swear* to it. It seemed like the kind of oath that you shouldn't break.

"Shall we gather wood for a fire, Baker?" Iliana suggested.

Hapless jumped up. "I'll assist."

"It's quite all right," Iliana said. "Aurelie gets distraught if we don't spend enough quality time together."

Aurelie rolled her eyes but followed Iliana nonetheless to a patch of trees a little removed from the clearing where they'd chosen to camp.

They had been gathering wood for several moments when Aurelie spoke.

"We're going a bit far out of our way."

"How do you know that? You've never been anywhere."

Iliana wasn't wrong, but Aurelie still bristled. "I know which way is north. And I know that the Scholar's City is north, and I know we're not headed in that direction. We could've turned around, gone back to the village, and left from there, all in a matter of hours. So why are we still in the woods?"

"I enjoy the scenery."

Aurelie wouldn't dignify her with a response. At least, not until she couldn't help but ask, "Who do you think was responsible for the ambush?"

Iliana tilted her head back and forth, considering. "Someone at Court, most likely."

"Why do you say that?"

"There's the proximity, for one. The uniforms, for another."

"Uniforms?"

"The attackers wore the uniforms of official palace guards. They're awfully hard to replicate and even harder to come by—made on-site and dispensed only by the palace clothier. Maybe those people weren't from the palace, but they had access to the uniforms from someone who is."

"But why would anyone purposefully imply that the attack came from the palace?"

Iliana shrugged. "To make a statement. To sow mistrust. The situation is . . . a bit untenable at Court, at the moment. King Gallant is respected, but there will always be detractors. People who want something done this way or that. People who want more for their districts or their tenants." She paused. "There's also the possibility of someone who's unhappy with their position or their circumstances, looking to upset the balance. Some act of resentment."

"Why would someone resent Hapless?"

"He wears clothes too well. Pure jealousy, I'd imagine."

"Be serious."

"I assure you, I'm quite serious." She smiled, but it faded upon seeing Aurelie's expression. "They might not resent Hapless specifically. But a life spent in the service of royals? It could certainly drive one to drastic measures."

"You don't really believe that, do you?"

Iliana adjusted her grip on the branches she had collected. "I believe we have a fire to build."

"Wait." Aurelie grabbed her arm. Iliana looked down at it, and Aurelie let go immediately. "Just tell me. Honestly. Why aren't we going north?"

"If someone is still pursuing the prince—which I suspect they are—they'll expect us to go straight to the Scholar's City," Iliana said quietly. "I'm taking us the long way 'round. The longer we're in the woods, the safer we'll be. Trust me."

"When I trusted you earlier, I got sucked into the ground."

"That was an unfortunate oversight. I can nearly guarantee that it won't happen again."

"*Nearly* guarantee?"

"Well, nothing is *entirely* guaranteed, is it? I'd look quite the fool if I *entirely* guaranteed it and then you went and got sucked into the ground again."

"Very reassuring."

Iliana smiled. "I try my best."

Eight

They sat around the fire later, eating a meal that Iliana had inexplicably produced from her coat—a baguette, some hard cheese. Quad pointed out some fruit growing from a nearby tree that was safe to eat. Iliana and Hapless both tried some, but Aurelie wasn't willing to risk it. *Pink stripes*, she thought, and bit down on a piece of (slightly stale) bread while Iliana waxed poetic about the fruit.

They recounted the ambush while they ate, Hapless praising everyone's quick thinking and levelheadedness and magic ability. Quad's first charm in particular garnered a rave review, and Hapless spoke in raptures of the "magical cloud" for some time.

"It was amazing," he concluded. "I wish I could do magic like that."

Quad just huffed, and Aurelie couldn't tell if she was pleased or embarrassed.

"That's my track, at the university," Hapless said. "Magic. I want to be a magic scholar."

"Really?" Aurelie couldn't help herself. It was a little hard to imagine the prince as a scholar of anything, besides maybe being good-natured or wearing very snug waistcoats. "It's just . . . I didn't know it was something people were still studying."

"Of course it is."

"Why did you choose it?"

Hapless tore off a piece of the loaf. "To put it simply, because my brother told me not to."

A smile pulled at Aurelie's lips.

"To put it less simply: I can't imagine knowing that magic exists and choosing not to take an interest in it. It's the most fascinating thing I can think of."

"Plenty of mortals choose not to take an interest in it," Quad said.

"Well, I'm not one of them."

"And neither is Baker," Iliana said.

Hapless looked over at Aurelie, eyes alight. "Do you do magic?"

"A little," Aurelie admitted.

"Baker trained in seeking," Iliana supplied.

"Seeking?" Hapless looked interested. "That's quite rare these days, isn't it?"

"I learned at school," Aurelie said. "But I don't do much magic anymore. I have my apprentice work."

"I suppose one could argue that a good riverberry tart is its own particular brand of magic," Hapless said. "My sister, Honoria, always looks forward to those when she judges mastery for baking."

"Have you awarded any masteries, Prince?" Iliana asked. "I

heard it's a whole"—she waved a hand—"process. Members of the Court looking at paintings and trying on jackets and eating consommé and the like, judging them as worthy or not worthy."

"I'm not actually allowed to declare it," Hapless said, looking a bit sheepish. "At first it was because I wasn't old enough, but since I've come of age, I know it's because no one trusts my judgment." He looked over at Aurelie. "What's it like being an apprentice? Do you enjoy it?"

"It's . . . dependable," Aurelie replied. It was the most diplomatic way she could think to describe it.

"Dependable?"

She shrugged. "I know what each day will look like."

"The same as the one before and the same as the one that will follow," Iliana said. "Honestly, I don't know how you bear it. You don't see nearly enough sunlight. That mentor of yours—"

"Yes, well, none of it is nearly as interesting as Quad's magic was today," Aurelie said, a very transparent change of subject.

Iliana cast her a look, but luckily Hapless was easily shifted. "It's true," he said, turning back to Quad. "You have a gift. I hope to be a fraction as accomplished one day."

"I'm sure you have gifts of your own," Quad said.

"Not really. Though . . . I suppose I can wink pretty well." He winked in Iliana's direction.

Iliana snorted in response. "That's nothing. Everyone can do that."

Hapless smiled winningly. "Maybe so, but can they *pull it off*?"

"What's the point of it?" Quad asked.

"It's a sort of . . . means to communicate without speaking," Hapless said.

"Silent communication." Quad considered this. "That could be useful. So you just shut one eye while keeping the other eye open?"

Quad looked at Aurelie, eyebrows raised, and then shut her left eye. It was still closed when Aurelie said, "I think . . . maybe that's too long? Brevity is better?"

"But it has to be long enough that someone knows that you're doing it on purpose," Hapless added, "and not that you've just gotten something in your eye."

"I'll practice," Quad replied. "I should like to master this wink."

"I've found it quite effective in certain situations," Hapless said.

Aurelie met his eyes for a moment. He winked again.

It was not effective. At least, that's what Aurelie told herself.

"All right, Prince Charming," Iliana said. "Give it a rest."

Hapless smiled. "He was my great-great-great-great-uncle, you know. Historically, he's actually the reason for the Court name convention. Aspirational naming and all that."

"When I was little, I used to think you picked your Court names arbitrarily," Aurelie said. She recalled children's games from school—playing Lady Thoughtful and Lord Kind to learn table manners and etiquette. But she also recalled the imaginary games they invented at free time, and being the Honorable Squash or Baroness Emergency.

"Well, some say it's meant to capture a quality one wishes to bestow, though others think it describes a natural inclination already possessed by the bearer. People have gotten creative in the past several decades. Even my own parents challenged convention with my sister, Honoria. It used to be purely adjectives, but now you can have an adverb or a noun and it's considered perfectly acceptable. Like Lady Softly or Lord Justice."

"Or Lady Pith," Aurelie said, sketching a look over at Iliana, who studiously ignored her.

"This fruit," Iliana said. "Have I mentioned how delicious it is?"

"Several times, in fact," Aurelie replied.

"Any progress with Lady Pith, then, Iliana?" Hapless asked with interest. "I seem to remember you speaking fondly of her—"

"I think we should talk about something else."

"Speaking fondly?" Aurelie asked. "How interesting."

"Heaven help me," Iliana muttered.

Hapless finished off his piece of bread and then brushed his hands together, away from himself to avoid getting crumbs on his clothes. "What about you, Quad? Any paramours? Are you currently in love, or have you ever been?"

"In love?" Quad's expression grew incredulous. "Me? I'm not old enough to be in *love*. I'm just a child!"

"What? You are?"

"But of course! Of course I'm a child!" Her expression was aghast as she regarded each of them in turn. "Isn't it obvious?"

"But . . . you said you were *older than many trees*!" Aurelie exclaimed.

"That's not very old for a troll! That's quite young indeed!"

"If you were equivalent to a mortal child, how old would you be?" asked Hapless.

"It's difficult to say. Mortal youth are rather stupid."

"If you're a child, then where is your family?" Hapless asked next. His tone was kind, artfully skirting *impertinent* and grounding the question as *merely curious.*

The mirth faded from Quad's face. "Well." She folded her arms across her broad chest. "It's not so similar to how it is with Commonfolk. We're independent, you see. My family, they . . ." She trailed off. "It's different."

"You just get to roam the Kingdom, having adventures? As a child?"

"Perhaps I'm . . . Perhaps I've been more independent than most."

It was quiet, the flickering of the fire casting a warm glow.

"Older than many trees but too young to fall in love," Hapless mused eventually. After another pause, he added: "I suppose I'm younger than many trees."

"But old enough to fall in love?" Quad said.

Aurelie couldn't help but look at Hapless then. He leaned back on his elbows and turned his eyes to the sky.

"Maybe," he replied. "I don't know." He smiled. "We mortal youth are rather stupid, you know."

Aurelie found it difficult to settle down that evening. Quad disappeared after their supper, and eventually Hapless stretched out a little ways from the fire, curled in on himself, and fell asleep.

Iliana sat with her back resting against a tree, reading a newspaper by the light of the fire. Eventually Aurelie crossed over and sat down next to her, for lack of anything better to do.

"Where did you get that?" She gestured at the paper.

"I had it delivered. Didn't you see the cart pass by?"

"Ha ha."

Iliana indicated her coat. "Brought it along. Naturally."

"Oh, naturally. For a bit of light reading?"

"Yes, in fact. Is that shocking?"

Aurelie never really thought about what Iliana might read in her spare time.

"I pictured you more of a Gothic romance sort."

"Who says I don't have one of those in here too?" Iliana said, and then turned back to the paper.

"Anything interesting?" Aurelie didn't feel ready to sleep yet. In fact, despite the day's walking, she felt more invigorated than she had in a very long time.

"Well, I'm only on chapter five, but I've heard that the tale of Blaise the highwayman and Isadora the innkeeper's daughter gets pretty lurid."

"I meant in the *paper*."

Iliana rolled her eyes, then shifted the angle of the paper so that Aurelie could look too. A series of headlines jumped out from the page:

CROP PRICES DIP DESPITE SOUTHERN TRADE DEALS

PRESSURE MOUNTS IN COURT AS KING PUSHES FOR NORTHERN PASS THROUGH UNDERWOOD

And at the bottom:

"COMMON KING" REASSERTS CLAIM OF ROYAL BIRTHRIGHT

"Common King?" Aurelie said.

Iliana made a noise of disapproval. "Sylvain Copperend. Have you heard of him?"

The name sounded familiar. From chatter in the bakery,

maybe, or one of Mrs. Basil's monologues. *Self-made, as one should be these days. There's honor in it, dignity, isn't there, rather than being* handed *everything.*

"He's New Rich," Aurelie said.

Amusement flickered in Iliana's eyes. "What do you know of the New Rich?"

Aurelie frowned, indignant. "I know things."

"Certainly. Your skills with bread are unparalleled. But I didn't think you kept up much with politics, or Court gossip, either. Copperend's a bit of both."

"Who is he?"

"In reality, he's a tradesman, and a rather successful one at that. But by his count, he's the rightful king."

"What?"

"He claims to be the late queen's long-lost older brother. It's utter rubbish. A blatant attempt at a power grab." She turned her gaze back to the page. "The worst part is, there are some who truly believe him."

"How is that possible?"

Iliana shrugged. "The queen did have an older brother."

"Valiant," Aurelie said. Maybe she wasn't acquainted with the latest news from the Capital, but she had studied the royal lineage in school like everyone else. Hapless's mother, Queen Noble, was indeed the second born, but her brother, Valiant, had died as an infant.

"Yes. Copperend claims that Valiant's death was faked. That he was spirited away and hidden in the countryside, raised rough-hewn and *for the people.*" She snorted. "Copperend himself is quite rich, though, so I don't know how acquainted he is with the actual circumstances of the people." She shook her head. "He's at best a fraud and at worst . . ." She paused, considering. "Well. He's of particular interest to me."

"Why?"

"His apprentice. Former apprentice. Someone you're a bit familiar with by now."

Aurelie frowned. "Elias Allred?"

Iliana nodded. "The very one."

"You think Copperend might have something to do with his disappearance?"

"I haven't ruled it out, that's for certain." Iliana closed the paper and folded it up. "We should get some rest."

"I'm not tired."

Iliana stood and took her coat off, spreading it out on the ground. "Just shut your eyes and you'll begin to get sleepy."

"I'm not a child."

"Oh really?" Iliana stretched out on the coat. "How many trees are you older than?"

"Honestly, I don't know why I put up with you."

Iliana pillowed her head on her arms. "It's because you crave adventure a great deal more than you're aware."

Aurelie didn't reply.

"Good night, Baker," Iliana said, and closed her eyes.

Nine

When Aurelie woke the following morning, the prince was gone.

She sat up abruptly, her blood running cold. He wasn't called *Hapless* for nothing, after all. Could he have been spirited away in the night? Did he stumble and fall into another earth-dweller's domain?

She looked over to where Iliana was still sleeping, entirely unaware. Her brow was smooth, her face soft. The transformation was remarkable. Iliana looked just her age when she was asleep, younger even, and totally unguarded.

"He went that way," Quad said.

Aurelie startled. She hadn't noticed her at all, but suddenly there stood Quad at the base of one of the larger trees. She looked a bit tree-ish herself.

"Perhaps you'll want to check on him," Quad suggested.

Aurelie nodded and got to her feet, heading off in the direction Quad had indicated.

She wound her way through the trees, the ground gradually

sloping downward, and realized it was leading to a small stream, water clear and sparkling as it burbled over smooth stones.

Hapless stood beside the stream. His boots were off, his pants rolled up. His waistcoat was strewn on a nearby bush, and he was bare-chested, holding up his shirt, head bent in examination of it.

The line of his shoulders in the morning light was . . .

Not something to be considered.

Aurelie turned back but stepped on a stick inadvertently— the loud crunch of it couldn't be ignored.

"Aurelie!" Hapless called, and when she looked back, he gave her a merry wave. "Good morning!"

"Is it?"

"I suppose so, don't you?" He gestured, indicating the stream, the willows bent toward it, the dappled light. Then he looked down and seemed to realize. "Ah. Sorry." He fumbled to get back into the shirt, which was fully wet. "Sorry. I was trying to do a bit of spot cleaning"—the shirt fell over his head—"but then I accidentally dropped it in the stream. Had to wade in to fish it out." His head emerged, and with it, a sheepish expression. "Got a knack for it, you know."

"Wading?"

"Dropping things."

"If only it was a sport," Aurelie said before she could stop herself. Hapless's face broke into a smile.

Aurelie stepped toward him. "I could—" she stopped short.

"What?" He moved a little closer.

"There's a transformation," she said, and reached a hand out. "I'd just need to . . ."

She placed her hand lightly on his shoulder and pushed

a little magic forth. The shirt grew dry under her palm, the dry spot spreading outward, water wicking away.

Hapless watched, transfixed.

"That's a great skill to have," he murmured.

"Hm?"

"Spilling things sort of accompanies the habit of dropping things."

Aurelie smiled.

And then the prince's shirt was dry, completely, and she was still touching him.

"Sorry." She pulled her hand away as if burned. That's how it felt, palms hot with magic.

"What will it cost?" he asked.

"Pardon?"

"That sort of spell. What's the consequence?"

Aurelie wasn't entirely certain. She used the spell on her own clothes every now and again and had never noticed any negative effect. "You're the one studying magic."

Hapless's expression faltered, his gaze shifting away.

"Yes," he said.

And then: "I am."

And then: "Doing that."

And finally: "I suppose."

"Sounds pretty definitive," Aurelie said, and the prince's lips twitched, a bit of mirth reappearing in his eyes.

"Well. The truth is, it's been . . . Things have been . . . School has not exactly . . ." He looked up at her now. "I barely passed my classes last year. I can't remember the theories. My enchantments are dreadful. Sometimes I think my feather test was a false positive."

"You did the feather test?"

"Of course. Every child in the Kingdom does the feather test."

Aurelie had assumed that royals were exempt from that sort of thing. That a royal's magical ability would simply be . . . observed, and then noted, doors would be opened, hands shaken, school acceptances bestowed. Wasn't that how it worked for people like Hapless?

Aurelie recalled her own test all too well—the headmistress's stuffy office, the lamps burning low in the late afternoon of winter. First-year students were called in one by one to sit in a spindly wooden chair in front of Headmistress's desk. Headmistress sat with her arms folded. Her dress was high-collared and pristine. Aurelie liked to imagine that Headmistress's clothes were too afraid of her to wrinkle.

Miss Ember had stood behind Headmistress, looking even softer and younger by comparison, and gently asked a ten-year-old Aurelie to look at the feather sitting on the otherwise empty desk and imagine it as something—anything—else.

"Why?" Aurelie had asked, because even though Headmistress was intimidating, Miss Ember wasn't the kind of teacher who would call it *impertinence*. She always encouraged questions.

"It's a game," replied Miss Ember. "We would both very much like to see you play it."

Aurelie thought it was a rather strange game. And rather unlike most games, which usually had rules, and actionable steps, and a reason to play. There no way to win at imagining a feather.

"Am I supposed to say what I imagine?"

Headmistress opened her mouth to speak, but Miss Ember was faster. "No. Just in your mind."

"But how will you know?"

"You'll make us see."

"Make you see?" Aurelie repeated. It really was a curious game. She had to think of the feather as being—say, blue or purple with white spots. It was jet-black currently, iridescent in the light from the lamps. Purple with white spots wouldn't do; it really was a beautiful black. Aurelie thought of the bird that must have shed it, lovely dark wings flapping against a midnight sky. She thought of the feather as it would have appeared, gleaming in the moonlight, and thought wasn't it a shame that the feather couldn't go join its fellows, that it had been discarded in this way. If only it could take flight and seek out the bird again, if only it could find its way home—

Miss Ember let out a soft breath. Aurelie looked up at her, but Miss Ember wasn't looking back. She was staring instead at the feather, which now hovered in the air above the desk. The three of them watched as the feather glided upward and then drifted toward the open window and quietly passed through it.

Aurelie was stricken. Headmistress's expression was not pleased.

"I'm sorry," Aurelie said. "I . . . hope it wasn't an important feather."

"What did you imagine?" asked Miss Ember, a note of something in her voice that Aurelie couldn't place.

Aurelie didn't speak. It must have been a very important feather.

"Answer, child," Headmistress said.

"I only thought of how the feather might like to rejoin its . . . its bird. The bird that it fell from. I thought of the bird in the nighttime, and—" It sounded so foolish, saying it out loud, but Aurelie continued anyway: "How nice it must have looked in the moonlight."

Maybe imagining the feather could make it reappear. Aurelie tried frantically to envision it floating back through the window and settling onto the desk. But it was no use— the feather didn't return.

Aurelie was dismissed from the room, and when the door closed behind her, she walked away loudly and then tiptoed back as noiselessly as she could. She had to know if she was in trouble for what had happened to the feather—or what the point of the game was in the first place.

Miss Ember normally spoke softly, but now her voice was raised slightly, impassioned. "She should be taken to the Scholar's City at once."

Headmistress, in contrast, sounded unmoved. "Her family can't afford the likes of that. They can barely keep her here."

"Surely there are scholarships—"

"What would you have her do when she arrived there?" Headmistress's tone was withering. "Join classes at the university? She's a child."

"There will be dedicated tutors there, for those with her gift. More resources to offer her than we have here—"

"Nonsense."

"We've seen fifty girls today, and of the mere handful demonstrating an aptitude for magic, not one, not *one* could even *approach*—"

"Ember—"

"She opened the window!"

Aurelie frowned. She certainly didn't remember doing that.

Miss Ember's voice softened, and Aurelie had to lean in to hear. "That was no mere transformation."

Headmistress's tone, in response, was crisp: "Nonetheless."

Silence followed. Aurelie worried that the conversation was over, that Miss Ember would leave and discover her in the hallway, so she hurried away.

She didn't even realize that what she had done was magic. Not until Miss Ember called her into her office the following evening and said, "I'd like to give you some lessons, outside of class. I'd like us to talk about magic. I think it's an important subject to learn about. Is that something you would be interested in?"

An important subject to learn about. Nobody really seemed to think that magic was important. But Miss Ember did.

"Yes," Aurelie replied, and thus her education in magic began.

The memory of it all made something squeeze uncomfortably in her chest as she stood with the prince in the Underwood. She pushed those thoughts from her mind and tried instead to imagine a school-aged Hapless, round cheeked and bright eyed, making his own feather dance or turn to jelly while some royal magician looked on in amusement.

"What happened to yours?" Aurelie asked. "Your feather?"

"I made it disappear," Hapless replied. "Or rather, I made it invisible. Clear? Or the same color as the table. I suppose there are a number of ways one could interpret it, but for all purposes, it was as if it had vanished. Only when the proctor reached out . . . Well, it changed back as soon as he made contact with it."

"Why did you make it disappear?"

Hapless shrugged. "No good reason, really."

"You must've thought of something in the moment."

He looked a bit sheepish. "I wanted to play. Outside, a real game, with Honoria or Gallant, and I thought to myself, if only this feather were gone, then I wouldn't have to be here, doing this. And then suddenly . . . it *was* gone. Like magic."

"Not *like* magic," Aurelie said. "Actual magic."

"I've thought about it since. Wondered if . . . if someone else in the room made it happen. I can hardly transform an acorn now. My mentor says it's a lack of focus. That it's not enough to want to do it. One has to *focus the desire*. Is that . . . ?" His throat bobbed on a swallow. "Is that how you feel? Do you think that's right?"

"I don't know."

Hapless cast a doubtful look.

"No, truly. I know there are theories, of course. Attempts to explain it or rationalize it, but . . . at the core of it, I don't know. You just . . . reach inside yourself and it's there."

"So one either has it or they don't."

"I . . ." Aurelie thought of the time Mrs. Basil went to the opera, how she spent the weeks that followed warbling arias in an uneven soprano. "I think it's like how some people are naturally good singers. And some people can take lessons."

Hapless looked chagrined. "You could train me for a thousand years and I'd never be able to sing Faustival from

Fugue and Fury. Some people are just hopeless." He shook his head. "I may in fact be the worst magic scholar who ever existed."

Aurelie smiled a little. "Well. At least you exist."

A small smile tipped Hapless's lips in return.

"Should we get back to the others?" Aurelie said. "Iliana will wonder where we've gone."

Hapless nodded.

They headed back toward the trees, Aurelie leading the way. She squeezed between several large cations, their trunks growing thick and close. She didn't spot the large root sticking out of the dirt—wasn't aware of it until her foot caught on it, and suddenly she stumbled—she fell—

And kept falling.

Ten

The feeling was the same as before—the slide of earth beneath her, the expectation of solid ground where there was none. It was a bit like thinking there's another stair on a staircase and stepping out onto nothing—yet it was gone in an instant. Aurelie squeezed her eyes shut, expecting the press of dirt, the feeling of hands gripping her, but when she opened her eyes, she was . . .

Not underground.

Also, decidedly no longer in the woods.

Aurelie was in a garden—a scraggly one, situated behind a building with a thatched roof and diamond-paned windows. A clear blue sky stretched overhead. She was standing in the center of an overgrown path that snaked between a bed of ornamentals and a vegetable patch.

There was an odd sense of unreality about it—to have been in the Underwood just a moment before, surrounded by trees and steps away from the prince, and now—

Aurelie took a step forward, and though she felt exceedingly foolish, reached out to touch a blossom on one of the flowering bushes. Was it real? Was this some sort of . . . illusion? A vision?

Before her fingertips could connect with the petals, someone spoke from behind her.

"Well, that was unusual."

Aurelie whipped around. It was Hapless.

"What are you—" she began, just as he said, "Are you all right?"

"How did you—"

"You disappeared," Hapless said. "Through the circle."

Aurelie looked down at where the prince stood. There, on the ground beneath his feet, was a seeking circle.

Without thinking, Aurelie grabbed his arm and quickly pulled him away from it.

He looked at her curiously but didn't shake her hand off.

(Aurelie really should've let go, but she didn't for a moment, and didn't want to ponder why.)

"You might fall back through," she explained hastily.

"I didn't fall through—*you* fell through," he replied evenly. "I jumped through."

"Why would you do that?"

"Because you fell through. Seemed a bit perilous. You could have been in danger."

"So could you!" She gripped his sleeve tighter for some reason. "You should've gone and gotten Iliana instead of jumping into *potential oblivion!*"

"Nothing ventured, nothing gained, that's what I always say," he said cheerfully. "And anyway—" He cast a look around. "Wherever we are, at least neither of us is here alone."

Aurelie released Hapless's arm and approached the circle. It was etched into the packed dirt of the path. The symbols were the same. Everything about it appeared the same as any seeking circle Aurelie had ever drawn herself.

She picked up a nearby pebble and tossed it into the circle.

It lay there in the dirt, unremarkable.

"We're no longer in the north," Hapless said. "That's curious."

"What? How do you know that?"

"Heartfruit." He nodded toward a stand of small trees at the edge of the garden. "They only bloom pink south of the Underwood. I'd say we're in the Meadowlands. Eastern, probably?" He gestured to the building. "They prefer shingles in the west, and farther south would take us toward the Capital, which tends more toward the modern styles, though right now there's somewhat of a classical resurgence. It's quite odd, people tearing down perfectly good houses just to build them back up to look centuries older than they are—"

As Hapless spoke, Aurelie knelt and tentatively reached out to rest her fingertips atop the circle. Nothing happened. She pressed downward into the dirt, but it didn't give. Nothing but solid ground.

"It doesn't work both ways," she murmured, and then looked at Hapless, her stomach clenching at the full realization: "We can't get back."

"Hm." A wrinkle appeared between his brows. "I suppose we'll have to . . . readjust our course?"

"That's putting it lightly."

"It's not such a hardship, is it?"

Maybe *hardship* wasn't quite right, but *disaster* might work.

Or *catastrophe.* Aurelie couldn't tamp down a growing sense of panic. "We've been *flung asunder*! We have no idea where we are!"

"I'd say we're at least a little *sundered.* Eastern Meadowlands and all—"

Aurelie climbed to her feet and cast a frantic look around, as if some other seeking circle with transportive abilities might reveal itself just down the path. It did not.

"Yes, on account of the roofing and the random trees," she said. "I swear, you must've taken the same strange course in annoyingly targeted clue-finding as Iliana—"

Hapless smiled, bright and brief, and then tried to look as if he hadn't.

"What?" Aurelie said. "What is it?"

"Nothing. It's just—you're funny, is all."

"I'm not trying to be funny."

"Maybe you can't help it. My sister says natural gifts just . . . manifest."

"We're stuck here." Aurelie could hardly believe the prince's nonchalance. Did he not fully grasp the situation? "Without Iliana or Quad. We have no way to get back."

"I'm sure everything will be just fine," Hapless said kindly.

"That's easy for you to say!" Aurelie couldn't stop the words from bursting forth. "You're royalty! All you have to do is flag down a carriage and make them take you wherever you please!"

"That's not how we generally conduct ourselves."

"Isn't it?"

His expression turned suddenly serious. "That's not how I conduct myself. I wouldn't just hop in a carriage and leave you . . . *asunder.*"

"There's literally nothing preventing you from doing so."

"Well, you saved my life," Hapless said. "Twice."

"Twice?"

"Once in the woods, during the ambush. And once here, when you pulled me out of the circle."

He sounded very earnest, which made Aurelie feel strangely . . . off-kilter. "You weren't in any danger of falling back through," she grumbled. "We established that."

"Nonetheless, the impulse was there. I'd say it still counts."

Aurelie regarded the prince—his expression open, his gaze unwavering—and then very quickly looked away. "Well, technically, you tried to save my life too," she said. "When you threw yourself through the circle."

"Rather heroically, I'd say."

"Foolishly, more like."

Hapless looked again as if he was suppressing a smile and succeeding rather poorly at it. "We're still two to one, which means I'm in your debt." He put a hand over his heart. "So I pledge that I won't abandon you. You have my word as prince, duke of the Northern Realm, and peer of the Scholar's City."

It made Aurelie feel better than she rationally thought it ought to. "Any other titles you'd care to add?"

"Well, I *am* the undisputed ruler of the back third of the Royal Gardens."

"Back third?"

"We divided it up when I was a child. I wanted the back third because it had the best climbing trees. Honoria got the middle third with the rose garden, and Gallant got the front third, with all the stuffy topiaries and classical fountains."

Aurelie couldn't help but smile.

"Let's have a look at the building," Hapless suggested. "I think it might be an inn."

"What annoyingly targeted clue makes you say that?"

"The moss on the back wall is a varietal that only grows on temporary lodgings."

"Truly?"

Hapless's eyes shone. "Certainly not. There's a sign hanging from the side entrance that says 'The Thistledown Inn.'"

Aurelie debated the propriety of smacking a member of the royal family on the arm, and then ultimately decided against it.

She and Hapless approached the building and had nearly reached the side entrance when Aurelie stopped short. "Wait. What if you're recognized? Iliana seemed to think . . ."

Hapless paused and turned to look at Aurelie. "What?"

"She seemed to think that you might still be in danger. That whoever was after you in the woods might . . . still be after you."

Hapless considered this for a moment and then answered definitively. "I'm quite sure I won't be recognized."

"Why?"

"Look around." Hapless waved an arm, encompassing the surroundings. The inn was the only building in sight. A road cut across the land in front of it, but otherwise, there were uninterrupted fields for as far as the eye could see. "It's rather remote, isn't it? I don't imagine many people in these parts are familiar with the royal visages. And anyway, my official portrait is frightfully out of date. Sat for it when I was twelve. I was about a foot shorter and not a quarter as good-looking."

Aurelie's lips twitched.

"I sat for another when I came of age," Hapless continued, "but it hasn't been released to the public yet. I've been in a terrible fight with both my sister and the royal portrait artist about it. The likeness is inadmissible."

"Inadmissible?"

"The distance between my eyes, the sheer *length* and *breadth* of my forehead—it's absolute lunacy. You'd think that I had mortally offended the artist! That I'd sentenced his family to ruin the moment before brush touched canvas!"

"How can you be sure it's not accurate?"

Aurelie couldn't help herself. It was like needling Iliana but maybe even more fun. Iliana often just ignored her, whereas the prince's eyes—which were a very nice brown and spaced to a perfectly reasonable degree—widened in surprise.

"Whatever do you mean by that?" he said.

"It's the rare person who sees themselves as they truly are."

"I've not known you very long, so I'm not sure what I've done in that time for you to say something so hurtful."

"I'm sorry. I haven't seen the portrait, so I suppose I can't truly judge."

"I'm widely thought to be handsome, you know."

"Really. Have you conducted a poll?"

Hapless looked at her for a moment, and somehow the indignation on his face melted into amusement. "You're quite unusual," he said.

"I've always considered myself to be rather ordinary."

"Well. It's the rare person who sees themselves as they truly are."

He smiled, and Aurelie couldn't help but match it.

"Even still," she said after a moment, remembering the matter at hand. "Even if no one here knows your face, you do look . . ." She waved a hand. Hapless peered down at his clothes, which were a bit shabby from a day's wear in the Underwood but still undeniably fashionable. "Conspicuous," Aurelie finished.

"I'm sure I'll blend in," Hapless said confidently. "I'm a little hungry, aren't you? Let's see what they have to offer." He crossed to the entrance and opened the door for Aurelie. "After you."

Aurelie fidgeted for the seventh or eighth time, running her fingers nervously over the embroidery on one of her apron pockets.

She and Hapless were seated at a table by a window that faced the wide lawn in front of the inn. A barmaid had brought them two bowls of soup, a loaf of bread, a wedge of cheese, and a bowl of fresh berries. Under other circumstances, Aurelie would've been thrilled to have such a meal, in such a place (she had never been to the Southern Realm before), and with such a person (the ruler of the back third of the Royal Gardens!).

But she couldn't bring herself to enjoy the meal. However unconcerned Hapless seemed to be about their situation, Aurelie knew it was not a good situation to be in. They needed to figure out a plan.

Hapless's plan, thus far, seemed only to consist of a second bowl of soup when the first one was finished.

"Isn't this lovely?" he said, tearing off a hunk of bread. "Just . . . being out among the people, enjoying the atmosphere and the good cheer? It's all very . . . pastoral and . . . *soul-satisfying*, don't you think?"

Aurelie's soul did not feel satisfied. It felt anxious. "For most everyone, it's just a normal day," she said.

"Yes, but not for either of us." He glanced up at Aurelie, and she suddenly felt compelled to look away. "What sort of business is that mentor of yours running, anyway? Sounds as if you never leave the place."

"Yes, well. The dough won't make itself."

"It must pay well."

"It pays in experience."

Hapless frowned. "Experience won't buy food or lodging."

"One day it will."

Hapless considered that for a moment and then turned back to his food with renewed vigor. "Is it your dream, then?" he said between bites. "To be a baker?"

"It's my goal."

"Is that different from a dream?"

"I'd say so."

It was quiet for a moment—just the murmur of the other diners, the clink of dishes and silverware. Aurelie cast a quick look around the room to make sure that they hadn't drawn anyone's attention. She couldn't shake Iliana's words from the evening before: *If someone is still pursuing the prince—which I suspect they are—*

But no one seemed to be paying them any mind. Aurelie picked a berry from the bowl and bit into it. It was delicious, even under the circumstances.

"I suppose I have neither," Hapless said eventually. "Dream nor goal. Truthfully, there's no reason I'd need either."

"Why not?"

Hapless took a large bite of bread and talked around it. "I'm third born. It doesn't quite matter what I do. So long as nothing happens to my brother and sister, I'm entirely superfluous."

He said it very matter-of-factly. Aurelie frowned. "You can't truly think so little of yourself."

"I don't think little of myself. It's just the truth. It's freeing, in a way."

Before Aurelie could reply, the barmaid appeared at their table.

"Is there anything else I can get for you?"

"No, thank you," Hapless said. "It's delicious. Fit for a king."

The barmaid's eyes lit up. "That's quite apt, today of all days." She leaned in confidentially, dropping her voice. "We just so happen to have royalty here at this very moment."

Hapless choked on his drink.

"Sorry?" Aurelie said, thrusting a napkin his way.

The barmaid's eyes shone. "The lost king Valiant is dining with us today."

The prince stopped coughing long enough to choke out, "Sylvain Copperend?"

"The very one. So you've heard of him too? I don't see how the rumors could be true, but his manner does make you wonder. . . . He's got an air about him, to be sure. *Silver-tongued*, my mother would say. I've never seen one of 'em myself—the royals—but I'm sure they'd be just of his ilk."

"Where is he?" Hapless asked.

"Dining in the back room. He's gathered up everyone with a bit of influence from the nearest villages. You should see Augustus Tailor—never looked so proud of himself. I've forgotten, did you say you'd be needing anything else?"

"We're quite well, thank you," Aurelie said, and the barmaid retreated.

Hapless set his napkin aside and went to stand.

"Where are you going?"

"I want to see him."

"Why?"

"Because he—"

"Eliza!" A booming voice cut through the dining room at that moment, and a crowd of men began filtering in. Among them was a man in an impeccably cut jacket and waistcoat. He was middle-aged or thereabout, broad-chested and tall, with shoulder-length hair that had just a bit of silver in it. It had to be Copperend. A glance at Hapless confirmed it—the prince's eyes had narrowed.

Copperend approached a woman and clasped her hands. He spoke loudly, like an actor onstage, aware of the audience. "Thank you for your hospitality, truly. A sumptuous feast. Far better than we deserve."

"Are all the matters of state settled, then?" The woman—the innkeeper, Aurelie assumed—said with a smile.

"We've made a start." Copperend turned and observed the patrons gathered at their tables, most of whom who were looking back. "It was a delight to dine among you."

His gaze swept the room. His eyes landed on Hapless and Aurelie.

Aurelie nudged Hapless under the table.

"I'm quite sure he doesn't recognize me," Hapless murmured.

After a moment, Copperend's gaze moved on.

He bade farewell to the innkeeper and the room as a whole and then headed out, some of the men going with him, others settling in at the bar.

Aurelie let out a breath. When she looked over at Hapless, his expression was troubled.

"It's not right," he said. "Putting about that sort of rumor. I don't know how anyone could believe him."

Aurelie didn't know what to say.

Hapless's expression cleared after a moment, and he turned back to his food. "We shouldn't let it spoil our meal."

"Certainly not," Aurelie said, reaching for a handful of berries. "After all, there's no saying when we'll get to have something so *pastoral* and *soul-satisfying* again."

Hapless's eyes twinkled. "Are you mocking me?"

"That would be improper."

"I can assure you, it's perfectly proper to mock a member of the royal family when the occasion calls for it. You should've seen the outfit my brother chose for the midsummer festival last year. It had a full-length cape."

"Is that worthy of mockery?"

Hapless looked affronted. "A *full-length cape?* For a daytime affair? I'd say so."

Aurelie smiled. "I'll keep that in mind for my next midsummer festival."

Eleven

Eventually, the meal drew to a close. Hapless would've had it go on much longer, sitting there in front of the window overlooking the Meadowlands. Sitting across from Aurelie, who was . . . far more interesting than the Meadowlands. Potentially more interesting than anyone Hapless had ever met.

She ate slowly and carefully, as if trying to make the food last as long as possible. (Hapless, in contrast, ate as quickly and indecorously as possible—if one is questing, one might as well enjoy oneself, etiquette be damned.) Aurelie peered out at the scenery often, but when her eyes met Hapless's every now and then, he couldn't help but feel it as a sort of achievement.

She was remarkably easy to talk to. And funny, Hapless thought, in a way that people didn't often allow themselves to be around him. And when the corners of her lips twitched at something he said—well, that felt like an even better achievement.

The luncheon couldn't last forever, though, no matter how many additional bowls of soup Hapless ordered. (Four, in total. Adventuring was hard work, after all.) Eventually, it was time to settle the bill.

This was something Hapless had not considered.

"What?" Aurelie said. It must have shown in his expression. Hapless had always lamented his face's ability to do that—to so easily project thoughts or emotions that he'd prefer to keep to himself.

"It's just . . . I don't often carry money."

Aurelie looked aghast. "Truly?"

Hapless shrugged, a bit sheepish. "Maybe they'll let us wash dishes."

"What was your plan when you sat down?"

"I was distracted. Focused on the meal and all."

Aurelie let out a sigh and then fumbled with something under the table for a moment before producing several bills.

Hapless's eyes widened. "Did you make those just now? With magic?"

Aurelie gave him a withering look. "You can't just *conjure* money. If you could, I'd have a team of racehorses from Ardent Fields by now."

"That's awfully specific."

"Blame Iliana." She stood. "Stay here."

Hapless did as he was told, casting a look around the dining room as Aurelie went to find the barmaid. The crowd had thinned, but there were still some men from Copperend's gathering sat here and there, drinking ale and looking self-important.

That was Copperend's method—traveling to far-flung

parts of the Kingdom and gathering supporters. He had requested an audience with Gallant not a month before, while the family was staying at Winsome House, the western estate. Gallant had gone as far as to meet with him. Hapless didn't know exactly what was discussed, but Gallant had been angry enough afterward that he broke two grass-ball rackets and a decorative bust of Great-Aunt Temperance.

Aurelie returned, and they took their leave. She and Hapless had just stepped outside when someone spoke.

"You could've saved me some fruit, at the very least."

It was Iliana. Casually leaning against the wall of the inn as if she were waiting for a carriage.

Aurelie looked stunned. "How did you get here?"

Hapless was less surprised. Iliana was, as Gallant would put it, *results-oriented.* Of course she would figure out a way to find them. "Indomitable, that's Iliana," he said with a grin.

"Where's Quad?" Aurelie asked.

"Here."

Hapless turned. Quad stood behind them, looking placid.

Aurelie looked even more shocked. "When did you—how did you—"

"All in good time, Baker," Iliana said. "For now, let's go somewhere a little more private, shall we?"

She led them to the grove of heartfruit trees behind the inn. Three of them settled down on the ground, but Quad stood, looking up at the branches overhead. She flicked a finger, and a piece of fruit fell into her open hand. She offered it to Hapless, but he shook his head. That fourth bowl of soup may have been slightly inadvisable.

"When we realized you both were missing, it wasn't hard

to track you to that circle," Iliana told them. "We debated the pros and cons of going through it ourselves—"

"We also conducted experiments," Quad added as she summoned several more pieces of fruit. "We threw a few things through first."

"Ultimately, we determined it was worth the risk, since we had very little else to go on to find you. Besides the seeking stones, of course, but it's not as if either of us knows how to use them. And anyway, it wouldn't do to lose a member of the royal family—my reputation would take years to recover."

"But you think it *could* recover." Hapless couldn't help but feel amused. "If you lost me."

"The circle doesn't work both ways," Aurelie said.

"I know," Iliana replied. "I don't suppose you could draw up one that would get us back?"

Aurelie shook her head. "I've never heard of that kind of magic before. I didn't even know it was possible."

"But you did it in the forest," Iliana said. "That's how your little tree friend got ahold of you, remember?"

Hapless frowned. "Tree friend?"

"A demon," Quad said.

"A *demon*?"

Iliana waved a hand. "It's reductive. Apparently."

"I didn't do it on purpose," Aurelie said. "Who knows what influence the forest has? That's why people shouldn't go into the Underwood."

"Well, we're not there anymore, are we?" Iliana said.

"We're in the eastern Meadowlands," Hapless supplied helpfully.

"I know." Iliana leaned back on her hands. "I'd reckon we're about a day and a half out from the Capital. At this point, it'd make a great deal more sense to return you to the palace than to try to head back north."

Hapless tried not to sound wounded in his reply. "I'm not a book that's been lent out. I don't need *returning*."

"No." Iliana looked at him evenly. "But someone ambushed your party, remember? Aimed all sorts of pointy weapons at you for reasons unknown?"

Hapless couldn't deny that.

"You'll be safer back with your family."

Hapless didn't love the idea of returning home. But he nodded anyway. "I suppose that's true."

"Excellent. We should get you properly disguised before we set out."

"I'll be fine," Hapless said. "It's not as if I'm on a coin or something. Though I have always thought I'd look dashing on a copper piece."

"Just copper?" Aurelie asked.

"Suits my complexion. Silver would wash me out."

Iliana looked amused. "We won't be in the Meadowlands forever, Prince. Someone will spot you eventually."

Quad led Hapless to sit at the base of one of the heart-fruit trees, his back against the trunk. She peered at him for a moment.

"You didn't do too poorly on your own," she murmured. "But mine will stick a bit better."

"Sorry?"

"Shh," she said, and hovered her hands over his face.

Hapless squeezed his eyes shut in anticipation of . . .

something. Some unpleasant prickling of magic. But there was only a gentle warmth from Quad's hands as she worked.

Hapless peeked through one eye. Aurelie had crossed over and bent down a bit, peering over Quad's shoulder as Quad worked.

"What should your name be?" Aurelie said. "You'll need a new identity to match your disguise."

"What's the opposite of a quadrille?" Quad asked.

"An uncontrolled fall to the floor, I suppose," Iliana said.

"Sounds apt," Quad said. "Maybe we could find a way to shorten it."

"How about Bastian?" Aurelie suggested.

Hapless smiled. Bastian Sinclair was the protagonist of *The Pauper's Play*, a scrappy orphan who grew into success and prosperity. "I like it."

"All done." Quad lowered her hands and stepped away. "What do you think?"

Hapless reached up and touched his face. It felt entirely the same. He supposed the magic wouldn't alter his features intrinsically, just change them to the viewer. The only difference he noted out of the corner of his eye was that his hair, normally brown, was now a somewhat lighter shade.

Aurelie was looking at him curiously, which led him to wonder if he was more handsome now. (Was that even possible? Did she like the disguise better? That certainly wouldn't do.)

Iliana gave him only a cursory glance. "Quite good," she said, and got to her feet. "We'll need to do something about your clothes, though."

Hapless looked down. He hadn't had the heart to abandon

his waistcoat in the woods the prior day—it was bespoke, after all. "I assure you, this is the very height of fashion."

"Yes, and we're in the middle of nowhere." Iliana produced a shirt from one of the pockets of her coat and threw it at him. "Try this instead."

"Do you have an entire wardrobe in there?" Aurelie asked as Hapless ducked behind a tree to change.

"Not an *entire* one," Iliana replied, as if a partial wardrobe were a perfectly reasonable thing to carry around in your pockets (which Hapless supposed it was, if one had the room for it. He would certainly do the same).

When Hapless emerged, Iliana took his proffered shirt and waistcoat and stuffed them into her coat. The coat somehow managed to still look perfectly normal from the outside, not lumpy in the least. Hapless told himself he needed to ask Iliana about her tailor at some point.

"Now that's all sorted, we should be on our way," Iliana said, and the four of them set off together.

Twelve

They journeyed through several small villages, then several larger ones, and stopped eventually at a bakery for a bit of food.

"You should feel right at home," Iliana said to Aurelie as they approached the small clapboard-covered building. But Aurelie didn't feel at home in the slightest; in the end, she waited outside. Something about stepping into a bakery made her stomach twist. It reminded her too much of the responsibilities waiting for her back in her village.

Hapless hung back too, standing out front with Aurelie as Quad and Iliana went inside.

"Lovely village," he said, peering up and down the lane of small shops.

Aurelie made a noise of assent.

She also couldn't help but feel a twinge of worry about going to the Capital. She had never been there before, but surely it must be a big place? Surely there was no way they could possibly run into Mrs. Basil?

"Reminds me of a poem from Carmine," Hapless continued. "'Down the Meadowlands, I heard a flower whisper—'"

"'Through village small and stately, through green wild,'" Aurelie finished, and a grin broke Hapless's face.

"I love her work," he said. "I took a class on poets from the Age of Indifference last semester. It was the only one where I got halfway decent marks."

"She was a magician, you know," Aurelie said. "Carmine."

"Really?"

Aurelie thought of Miss Ember. "One of my teachers had a big book of her poems. She would read them to us in class sometimes. There wasn't much about magic in our normal lessons, so she tried to point out places where it intersected."

"I would've liked to have a teacher like that," Hapless said. "My tutors were always so rigid in their—"

It was at that moment that Aurelie happened to catch sight of a newspaper discarded on the ground, and the headline emblazoned across the front:

PRINCE HAPLESS MISSING: KIDNAPPED IN THE UNDERWOOD! SUSPECTED DEAD?

"Oh no," Aurelie breathed.

"What is it?"

She picked up the paper, and Hapless leaned in to take a look. The warmth of him standing so close shouldn't have affected her.

Shouldn't have, but did. Aurelie's stomach gave a sudden swoop that was both very pleasant and also unsettling, like she had been set off-balance somehow. She tried to ignore it as she began to read:

FROM THE CAPITAL: Notoriously gormless
Prince Hapless was the unwitting victim of an
ambush and kidnapping in the treacherous
Underwood just yesterday morning.

"Notoriously gormless!" Hapless exclaimed. "A bit edito-
rial, don't you think?"

While traveling through the woods, the
prince was ambushed and taken away—

"And anyway, Lord Gormless was my great-aunt's second
husband—"

"Shh," Aurelie said.

The Palace reports that Uncommon magic
was used to persuade the prince from
the company of his party. The prince's
whereabouts are currently unknown. He is
thought to be either living or dead.

"I'm pretty sure everyone who ever existed is thought to
be either living or dead," Hapless scoffed.

Aurelie huffed a laugh, in spite of herself.

Iliana and Quad appeared then, each holding two pasties.
Iliana handed one to Hapless and then frowned, catching sight
of the paper. "'Suspected Dead?' That's a dreadful headline.
You can't just throw any wild assertion out there as a question."

"Exactly," Hapless said. "It's like saying, 'Southern Crop
Blight—Pixies Responsible?'"

Quad took a large bite of pasty. "Pixies would never be interested in something as pedestrian as crop blight."

"Is no one concerned by the contents of the article?" Aurelie said, shaking the newspaper. "They think *we* kidnapped Hapless!"

A description of the kidnappers is as follows:
ONE Common girl, age approximated
between 14–16, small and unremarkable.

"I'm seventeen, for the record," Aurelie muttered.

ONE Common girl, age approximated
between 18–20, wearing a large overcoat.
Dashing and competent.

"I don't know who wrote this, but I like them," Iliana said.

ONE Uncommonfolk, age unknown,
appearance unknown.

"Now, how did you pull that off?" Iliana asked, and Quad shrugged.

"Your magic wore off, though," Aurelie said. "Whatever you did to the steward to convince him to let Hapless go, it doubled back and made him twice as suspicious!"

"That's not how our magic works," Quad said.

"Well, that's how it worked this time! They think we're kidnappers! Look at this—'Palace guards have been dispatched toward the Underwood in search of the prince.' They're looking for us right now."

They all looked around then, but the street was mostly empty, aside from a woman passing by with a small child in tow, who was clutching an over-large cinnamon roll. Hapless beamed at the sight of them and gave a small wave. The little boy waved back.

"Stop that!" Aurelie hissed. "Don't draw attention to yourself!"

"It's fine," Hapless said. "If we're approached by guards, I'll simply explain to them what happened."

"You're forgetting something," Iliana said, and Hapless looked at her expectantly. "The people who ambushed you in the woods were just that—*guards*. They were wearing the palace livery. So who's to say that all the guards out there looking for you right now are legitimate ones? What if the same ones with nefarious intentions are mixed in?"

"And we hand you over to them, and then you really are kidnapped," Aurelie finished.

"Hm." A small crease appeared between Hapless's eyebrows. "What do we do?"

"Well, first of all, we stop having this conversation in the middle of the street." Iliana ushered the whole group ten steps to the left, into an alley between the bakery and the building next door.

"Yes, this is much less suspicious," Aurelie said.

"*Second*," Iliana continued, ignoring her, "we consider the positives—Hapless is disguised, so that's good."

"But they have descriptions of us!" Aurelie said.

"'Small and unremarkable'? The level of detail staggers."

"You need to take off your coat."

"I don't see why that would be necessary," Iliana replied,

looking affronted. "Can't you . . . glamour it or something?"

"Glamour it?" Aurelie repeated. "Uh, maybe I could *a hundred years ago.*"

"Astonishing, you don't look a day over fourteen."

"It's true, no one teaches glamours anymore," Hapless said. "It's well accepted that advances in face paint and wig-work have been significant enough to outweigh the possible consequences of glamouring—"

"What would you call what Quad did to you?" Iliana asked.

"I wouldn't call it a glamour," replied Quad.

"Sounds definitive," said Hapless.

Iliana threw her hands in the air. "Yes, fine, I'm hopelessly out of touch with magical convention. Can we proceed here?"

"Yes. Take off your coat," Aurelie said.

"The coat is inconsequential!"

Aurelie shook her head. "*One* unremarkable baker. *One* dashing, *coat-wearing* idiot—"

Iliana frowned. "Unwarranted."

"And *one* Uncommonfolk, along with, well, what do you know—a slightly blond version of the missing, kidnapped, suspected-dead prince!"

"You know, if you had criticisms of my disguise-work, you could've raised them earlier," Quad muttered.

"Would we call this blond?" Hapless asked, trying to inspect a lock of hair.

Aurelie let out a strangled sound.

"More of a sandy blond," Iliana replied, and then turned to Aurelie. "Baker. Please. I know this is stressful—"

"I'm going to get *thrown in jail!*"

"I won't let that happen." Hapless's expression turned suddenly serious. "Truly. We'll sort everything out."

"How?"

"We'll proceed to the Capital," he said. "In the next larger village, we'll find transportation. We can stay out of the way overnight and reach the city by midday tomorrow. Quad will . . . *tweak* . . . my disguise, and we'll be sure not to call attention to ourselves. It'll be fine. No guards—legitimate or otherwise—will find us."

It sounded reasonable, if you put aside everything that was completely unreasonable about the entire situation.

Aurelie took a breath. Then she nodded. "All right."

Hapless smiled. "Excellent."

Thirteen

In the next large village, they caught a hackney cart headed southward. They purchased passage in pairs—Iliana and Quad, Hapless and Aurelie—and were seated accordingly in the large horse-drawn wagon, a handful of other folks between them. No one gave Aurelie and Hapless a second glance, except for a young woman sitting across from Hapless who kept darting her eyes in his direction and then smiling shyly and looking away. For a moment Aurelie wondered if the young woman had recognized him, but Quad had gone back in with her not-a-glamour and lightened Hapless's hair further, altered the planes of his face to be a bit more angular, and sprouted some stubble.

So it wasn't that the young woman recognized him. It was simply that Hapless was universally appealing, no matter what he looked like. Aurelie remembered what her mother had said about Queen Noble's "glow." *She wasn't beautiful, but she was very striking. The way a piece of art ought to be.* Hapless wasn't like a piece of art at all—something you could admire but never touch. There was a sort of radiance about him, to be sure, but his open and friendly nature made it accessible and therefore all the more appealing.

Right at that moment, he was talking jovially with a man seated on the other side of him—a woodworker from the Middlelands who was heading toward the Capital in hopes of selling some wares.

"I think I'll get a decent price at the Upmarket," the man said. "What do you reckon, one silver for the small bowls, three for the large?"

"Seems fair," replied Hapless, who had clearly never purchased a bowl in his life. He probably didn't even know what a loaf of bread cost.

"I use only the finest wood, of course." The man obviously sensed an opportunity for a sale. He pulled a small wooden bowl out of his pack. It really was beautiful—the wood grain was smooth, and a simple circular design was etched into the outer rim. "For your lovely companion, perhaps?"

"Ah," Hapless said, eyes darting to Aurelie. "She is—that is to say, we are—"

"Hopelessly in debt," Aurelie said. "From all his spending. But thank you. It's fine craftsmanship."

They left the coach after several hours' ride. Iliana thought it was best to take rooms for the night and continue on in the morning. Twilight had fallen, and the sky was streaked pink and gold, melting into purple dusk.

"Thank you for the conversation," Hapless said to the woodworker before he disembarked. Aurelie saw a flash of silver in

Hapless's palm as they clasped hands, and it was no surprise when he approached her in possession of the small bowl.

"I thought you didn't have any money," Aurelie said as they started down the wide road through the village center. Quad and Iliana walked ahead of them, heads bent in conversation.

Hapless looked rather proud. "I found it in my boot."

"We could've used that to pay for our food this morning!"

"I didn't know it was in there then." He extended the bowl toward her. "For you."

Aurelie blinked. She wanted to take it and clutch it to her chest, but at the same time, she also felt the urge to hit him over the head with it. "What am I meant to do with that?"

Hapless shrugged. "Put fruit in it?"

"It's too small for fruit."

"Depends on the fruit," Hapless replied, eyes shining. "Anyway, maybe it'll come in handy. And if it doesn't, at least it's beautiful."

Aurelie swallowed. "I'm afraid I have little use for things that have no purpose."

"Why not have something just because it brings you joy?"

Anything Aurelie got, Mrs. Basil would take. *Everything under my roof belongs to me*, she was fond of saying. Aurelie would rather give up Hapless's gift than have it go to Mrs. Basil.

It wasn't worth explaining, so Aurelie just said, "Give it to Iliana. She can keep it in her coat."

Disappointment flashed across Hapless's face, but he managed a smile in spite of it. "You know, one day you may wish you had a bowl."

"I'll think of you if that day arrives."

The smile turned brighter. "I do hope you'll think of me before then."

There was only one inn in the village, and only one room available that evening.

"Sorry, miss," the clerk told Iliana. "There are many folks traveling for the season."

"It's fine. One room will suffice," Iliana said. "For me and . . . my brother." She gestured to the prince. "And his wife." Indicating Aurelie. "And . . . my wife." She gestured to Quad. "That's us. Just . . . one big family."

They received the heavy metal key to the room and were heading up a rickety flight of stairs when Quad turned to Iliana.

"Why am I your wife?"

"No one would believe for a second that I'm Hapless's wife, " Iliana said.

"Why does anyone have to be anyone's wife? None of us is married."

"Don't say that so loudly—the innkeeper will be scandalized."

"I thought you were supposed to be good at subterfuge," Hapless said with amusement.

Iliana glared at him. "It's been a long day, and I don't see anyone else stepping up with credible cover stories."

"Why do we need a cover story at all?" Quad asked. "Why couldn't we just have a room?"

"People would talk. Four unmarried people sharing a room with—"

She swung the door open to reveal—

"One bed. How quaint."

"I'd rather sleep outside," Quad said.

"Well, I'd rather we all stay together," Iliana replied, crossing the room and drawing the window curtains shut.

"I'll sleep on the floor," Aurelie offered.

Hapless looked somewhat alarmed. "No, you shouldn't—"

"I'm used to it," Aurelie said. "I prefer it."

"At least use my coat," Iliana told her. "It's remarkably comfortable to sleep on."

"Of course it is. And at the full moon it sprouts axles and wheels and turns itself into a carriage, doesn't it?"

"It's a remarkable coat," Iliana said loftily.

"So you've said."

Iliana laid the coat on the floor, and when Aurelie sat down on it, she was both surprised and annoyed to find that it was indeed comfortable.

"I'm going out," Iliana declared, "for a short while. I trust you can all stay out of trouble. Quad, you're in charge."

The door shut behind her, and suddenly it was quiet.

Hapless spoke first. "One of you should take the bed."

"I have no need to recline," replied Quad.

"And I've just said I'm quite fine on the floor," Aurelie said.

"Well, I certainly can't sleep on the bed if you're sleeping on the floor."

"Why not?"

Hapless looked offended. "It wouldn't be right! Quite ungentlemanly!"

"Why don't you share it?" Quad said lightly, and Aurelie glared at her.

"That would be . . . Well, I suppose that it's—" Hapless glanced at the bed and then shook his head forcefully. "No, that would hardly be any more . . . gentlemanly. . . ."

"I'm going to sleep," Aurelie said, and made a show of stretching out atop the coat.

"So am I," Hapless said, and sat down on the floor near the fireplace.

"You could at least sleep in the chair if you're going to be stubborn."

"So could you!"

"If you're both going to sleep in the chair, you might as well both sleep in the bed," Quad murmured. "Rather more comfortable, I'd say."

"Good night!" Aurelie said loudly, turning on her side to face the wall.

Quad gave a short exhalation that wasn't definitively a laugh. It wasn't *not* a laugh, either.

Aurelie couldn't sleep.

Iliana had been gone for some time. Hapless was snoring on the floor near the fireplace. Quad was still in the corner—at least, Aurelie thought so. Quad was so motionless, she might as well have been the grandfather clock.

Aurelie heaved a sigh. There was no use in trying. She sat up and contemplated Iliana's coat.

If Iliana could be believed—Aurelie was unsure of that on any count—there was a romance novel in there somewhere. Or, at the very least, a newspaper. Aurelie just had to find it.

The fire had burned low, and it was relatively dark in the

room. So Aurelie did a small enchantment, one of the first she had learned from Miss Ember: she brought a light forth to the ends of each of her fingertips. It didn't break through like a flame, but instead glowed orange under her skin, the same way the outlines of your fingers looked if you held your hand up to the sun to shield your eyes on a bright day. The soft glow would cast enough light to read, or in this case, to search.

The inside of Iliana's coat had a dozen or more pockets sewn into the lining. When Aurelie reached into one, she found that it had much more space than it appeared—so much so that her arm could fit inside, nearly up to the shoulder.

She explored a number of the pockets and found among them a loaf of bread, a handful of coins, a glass bottle (empty), the seeking stones, and curiously, a set of knitting needles and a ball of spun wool.

It was in the sixth pocket that she found a knife.

It wasn't one of the daggers that Iliana wore at her sides or one of the smaller blades normally strapped to her legs. This one had a jet-black handle, unadorned. The blade itself had a design etched into it, a series of loops and spirals. When Aurelie gripped the handle, it seemed to accommodate her hand perfectly. The blade seemed almost to hum.

Aurelie couldn't explain why, but it made her feel uneasy.

She carefully slipped the knife back into the pocket where she found it and continued with her search.

It was in the next pocket that Aurelie discovered a handful of parchment pieces, folded into small squares. They all bore different seals, already torn open—a circle of red and gold wax, a stamp of a tree in black ink, its leaves bare.

She unfolded one square, which revealed two sheets of paper. In spidery script across the center of the top sheet, it read:

> *LEONINE FIEZEL*
> *5G, 10S, 15C*
> *LoD*

On the second sheet of paper was a sketch, and Aurelie realized she had seen it before—a rendering of a person with a bald head and a grim-set mouth.

She opened another, and another, and then two more, and found that they all bore names and denominations. Some had sketches but some didn't—a short description was provided instead. Aurelie thought of her consultations with Iliana—*the man has a scar above his left eye. The lady in question wears a peacock-feathered hat.*

These were bounties.

Aurelie was staring at one when Iliana returned eventually. She stumbled just a little as she stepped into the room and shut the door behind her, not as noiselessly as she probably intended.

"Iliana?"

"Yes, I'm here," she whispered, too loudly.

"Are you drunk?"

"Me? Not at all." She bent over, fumbling with the laces on one of her boots. "It's just that the wine is significantly better in the south. I had to have a glass."

"One glass?"

"Or two. That mulled stuff up north—it doesn't suit me.

It's much fresher here. This one had a"—she struggled with the laces but somehow couldn't figure out how to unfasten them—"brilliant bouquet."

"A what?"

"Never mind. You're glowing—are you aware?"

"I am."

"I mean that in a literal sense, rather than a figurative one."

"I got that."

"Not that you don't have your odd moment of figurative glowing."

"Do I?"

"Occasionally. Very rarely." She plopped down next to Aurelie, loosening one of her boots enough to kick it off, and then starting on the other. "What have you got there?"

Aurelie held up one of the bounties.

"Poking around in my coat, I see."

"I was looking for a book to read."

"Fifth pocket, left side."

"*Blaise the Highwayman*?"

Iliana nodded. "Isadora is far too good for him. Frankly, her father is setting her up for disaster at that roadside inn of his. She should turn Blaise into the authorities, take the bounty, and set up her own inn somewhere else."

Aurelie smiled a little.

"Who do we have here?" Iliana peered at the paper in Aurelie's hand. "Ah. Him."

It was the sketch of Elias Allred. And the accompanying bounty, which Aurelie had never been privy to before.

30000G, 50000S, 80000C, LoD

"Thirty thousand gold." The number was unfathomable. "Fifty thousand silver. Eighty thousand copper."

"Yes," Iliana replied evenly.

"And *LoD*?"

"Living or dead."

Aurelie spoke delicately. "As in, dead when you found them, or . . . dead because you . . . made them that way?"

"Upon finding," Iliana said, looking aghast. "Goodness, Baker, after this long together, I didn't think I'd have to assure you that I'm not in the business of assassination."

Aurelie felt a bit foolish. "Have you ever found someone who was . . . ?" She shook her head. "No, never mind. I don't want to know."

Iliana took the paper from Aurelie. "If I find someone in that condition, I won't pass up the bounty. And anyway . . ." She considered the sketch for a moment. "People want to know, either way. Where they are. What became of them." She swallowed. "Now, this particular bounty has been a real challenge, as you're well aware."

"Do you think he's dead?"

"I don't know," Iliana said, with surprising candor. "We can't find him by seeking, which may indicate that he is. You yourself told me the departed can't be found that way. Though I suspect you said that just to make me go away."

It was quiet and comfortable with just the orange glow from her fingertips, so Aurelie didn't bother to look sheepish. "I did."

"I can't say I entirely blame you. I can be—what is it my mother says?—an absolute trial."

"I should keep more of that southern wine on hand. You're rarely so honest."

"I'm honest to a fault," Iliana said. "You're the one who holds back."

Aurelie didn't speak.

"Anyway"—she set aside Elias Allred's bounty—"whether you can seek those who have passed on or not, we both know Elias Allred turns up nothing. He just . . . vanished." She picked up another piece of parchment. "This one, on the other hand"—It was the one labeled LEONINE FIEZEL—"I found him inside three hours."

"How did you manage that?"

"You," she said. "You told me he was in a room with white-washed floors and a gold ceiling. Do you remember?"

Aurelie did, in fact.

"I knew that was the taproom in Upper Abling. I'd been there not a week before. That's the thing about seeking. It's only as reliable as one's interpretation of it." Iliana began folding the bounty back up into a little square. Aurelie wondered if they came that way or if Iliana just made a habit of it. "My brother fancies himself something of a scientist, and he says that it's not enough to collect data—you have to be able to interpret it. Lucky for us, Baker, you're very good at seeking, and I'm very good at interpreting."

"You have a brother?"

"Yes. He's insufferable."

"Is he your only sibling?"

"He is." Iliana looked over at her. Her face was flushed, a rosy bloom high in her cheeks. It was odd to see her this way. "And what about you? Any little baker siblings running around, crafting pies and making things glow?"

"Just me."

"Don't see your parents often, do you?" Iliana asked, and Aurelie shook her head. "Do you miss them?"

"No."

"Do they miss you?"

Aurelie smiled a little. "No."

She wasn't sure what compelled her to continue. The quiet in the room, maybe. That uncharacteristic openness in Iliana's expression. "My parents never seemed entirely reconciled with the notion of my existence."

Iliana frowned. "What does that mean?"

Aurelie shrugged. "It's not as if they were cruel or negligent or any of that. They were loving, of course, but they were also . . . careless. They like going to the pub in the evenings, traveling, gambling. I just didn't fit in. They sent me away to school as soon as I was old enough, and I suppose they would've kept me there as long as possible if they hadn't run out of money for tuition. Did you happen to find out about that during any of your investigating? The *grand tour* that meant the end of my education?"

"No," Iliana said. Aurelie was certain that Iliana wouldn't have admitted it under any other circumstances. "I only knew that you left to apprentice."

We've made plans for the most delightful grand tour, dearest! We'll spend the whole of the winter season away and will be thinking fondly of you all the while. It was one of the last letters Aurelie had received from her parents at school. In reality, their grand tour was far grander than it ought to have been, and Aurelie was left with the consequences. It seemed strange to think that people believed only magic had reactionary consequences, when in fact, everything did.

Aurelie examined her hands. "I can't blame them. Not really. Sometimes you can't save people from themselves."

It was quiet for a moment. Just the sound of the prince's slow breathing, the rustle of movement as he shifted onto his side.

And then Iliana picked up one of the parchment squares and held it out to Aurelie. "Here. Why don't you keep this one?"

It was the Elias Allred bounty. "Why?"

She shrugged. "You can practice with it. If you find him, you'll get the thirty thousand gold."

Aurelie considered the parchment for a moment. "What happened to him?"

"No idea. Hence the search. Goodness, Baker, one would think you weren't listening in the slightest."

"What were *the circumstances of his disappearance*?" Aurelie said flatly. Iliana was vexing enough as it was, but drunk Iliana was even more to reckon with.

"He was traveling with Copperend when he disappeared," Iliana said around a large yawn. "In the Underwood, of course."

"Why 'of course'?"

"That's where people disappear, isn't it?"

"We didn't disappear there."

"That's different. We had Quad. And me, and you. And Hapless, for morale."

As if in response, the prince let out a particularly loud snore.

"That's true," Aurelie said after a pause. "And we had your armory as well, just in case."

"My armory?"

"I came across a few of your weapons in my search for Isadora."

"Ah, yes. Well. Preparedness and all that. One can never be overdressed or overarmed."

"Is that something people say?"

"It's something I say."

Aurelie smiled briefly but then looked away. "One knife in particular was . . . odd. The one with the black handle?"

"I suppose you'd find that one, wouldn't you?" Iliana reached into the coat, and after a moment of searching, pulled out the strange knife with the etchings.

"Where is it from? And why is it . . ."

"Unsettling?" Iliana supplied. "Good to know it's not just me. I thought my lack of magical ability might be . . . Well, regardless—this, Baker, is an Impossible knife."

"What makes it impossible?"

"Impossible weapons aim true. They never miss their mark. And if you're about to say 'that's impossible,' the answer is yes—that's where the name came from."

"They're enchanted?"

"Very heavily so."

"Where did you get it?"

"I took it," Iliana said. "From the scene of the ambush."

"What? Why?"

"For evidence, of course. And also because I wanted it."

"Oh, of course."

"They're particularly hard to come by," she added a bit defensively. "A combination of expensive and rare that's truly prohibitive for collectors of fine weapons such as myself."

"Why would the attackers have Impossible weapons?"

Iliana's expression turned serious. "I suppose they meant to kill the prince."

"But they didn't. They missed. Why would you aim true and then miss?"

"I don't know," Iliana said. "It's been troubling me." She considered the knife for a moment, its blade catching the light from Aurelie's fingertips, and then she slipped it back into her coat. "A mystery for another day. Did I mention you're glowing, Baker?"

"You did mention that."

"You know, if we were all going to sleep on the ground, we might as well have stayed outside." Iliana clambered to her feet. She wobbled only a little. "He's far too gallant, and you're far too obstinate."

"By all means, take the bed, Iliana."

"Don't think that I won't," she said, making her way over to it and collapsing on top of the covers.

Fourteen

The following morning—not early in the least for Aurelie, trained as she was in waking before dawn—the group emerged from the inn and spotted a pair of palace guards at the end of the lane.

The guards were standing with a woman and referring to a piece of parchment, gesturing as if to indicate a height.

"What do you want to bet that's a picture of you, Prince?" Iliana murmured.

Aurelie looked over and found Quad examining Hapless, eyes narrowed, as if to assess whether he was in fact the height indicated.

"Hopefully not the official one from the palace," Hapless replied. "The portrait I sat for my coming of age turned out dreadfully—"

"Heaven help us, not this again," Aurelie said, though it wasn't without a bit of amusement.

"They didn't capture me anywhere *near* accurately."

"Well, we're hoping they don't capture you at all,"

Iliana said, and they quietly slipped off in the opposite direction.

However, when they rounded the corner onto the next street, they were greeted with the sight of a second set of guards standing together in discussion. Before they could turn back or even move, one of the guards looked up, his gaze locking onto the four of them.

Aurelie's heart jumped into her throat.

"Don't worry," Hapless said quietly, and then he strode over to the guards with a hearty "Hello there, friends!"

Like a stone sinking into a pond, Aurelie's heart rapidly plummeted.

"What is he doing?" Iliana moaned.

"What fine weather we're having!" Hapless bellowed as he reached the guards. "This is the Meadowlands at their best, wouldn't you say?"

One guard appeared to be of middling years, his great red beard flecked with gray. The other was younger, a tall woman with a broad face. They both regarded Hapless warily.

"It is quite fine," the man conceded.

"What brings you to our humble village?" Hapless asked, and then pointed to the parchment that the woman held before taking it directly from her hands. "May I? Thank you, most obliged—oh, here's a dashing young lad." Hapless's eyes widened. "Is this the prince? You know, I've heard he has a much better aspect in person. This old style of portraiture so rarely suits—"

"Sir—" the woman began.

"Is he missing?" Hapless looked suddenly dismayed. "Dreadful news, that is. You know, the public would be a lot more familiar with his face if he were on a coin. If you ask me, he'd suit the copper quite admirably."

"We are indeed looking—"

Hapless lowered the parchment. "How can I help? Tell me what I may do. Anything in service to the crown. An honor, really, to have you in our little corner of the Kingdom. Is he honestly thought to be here? Who could imagine it! Royalty, just strolling down the street! Cheek by jowl with our own friends and neighbors!"

The man cut a look over to where Aurelie, Iliana, and Quad stood.

"May I ask—" he began.

"My lovely family, of course," Hapless said, waving a hand. "Mother, and my wife, and our dear little girl—"

What are you doing?! Aurelie wanted to cry. She could feel Iliana stiffen next to her.

"Just six she is, just this past spring! Wave to the guards, darling," Hapless said, and next to Aurelie, Quad tentatively raised a hand. "Oh, quite shy in the presence of real, genuine palace guards!" Hapless looked back to the two of them, smiling amiably, though Aurelie could see a glint in his eyes. "You are real, genuine palace guards, aren't you?"

"Yes, of course—"

"You hear the most awful things in the news lately," Hapless said. "All manner of impostors, crimes—please, tell me how I may be of assistance. Shall I go door to door with this?"

"That's quite all right—"

"I'm very well connected in the village. I can call for an assembly—"

"That won't be necessary."

"Do you require food or drink? Lodging? Our home is rather small—Mother sleeps under the stairs, bless her soul!—but we would be happy to accommodate you—honored, really—"

"Sir—"

"Such formalities! My name is Bastian, and I'm delighted to serve as your ambassador here—"

When the woman spoke, it was very rapidly and with no small amount of impatience. "Truly, we're just looking for any information on the prince's whereabouts."

"I can't say that I have any of that at the moment, but I can certainly work on winnowing some out! How should I contact you once I've thoroughly investigated?"

"I think we've got everything pretty well at hand—"

"Well, certainly not, with your prince missing," Hapless said.

The man looked flustered. "He's not missing on our account—"

"Isn't he? Where were you when he was taken? Back in the Capital, I suppose, doing the hard work of protecting the rest of the royal family. Suppose you can't be faulted for that, I imagine it's an incredibly demanding job—"

"Thank you for your help," the woman said, forcibly wresting the parchment from Hapless's hands. "We'll be on our way."

"More of the village to scour! Shall I accompany you?"

"No," she said. "In fact, I command you to stay right where you are."

"And continue to maintain surveillance here," Hapless

replied solemnly, tapping the side of his head. "I understand perfectly."

The guards quickly headed off in the opposite direction as Hapless called after them. "Report back at midday! We'll compare what we've found!"

The guards reached the opposite end of the street and disappeared around the corner.

Hapless turned and regarded Aurelie, Quad, and Iliana.

"Well, they were lovely, weren't they?" he said with a grin.

Fifteen

Hapless couldn't quite explain it, but that was nothing new. There were plenty of things he couldn't explain—why he found strawberries to be delicious but heartfruit to be abominable. Why some things (like the fundamentals of magic) went in one ear and out the other, but other things (like poetry from Carmine) stuck in his mind with permanent clarity.

So as for how he convinced the guards to see what he wanted them to see—he had no idea.

Quad offered an explanation as they fled the village to catch a passenger boat on the river. Iliana led the way, Aurelie nearly in step with her, while Hapless followed behind with Quad.

"You charmed them," Quad told him. "With surprising efficiency."

Hapless managed a smile. "Well, I've heard I do have the rare moment of charm. At least, my mother used to say—"

"Not like that. You *charmed* them. Literally."

Hapless shook his head. "I barely have magic in the first place, and that's to speak nothing of Uncommon magic."

"Not Uncommon," Quad said. "Just . . . forgotten. Like most mortal magic. Set aside."

Iliana arranged their fares on the large passenger boat, and when they were seated in a foursome toward the back—they were on the roof of the two-story vessel, a wide-open top space populated with clusters of chairs, perfect for the summer weather—she looked over at Hapless and said, "Try it again."

"Try what?"

"Your magic." Iliana frowned suddenly. "Why did I have to be your mother, by the way? I at least had the decency to make you my brother at the inn."

"Yes, but that wasn't an enchantment," Quad said. "It was just a lie."

"Same difference!"

"It's not," Hapless said, and then looked sidelong at Quad. "Right?"

Quad nodded. "Give it a try."

"I can't. I don't even know what I did."

"You were just talking," Aurelie said. She hadn't spoken much since the scene in the village. Right now she was looking out over the water, her expression contemplative.

"Exactly," Hapless said.

"No, I mean . . . it was like a spell that you cast just by . . . speaking with conviction."

"Speak now, Prince," Iliana said. "With extra conviction."

"Um." Hapless looked around. "This is a lovely day."

"Well, that's just stating the obvious."

"I don't know!"

"Tell us something," Aurelie said, and when Hapless looked at her, there was a surprising intensity in her eyes. "Make us see it."

Hapless shook his head, at a loss. He turned his gaze to the water, the riverbanks sliding by on each side. All of a sudden a random memory struck him: Gallant's sixteenth birthday. Being Gallant, he had decided that he wanted to celebrate with a *grand regatta.* Small, intimate family affairs just weren't in his nature. (Nor were they in Hapless's nature, either, if he was honest with himself. He had turned seven that year and wanted to celebrate with, in his words, "a pony spectacular.")

On the day of the birthday regatta, standing on the bank of the river in the Capital, Hapless had begged his mother to allow him to ride in Gallant's boat. The queen had refused.

"I'll do everything right!" Hapless had pleaded. "I'll listen to Gallant! I'll do whatever he says!"

The queen had just smiled knowingly, likely with amusement at the fact that Hapless rarely did what *anyone* said, least of all Gallant.

Hapless glanced over at his traveling companions now and then out at the water. "That's a lovely boat," he said, before he could think about it.

"Where?"

"Pulling alongside us, just there." He stood and crossed to the railing, the breeze whipping his hair back. "White and gold sails, a swift little thing—the newest and most fashionable, of course, nothing but the very premier model will do." His brother at the prow, calling instructions. The boat had whipped by them—Hapless had barely had time to wave—but he remembered the sight of Gallant clearly, his shirt billowing out, head thrown back in laughter.

"I've never seen a boat so fast," Hapless murmured. "We'll never keep up at this rate."

"I don't see it," Aurelie said, a bit apologetically, and Quad shook her head. Iliana peered out at the water with a frown.

Hapless couldn't help but deflate. "That's because I don't know what I'm doing."

Iliana clapped a consoling hand on his shoulder. "Don't worry, Prince. Neither do the rest of us."

Soon enough—far too soon, in Hapless's opinion—the architecture on either side of the river melted into the familiar. They were nearing the Capital.

He would've had the journey stretch on longer. Much, much longer.

As a child, Hapless sometimes felt sad the day before a holiday or a birthday celebration, and no one could quite understand his explanation why—how the fact that it had nearly begun meant that it was essentially finished.

Hapless's adventure would soon be over, which meant it was basically over now.

He tried to push the melancholy back as he took a turn around the boat to stretch his legs. He found a secluded spot on the lower level to gaze out at the water. To *think great thoughts* in solitude, as he had dreamed of doing on his quest. But none of his thoughts felt that great.

He was watching the peaks of the Capital draw nearer

when Aurelie sidled up next to him and rested her forearms on the railing.

"I wouldn't worry," she said.

"Hm?"

"About the enchantment. About not being able to replicate it."

That wasn't chiefly on Hapless's mind, but it was there also. That unusual bit of magic. "It's just odd, isn't it?"

Aurelie shrugged. "Everyone starts by doing magic they don't understand. That's sort of the whole point of the feather test, isn't it? It just sort of . . . happens. The understanding comes later, I suppose. If you're lucky." She peered out at the water. The boat cut through the water slowly, leaving a wide path of white foam in its wake.

"I always wondered about people whose tests were never followed up on," she said. "People who were magic but barely even knew it. Or didn't care." She paused. "Miss Ember—my teacher, the one who read us Carmine? She believed magic was important. She taught me everything I know about it. I'll always be grateful to her for that."

Hapless glanced over at Aurelie. "You should be the one studying magic." It was the truth. "It's all fairly wasted on me."

"Are you feeling sorry for yourself?"

"Maybe a little." His lips twitched. "I suppose I don't want the adventure to end. Wouldn't it be nice if we could just keep on questing together?"

Aurelie didn't answer right away. When Hapless looked over at her, her expression was hard to read. "We're not questing. Or . . . if we are, then delivering you is the quest."

"Maybe we need a new quest, then."

"Maybe all good quests come to an end." She smiled a little. "Maybe that's what makes them good quests."

"Ah, yes. Beauty in the ephemeral and all that."

Aurelie made a face.

"What?"

"My mother used to say something like that. Maybe I'm more like her than I think." She straightened up. "I'll try to redeem myself. There is beauty in the ephemeral, certainly. But there's beauty in permanence, too, isn't there?"

"You mean . . . buildings and monuments and such?"

"I suppose. Though those sorts of things can still fall."

"What's something truly permanent, then? Love?"

She let out a breath of laughter. "Love least of all, I'd say."

"Why would you say that?"

She shook her head. "Sorry. I'm . . ." She looked a bit sheepish. "I'm no authority on the topic. Sometimes I think even if love stared me in the face, I wouldn't know what it looked like."

Hapless thought about what Aurelie had said about her parents to Iliana last night at the inn: *They were loving, of course, but they were also . . . careless.*

She didn't know that Hapless had been awake. He wasn't *eavesdropping*, certainly not, but he had just so happened to wake up and hear. It was unavoidable in such close quarters; he couldn't be blamed for it. . . .

And he couldn't be blamed for wanting to know more about Aurelie. Or for the twinge in his chest at the thought of how reasonably she spoke of parents who didn't pay her much mind, of a childhood coming second best to traveling and gambling.

When Hapless looked over at Aurelie again, she met his gaze. For a moment he felt . . .

Suddenly her eyes slid to a point over his shoulder and widened.

Hapless frowned. "What is it?"

"There are guards waiting on the dock," Aurelie said quietly. "Don't look!" She grabbed Hapless's shoulder as he went to turn. "Just look at me."

The boat began to slow, approaching the pier.

"It's all right," Hapless said. "I'm disguised."

Aurelie shook her head minutely. "It's starting to wear off."

"Is it? What color is my hair?" He grimaced. "Is it quite bad?"

Aurelie ignored him. "Give your magic another try. Disguise us."

"It won't work."

"Well, not with that attitude." Aurelie tightened her grip on Hapless's shoulder. "They're looking at us," she said, and then, "Please forgive me."

And then she kissed him.

Sixteen

Hapless was being *kissed*—by Aurelie—and in an instant, he was kissing back.

It was—well, words weren't—

Every bit of him felt lit up from the inside. He had read stories of kisses that saved lives. *True love's kiss.* Surely this was one of those kisses. Surely they felt just like this—

One of his hands went into Aurelie's hair.

"Pardon me!" someone called from nearby.

They split apart, and for a second, all Hapless could see was Aurelie's face, her bright eyes peering up at him. They were a warm hazel. Hapless knew at that moment that it was a color he would never grow tired of.

She blinked, and then her gaze slid in the direction of the person who'd spoken. She called back, "Yes?" in a voice that was about as breathless as Hapless felt.

A uniformed guard stood on the deck nearby, her expression a mix of amusement and disapproval.

"Have you seen two people pass this way? One in a coat? One was Uncommon?"

"No." Hapless's voice sounded strange to his own ears. Off-kilter. "No one."

"I suppose neither of you would notice even if they had," the guard said. "It's a little early in the day to be courting, you know."

"Love knows no hour," Hapless declared, before he could even think about it. The balance in the guard's expression tipped more toward amusement.

"Even still. There's propriety to consider."

"Yes, ma'am."

"If I pass by this way again, I won't see the two of you here, will I?"

"Certainly not," Aurelie replied.

"We'll have found somewhere much more discreet by then," Hapless added, and Aurelie nudged him with her elbow.

The guard just smiled. "Aye, I'm sure you will." And she headed off.

For a moment the two of them just stood there. Hapless's heart was pounding, and he wasn't sure if it was the threat of discovery or—

Aurelie stepped away, putting more distance between them than Hapless would like.

"I'm sorry," she said. "I didn't—"

"Did you feel it? That was . . . I've never . . ." There were too many thoughts running through Hapless's mind. The concern in Aurelie's expression. The feeling of her lips. "Aurelie." He felt like laughing. "That was . . . I mean, that was . . ."

"Magic," she said.

"Yes!"

"No, I mean, it *was* magic. I . . . enchanted you. That was an enchantment."

Hapless blinked. "What?"

"I'm very sorry. I didn't mean to." She shook her head. "I wasn't thinking. I wanted to disguise us, and I must've . . . I put a bit of magic into it." She gave an uneven smile when she looked back at him. "I'm afraid you'll hate me double within the hour now."

"Surely you don't mean—"

"Psssst," someone said, and they both turned. Quad waved from farther down the deck. "This way," she whispered. Iliana was crouched behind her. Aurelie crossed over to them immediately. Hapless had no choice but to follow.

Seventeen

We were spotted as the boat pulled into port," Iliana explained as they wound their way through the streets of the harbor district. They had just narrowly managed to avoid the guards, camouflaged by the crowds disembarking at the Capital.

"I told you to take that coat off," Aurelie said.

"And I told you that was absolutely unreasonable."

"It's summer! You completely stand out!"

"Let's not cast any undue blame on outerwear. We made it out safely, didn't we?"

Aurelie didn't reply. Truthfully, the narrow escape wasn't what weighed on her mind at the moment. She couldn't stop thinking about the kiss.

She had *kissed* the *prince*.

It hadn't been premeditated. Not in the slightest. In fact, Aurelie had never done anything in her life with less thought than when she met Hapless's lips with her own.

And the way it had felt . . .

Hapless was right. It did feel like magic. Which is why it must have been. There was no way the prince could be so moved by a kiss—by *her* kiss—without magic.

Guilt pooled in Aurelie's stomach. She had only wanted to keep Hapless from the notice of the guards. That was all. A distraction. A cover. And of course she had to go and accidentally perform an enchantment.

Her lips tingled, even now, with the memory of it.

From the harbor, they traveled inland, where the buildings were packed close together, cobblestone roads branching off into narrow alleyways. They moved through a bustling market district that then gave way to neighborhoods of large, stately homes with neat lawns and manicured gardens.

It was Iliana who stopped them short of the road leading to the palace and said, "This is where we leave you, Prince."

Surprise flashed across Hapless's face. "Surely you'll come to the palace. All of you. It's the least I can do. You can be my particular guests."

"Your particular guests accused of kidnapping you?" Quad said.

"Now that we're here, I'll explain just what happened. It'll be no matter."

Aurelie, Iliana, and Quad exchanged a look.

"I *would* like to see a palace," Quad admitted. "Mortal invention and all that. I suppose it's meant to be the very pinnacle of your architecture."

"It is! Quite the pinnacle!" Hapless agreed. "Iliana? Aurelie?"

Aurelie met the prince's gaze for a moment and couldn't

quite deal with the openness—the hopefulness—that she found there.

It was a bad idea, to be sure. But she couldn't help it. "All right."

Hapless grinned. He looked to Iliana, his eyes shining. "You know, I think Lady Pith may be in residence at the moment."

Iliana rolled her eyes. "You're hopelessly transparent, you know."

"I know. It's one of my best qualities."

Iliana smiled begrudgingly. "Fine, then, Prince. Lead the way."

Everything about the palace was grand, though Aurelie supposed that was to be expected. But nothing could have quite prepared her for the level of detail—the frescoed ceilings, the immaculately polished floors, the sumptuous velvet drapes tied back with thick gold cords, the elaborate crystal sconces. The cost of one doorknob could probably feed a family in Aurelie's village for half a year.

Aurelie, Iliana, and Quad followed Hapless through a series of large hallways with tall, vaulted ceilings while he told them about their surroundings ("This fresco was recently restored, despite Honoria's best efforts—she says it's ghastly") and pointed out locations of particular interest ("This is the spot where I threw up on Duchess Pious when I was five. I can't say she was particularly pleased, but she was definitely surprised, which is at least something!").

They were making their way across a large central lobby

when a woman emerged through an archway opposite them. She wore an exquisite dress of pink silk, resplendent with ribbons and embroidery and little round jewels that caught the light and winked. Her dark brown hair was pinned into an elegant coiffure. The woman stopped short for a moment at the sight of the prince, but then elegantly strode over.

"Your Highness," she said, dropping into a deep curtsy.

"Duchess Bright." Hapless inclined his head in return.

The woman—the duchess, apparently—straightened, and her gaze swept across them and landed on Iliana.

"Darling," she said. "I didn't know we were expecting you."

"I've just come to deliver the prince," Iliana replied, and there was a note of petulance to her voice that Aurelie had never heard before. The confidence, the assuredness, her usual swagger had all but evaporated. Iliana looked suddenly . . . chastened, like a child caught sneaking sweets before dinner.

"Well, that's no way to speak of His Royal Highness, is it?" Duchess Bright said.

"I've come to deliver *His Royal Highness*," Iliana said, emphasizing the words, and then she added, "the prince," in an undertone.

"Please, we're beyond all that, aren't we?" Hapless said. "Just Hapless is quite all right."

Duchess Bright's elegant eyebrows raised. "How lovely to hear that you two have achieved such a . . . familiarity." She sounded delighted by the prospect. "And how good to see that you're well, Highness. We've been hearing the most dreadful things."

"I'm very well," Hapless said with a dazzling smile. "Not kidnapped or dead in the least."

Next to Aurelie, Quad made a noise in her throat that could have been the beginning of a laugh.

The duchess didn't appear to notice, instead turning to Iliana. "Well? Are you going to give mummy a kiss, or are you too *independent* and *worldly* for that?"

Iliana let out a short breath and then dutifully stepped forward and kissed the air alongside Duchess Bright's cheek.

It came as more of a confirmation than a surprise to Aurelie. Of course Iliana was nobility—she could only do what she did because of it. Certainly Iliana worked, but anyone else would have to work for ages to get to where she was—hardly older than Aurelie and running around the Kingdom self-sufficient, having adventures, doing as she pleased. There was a lightness about Iliana, one that Aurelie couldn't have defined before this moment, that spoke of a lack of burden—financial or societal.

Iliana didn't look at Aurelie or Quad as she stepped away from the duchess. Instead, her gaze darted across the lobby to a young man who was now approaching. And then she rolled her eyes harder than Aurelie thought was even possible—it looked like some sort of demonic possession.

The young man wore a beautiful black jacket and waistcoat, shot through with silver embroidery. His dark hair fell just above his shoulders, smooth and lustrous, and his face was handsome, his manner assured. He approached Iliana and the duchess with his arms outspread.

"Defiance," Duchess Bright said warmly, stepping forward to embrace the young man. "Your sister's just arrived."

Iliana's face had sunk into a scowl.

"How fortunate!" Lord Defiance said. "A family reunion."

"I'm sure you're just delighted," Iliana muttered.

"And who do I have the pleasure of addressing?" He turned to gaze upon Aurelie and Quad, bypassing Hapless with just an incline of his head. "Your Highness."

"This is Quad, and Aurelie the baker, both of the Northern Realm," Iliana said.

Defiance bowed over each of their hands. He lingered over Aurelie's, looking up at her with an unnervingly keen stare. The kiss he pressed to the back of her hand made something in her stomach squirm uncomfortably. She felt oddly relieved to take her hand back.

"Any friend of my sister is a friend of mine," he said.

"Oh really?" Iliana said with false brightness. "In that case, I'll be sure to curtail all future introductions."

"You'll do no such thing," the duchess said. "It serves your brother well to meet new people. He spends far too much time with his books and his experiments."

"Are you a student?" Hapless asked.

Defiance gave him an odd look. "Yes. At the university. We took entry-level composition together."

Hapless regarded him vaguely. "Ah, yes," he said, and then eyed him closer. "You sat by the windows, I believe?"

Lord Defiance's expression was sour. "Yes, that's correct."

"Don't worry, Prince," Iliana said. "People have always thought Defiance has a highly *forgettable* face."

Aurelie sincerely doubted that. Lord Defiance was worryingly good-looking in the exact same way that Iliana was.

"You sat in the front, didn't you, Your Highness?" Lord Defiance said. "To better *absorb* the knowledge, I imagine?"

"Defiance—" Duchess Bright began.

"Perhaps you sat too close," Defiance continued. "And that's why it just"—he made a soaring motion with one hand—"passed right over your head."

Hurt flashed across Hapless's face. He really was hopelessly transparent.

Aurelie spoke before she could even consider the words, or any potential consequences. "You must have positioned yourself similarly during your etiquette lessons, Lord Defiance."

Hapless let out a sound that turned into a cough.

Defiance kept his gaze on Aurelie as he addressed Hapless, his tone clipped. "Forgive me, Your Highness. I speak only in jest."

Iliana looked openly gleeful.

"Well, not that this hasn't been *delightful*, but we should be on our way, shouldn't we?" she said. "Mustn't detain the prince. Plenty to see and all that—"

"Speaking of," Hapless said. "I should make the rounds—my family, Steward, et cetera. Should probably sort out this whole 'suspected dead' kerfuffle, you know how it is—"

"I can't say that I do," Quad muttered, and Aurelie smiled.

"I'll find you a sitting room and some refreshments—" Hapless continued.

"We'd just as soon eat in the kitchens," Aurelie said.

Quad gave her a nudge. "Speak for yourself."

"I'll handle it," Iliana told the prince.

"I'll join you shortly, then." Hapless gave them all a wave as he backed away. "Very shortly!"

They watched him cross the lobby and disappear through an arched doorway.

"I should take my leave as well," Lord Defiance said. "Business to attend to."

Iliana eyed him askance. "What kind of business?"

"The kind that's none of yours," Defiance replied. He sketched a bow in Aurelie and Quad's direction. "Delighted to make your acquaintance." His smile was a little too sharp. "Mother, *dear* sister, I'm sure I'll have the pleasure of your company again soon."

"Don't be so certain about that," Iliana muttered as Defiance's footsteps retreated. She turned to the duchess. "We should be on our way too. Famished from the journey and all that."

Duchess Bright frowned. "You never did say how you—"

"We'll see you soon."

"You're coming home, then?"

"We'll see you . . . eventually," Iliana corrected, and then ushered Aurelie and Quad away. Aurelie caught one last glimpse of the duchess in the lobby before Iliana swept them through a doorway.

"Not a word," Iliana said as they fell into step with each other.

"You're just full of surprises, aren't you?" Aurelie replied.

"You're not surprised in the least."

Aurelie bit down on a smile. "Not really."

"I'm a little surprised," Quad said.

"Are you?"

"Yes, by how poorly you disguised your noble birth."

"Excuse me? I could just be . . . eccentric!"

Aurelie's lips twitched. "You once told me that *any proper household should include grapefruit forks among their flatware.*"

"Well, that's just common sense."

"One time you suggested I get a hobby, like *raising orchids.*"

"That's a very reasonable hobby!"

"I won't even bother mentioning your thoughts on horse racing."

"Just because I said a team from Ardent Fields is *essential*—"

"Honestly, you may be the worst undercover noble ever."

"Worse than Bastian the boy prince? Waving his arms around in the marketplace and loudly declaring that the sleeves of his work shirt would be *vastly elevated* by lace edging?"

Aurelie couldn't contain it any longer—she let out a snort, and the appalled look on Iliana's face was incredibly gratifying.

"I'm so sorry, was that too *indecorous* for you, Your Ladyship?"

"I swear on all that is holy—"

"Not very courtly of you, is it?" Quad said.

"I hate you both."

Eighteen

apless wouldn't say that his sister looked particularly *pleased* to see him. The expression on Honoria's face when he appeared in the doorway of her sitting room was primarily one of relief, but it wasn't without a strong undertone of exasperation.

"Surprise," Hapless said a little sheepishly.

"I could honestly clobber you," Honoria replied, before crossing the room and hugging him very briefly but very tightly. She then pulled back and held him at arm's length, assessing him in that direct way of hers that made him feel a bit like a specimen under glass, pinned for examination. "You're all right?"

"I am."

"Completely and totally? No curses, no hexes, no head wounds, no gaps in consciousness—"

"None."

"Good." Something softened in her eyes. "I don't know what we're going to do with you. Kidnapped!" Then the *something* in her eyes hardened back up. "And right before my engagement is announced!"

"You're engaged? Was no one going to tell me?"

"You were on your quest! How were we meant to reach you?"

"By letter?"

"Oh yes, I'm going to send some poor courier out into the wilds of the north just to tell you that I've decided to get married."

"We were hardly in the *wilds*. We didn't even make it past the Underwood."

"Yes, because you went and got yourself kidnapped."

"I wasn't *kidnapped*."

"You were ambushed and secreted away, Hapless, of course you were kidnapped."

"Why would my kidnappers be my friends?"

"That's a common delusion following a kidnapping. Sympathy for the perpetrators. You're probably in shock."

"I'm perfectly fine. Everything's fine. I've even brought my friends to join us—"

"You brought your kidnappers *here*?"

Honoria's maid, Noelle, entered then with a tray of tea and sandwiches.

"Honoria, they are *not* my—"

"It's true, the kidnappers are in the east wing. I've just heard it from Felizia." Noelle bobbed a cursory curtsy to Hapless. "Pardon the interruption, Your Highness." Noelle was more friend than maid to Honoria, and rather prone to interruptions.

Hapless waved a hand. "If you'll let me explain—"

"Have you seen Gallant yet?" Honoria asked. She was prone to interruptions herself.

"No."

"Go and see him; he's been worried to bits."

"Really?"

"Yes, and as long as you're certain you're fine, tell him everything and leave me alone to prepare for this evening. Adam and his family will be arriving at any moment, and we need to make a good impression."

"I think it's probably the other way around," Hapless said. "Shouldn't they want to make a good impression on us?"

"His parents are *academics*. They're not impressed by titles or jewels or . . ." She waved a hand, encompassing the room, which was decked out in the latest and finest in interior design. At least, that's what Honoria insisted. Hapless didn't follow the trends in furniture the same way he did in fashion. "Any of this. And neither is Adam, which is why I want him."

Hapless considered this for a moment. Maybe Honoria knew a bit about love. He couldn't help but ask, "How do you know if a kiss is true love's kiss?"

She looked at him askance. "Who did you kiss?"

Hapless ignored the question. "How do you know?"

"You just know."

"So if I *think* it is, then that means it probably is, right?"

"Who did you kiss?" she asked again.

"Felizia said that Duchess Bright's daughter is among the kidnappers," Noelle supplied helpfully.

"Duchess Bright's—oh, Hapless, truly. You know you're not exactly her type."

"That's not—anyway, I just want to know. Surely you must have felt it with Adam."

"I hardly think it's proper to discuss that sort of thing."

"You discussed it with me," Noelle said, and Honoria shot her a look.

"Go see Gallant," Honoria told Hapless firmly, putting the conversation to rest.

So Hapless made his way to Gallant's study. The family's private chambers were in the south wing of the palace. Honoria loved it in particular for growing plants indoors— she said southern light was essential. It boasted the best views too—in the distance, one could see the river, which fed into a large bay at the southern edge of the Kingdom. Hapless had always loved watching the longboats sail by as a child.

The door to Gallant's study was slightly ajar. Hapless had to knock twice before Gallant gave a distracted, "Come in."

Gallant's study was untouched by Honoria's enthusiasm for interior design. It looked nearly the same as it had when it was their mother's study—a massive desk done in dark wood sat across from a wall of bookshelves that stretched from floor to ceiling. Large windows lined one side, but Gallant often left the heavy drapes shut. *The sunlight will damage the books*, he said.

Then move the books, the kingfather often replied. *You need sunlight yourself.*

The main change was the painting of their mother, which Gallant had moved into the study from the portrait gallery when he took the throne. It had been commissioned upon the queen's coronation—she was just twenty at the time, her face rounder than when Hapless knew her, her eyes bright. She sat in a chair, holding an apple in one hand, a golden chalice in another.

I couldn't for the life of me figure out what to do with my hands, she said once. *The artist wanted me to keep them folded, but it was impossible.* She was always in motion—Hapless had very few memories associating stillness with his mother (not until the final ones, which he kept packed away). *He was nearly ready to quit, until your aunt came to keep me company and handed me part of her lunch!*

Gallant was the opposite—more like their father. Grounded. Unyielding. He was always best at playing statues when they were younger. Not that he played very often—he was eight years older than Hapless, after all, and besides that, he had always been due for succession. Hapless couldn't imagine being the oldest. Living one's life—one's childhood!—knowing that someday you would have to rule the entire Kingdom. The notion made Hapless's stomach turn. He couldn't even keep a pet. The cat had been a disaster—Steward had had to adopt it.

Right now, Gallant sat at his desk, which was covered in stacks of books and rolls of parchment and piles of newspapers. Hapless had in general avoided looking at newspapers after once seeing one with a rendering of his brother, his sister, and himself on the front with a headline reading: THE HEIR, THE SPARE, AND THE WHO CARES? He would be the first to admit that it probably wasn't wholly inaccurate, but it was something of a blow to one's ego to have it splashed out there for all to see.

Gallant glanced up from his papers, then down, then

sharply back up again in recognition. "Hapless. You've returned."

"I have."

Gallant stood abruptly. "Are you—what happened? Are you all right?"

Hapless nodded. "It was nothing. Well, it wasn't nothing—there was an ambush—"

"I heard." Gallant shook his head. "It's what I've been saying all along—those woods aren't safe. To be taken from your party like that, in broad daylight—"

"But it was my friends that I left with. They protected me. They thought I would be safer in their company." Hapless stepped toward the desk. "Have you questioned the attackers yet?"

Gallant frowned. "None of the attackers returned here. Only the members of your party. Steward and the guards—"

"The guards *were* the attackers!"

"Are you saying your party turned on you?"

"Not my party as it stood, the additional people who came—" Hapless shook his head. "Didn't Steward say? They wore the palace livery. They were charmed asleep—"

Gallant's expression was uncomprehending.

Something prickled at the back of Hapless's neck. The attackers in the Underwood—what had become of them? How did his party *lose* the fake guards between the woods and the Capital?

Or did they let them go? Did the attackers overtake the guards and take their places? If so, what about—

"Steward," Hapless said. "Where is he?"

Gallant waved a hand. "Off doing whatever he usually does when you're away."

"Which is?"

"I can't say I keep apprised of his schedule," Gallant said, in full *His Majesty* tone. It was one of his most annoying tones. "We'll follow up with him, if you'd like. Maybe you were mistaken about how things fell out. You do have a penchant for these kinds of scrapes, and you know how you are sometimes—"

"How am I?"

Gallant's expression softened. "Prone to confusion," he said. "Occasionally. And it's understandable. No one blames you one bit—"

"Don't patronize me."

"I'm not. I'm just saying, maybe when your . . . *friends* . . . arrived, you became confused—"

"All three of them saw what I saw," Hapless said. "You can speak to them about it; they're here with me."

Gallant paused. "Here?"

"Yes. They escorted me back. Go and speak with them and you'll see—"

Gallant shook his head. "That won't be necessary." He came out from behind the desk, strode over to Hapless, and clapped a hand on his shoulder. "We'll get this all sorted out. For now, don't think of it."

"How can I not think of it?"

"You're back now and you're safe. Let's be thankful for that and brace ourselves for the next traumatic event on the horizon."

"Which is?"

Gallant smiled, a little crooked. At that moment, he looked younger than he usually did.

"Honoria's wedding, of course. The engagement is just the beginning, you know. Soon all manner of preparations will begin. The outfits she's going to make us wear! The obscure relatives we'll be forced into conversation with!"

Hapless tried, but he couldn't quite smile back.

Nineteen

Aurelie, Iliana, and Quad took tea in an aggressively purple drawing room. Purple walls, purple carpet, purple furniture. There was even a large painting of a woman in a dress of purple satin. Aurelie wondered if it had been commissioned for this room specifically, or if it had served as the overall inspiration. There was something charming in the purple woman's expression—like she knew an excellent secret and was five seconds away from telling it to you.

Aurelie considered the painting while she, Iliana, and Quad made their way through a tray of tea sandwiches that a groom had brought them. She was into her fifth cucumber sandwich when Iliana glanced over, a teacup nearly raised to her lips.

"Are we going to talk about it?" she said, before taking a sip.

"About what?"

"How you kissed the prince."

Aurelie nearly dropped her sandwich. "How did you—"

Iliana set the teacup down on her saucer far more deli-cately than Aurelie could have ever imagined she was capable of. "Honestly, Baker, you must know by now. I'm prescient. All-knowing. Of course I saw."

"We'd already been made and were looking for the two of you," Quad explained around large bites of scone.

"I was trying to keep the guards from noticing us," Aurelie said.

Iliana looked too amused. "And you thought your lips were the way to do it?"

Aurelie colored. "I panicked."

There was a knock at the door. A footman entered and announced: "The prince's steward."

The man from the woods—Elias Allred's father, accord-ing to Iliana—appeared and acknowledged them with a bow.

"I'd like to thank you all for seeing His Highness back to the palace," he said. "As you can imagine, his safe return was most desirable."

"Oh yes, *most* desirable," Quad said, raising her teacup in the air, and Aurelie had to choke back a laugh.

The steward appeared unruffled. "The prince's arrival today is also most fortunate, as Princess Honoria plans to for-mally announce her engagement."

Aurelie glanced over at Iliana, who looked a little sur-prised. *Prescient and all-knowing, my foot*, Aurelie thought.

"As His Highness has family affairs to attend to," Steward continued, "I would kindly offer you transportation to wher-ever you desire. After you've dined, of course, and quite at your leisure."

Iliana frowned but nodded nonetheless. "Certainly."

"Her ladyship is most welcome to attend the engagement ball," Steward added, inclining his head in Iliana's direction.

Iliana's expression hardened. "I'd just as soon poke my eye out with a—"

"Thank you," Aurelie cut in. "For your hospitality."

Steward gave another bow and then departed.

"*Her ladyship,*" Quad said with a snicker.

"Don't." There was a dangerous look in Iliana's eyes as she stood and pocketed a few scones. "We should be on our way."

"But he said we were *at our leisure,*" Quad said.

"I can assure you, in royal speak, 'quite at your leisure' means 'as soon as humanly possible.'"

"But Hapless said he'd—" Aurelie began.

"He's among his own people now, Baker. It's nothing to take personally."

"What about what happened in the Underwood? Is he even safe here?"

Iliana looked conflicted for a moment, but then shook her head. "I'm sure the king will investigate. Nothing will happen to the prince under his watch."

Even though Aurelie knew Iliana was probably right, she couldn't help but feel a stab of apprehension. And beneath that, an undeniable sense of disappointment. They were going to leave without seeing the prince again. Without even saying goodbye.

It shouldn't have mattered, yet somehow it did.

Twenty

Hapless was on his way to rejoin his friends when he was intercepted by Honoria's maid.

His mind was full of the conversation he'd just had with Steward. *I have no recollection of transporting the attackers*, Steward had said, when Hapless tracked him down. *I recall only the party that took you.*

I wasn't taken. I left with them of my own accord—

One can never be sure, when Uncommon magic is involved.

Maybe it was what Aurelie had said—that Quad's magic had doubled back and made Steward twice as suspicious. Maybe it had affected his memory somehow. But Steward seemed convinced that Hapless was safe within the palace. *I have no doubt your brother will do the utmost to ensure your safety.*

Hapless barely noticed when Noelle appeared at his side. The clipped tone of her "Your Highness" implied that it wasn't the first time she had attempted to draw his attention.

"Pardon?"

"Lord Adamant and his parents have arrived early," she

explained hurriedly. "Her Highness is in a bit of a state. She sent me to find you."

So Hapless dutifully returned to Honoria's sitting room, where a well-groomed, somewhat nervous-looking young man was now perched on one of the sofas. An older couple sat on the sofa across from him, and Honoria sat stiffly in a gilt chair.

"Hapless," she said with a shade too much enthusiasm when he appeared. "How lovely that you've joined us!"

Hapless didn't think it wise to point out that he had seemed to have little choice in the matter. "It's my pleasure."

"Hapless, this is Lord and Lady Brash, and this is their son, Lord Adamant."

"Ah, yes, of course!" Hapless said, as curtsies and bows were exchanged. He cast his mind back to when Honoria first started mentioning this particular lord. "You and Honoria met . . . when she was traveling in the Eastlands, didn't you, Adamant?"

"Please, Your Highness, Adam will suffice."

"Adam, yes, certainly."

"We did," Adam said. "And we've been corresponding ever since." He cast a warm look at Honoria. "I thought the princess might feel it too bold of me to ask for such a correspondence, so I was of course delighted when she initiated it herself. . . ."

It was then that Hapless caught sight of the window, which looked out over the courtyard below.

"Correspondences are lovely things," Hapless said, distracted. Outside, he could see Aurelie, Iliana, and Quad making their way across the courtyard. "You send a letter, and they send a letter, and you . . . get to know each other . . .

over the course of the writing. . . . Would enjoy a bit of corresponding myself, I think."

"Would you?"

When he looked back, Honoria's expression was both amused and faintly embarrassed.

"Pardon?" Hapless said.

"You were just expounding the virtues of correspondence."

"Well, yes. Got you two together, didn't it?" Hapless crossed over, clasped Adam's hand, and gave it a firm shake. "Honored to welcome you to the family, Adam. Delighted to make your acquaintance, Lord and Lady Brash." He then chucked a kiss to Honoria's cheek. "Terribly sorry, must run. Looking forward to the"—he waved a hand—"announcing and whatnot."

"Hapless—"

"Dreadfully sorry!" The footman just managed to catch the door as Hapless reached it, and he only barely sketched a bow before Hapless had sprinted off down the hall.

They were leaving the palace, and Aurelie was trying very hard not to regret the fact that she would likely never see the prince again.

And then suddenly, as if she summoned him (had she? Could she?), Hapless appeared in the archway across the courtyard, one of the large oaken doors falling shut behind him as he strode over to where Aurelie, Quad, and Iliana stood.

"What are you doing?" He slowed to a stop, a bit breathless. "Are you leaving?"

"Yes," Iliana said. "You've got family affairs to attend to—"

Hapless waved a hand. "There are always affairs to attend to."

"Well, sooner or later we need to get Aurelie back north. Before her heinous mentor returns."

Hapless's eyes met Aurelie's. There was something a little wild in his expression, not to mention that he looked as if he had sprinted from somewhere far off. "Could I just . . . a private audience . . . with Aurelie . . ."

Iliana's eyebrows shot sky-high. "Certainly."

"But—" Aurelie began.

"We'll wait for you near the fountain," Iliana said. "The ghastly one with the chopped-off arms."

"Honoria commissioned that fountain," Hapless said with a grin.

"Did I say ghastly? I meant . . . aesthetically challenging."

"Is that better than ghastly?" Quad asked as she and Iliana retreated.

Aurelie watched them go, feeling . . . uncertain of just how she was feeling. Lit up inside, suddenly. Aware of everything. Her hands hanging at her sides, the smudges of dirt on her apron, the frayed stitching on the side of her left shoe.

Hapless's eyes. Brown and intent. And his tentative smile.

"Sorry," he said. "Bit abrupt and all that. But . . . do you really have to leave now?"

Aurelie nodded. She didn't entirely trust herself to speak. Iliana was right—she had to return to the bakery. Prolonging things wouldn't change that.

"If you stayed just a little longer . . ." Hapless swallowed. "If you stayed, we could travel north together when I return to school."

Another adventure. *Together.*

It was a different shade of the same thing he had said on the passenger boat: *Wouldn't it be nice if we could just keep on questing together?*

It was jarring, how much Aurelie realized she might want that.

But the truth fell from her lips unbidden, a reflex that couldn't be denied. "I have to get back to the bakery. To my apprenticeship."

Hapless drew in a breath and then took a step closer. "Aurelie." He reached out as if to take her hand, but he hesitated at the last moment, his fingers catching on air. "I . . . I know what you said about what happened on the boat. But didn't it feel as if—" He shook his head. "Don't you feel as if . . ."

Aurelie was struck suddenly with the memory of the time she had accompanied Jonas on a visit to Chapdelaine's, the rival to Basil's Bakery. She remembered the full force of Jonas's smile as he spotted Katriane through the front window of the shop. The glowing smile that had blazed across Katriane's face in response had been something close to magic.

That look between them—each of their smiles, mirroring the other—had grown into something strong and meaningful. Something of utmost value. That was the potential, in that sort of look.

But there was also the potential for a lot else—for ruin.

Aurelie spoke. Softly and not unkindly. "It was just an enchantment."

"Then why do I want it to happen again?" Hapless asked. "Why haven't I stopped thinking about it?"

Aurelie shook her head. "I'm afraid we really must be going."

She forced herself to turn away. To take several steps, until—

"I'll write to you!" Hapless burst. "If you'd like."

When Aurelie looked back over her shoulder, she was met with the prince's painfully earnest expression.

"Would you?" he said. "Like that?"

She couldn't help herself. "Yes."

Hapless looked resolute. And much happier than he had a moment before. "Then I will."

Aurelie wanted it so badly, she was loath to undo it with what she said next: "But . . . at the bakery, Mrs. Basil reads all the mail. I can't receive anything there that she won't read first. And I don't . . . leave the bakery often, so I couldn't—"

"I'll send a courier," Hapless said. "We can make a code or some such, like the spies in the Court of Intrigue novels." His eyes were so bright. "They'll come one day with a letter and then come back the next day and ask for a response, if you have one. Is that . . . does that sound suitable?"

Bad idea, bad idea, bad idea. "Yes."

Hapless smiled, a blaze of sunshine. "Excellent."

INTERLUDE

In Which Letters
Are Exchanged

Twenty-One

*D*ear *Aurelie,*
    I wanted to fulfill my promise
to write as quickly as I could. My
sister, Honoria, says that correspondence is
like a game of grass ball—one should strive
to get a volley going as soon as possible. As
it so happens, you have not yet been gone a
day. I hope your journey is going well. This
letter will follow your course north and
hopefully arrive shortly after you reach your
bakery. I hope it will be happily received.

    I will very soon leave for school, but in
the meantime, preparations for Honoria's
engagement are underway. There will be
a ball to celebrate the announcement in
two days' time. My sister insists on referring
to it as a "small, intimate affair," though
the guest list is no less than two hundred

people long. I shudder to imagine what the actual wedding will be like. "Tasteful" is what Honoria replied just now when I asked her about it. We are both currently in her sitting room, which has in it a lovely writing desk that overlooks the gardens. Unfortunately, it also has a terrifying painting that features a flock of sheep with eerily humanlike faces. Each of them peers out at the viewer as if in silent judgment. I swear that the one on the far left wishes me actual bodily harm.

(I also asked Honoria about this painting, and she maintains that "it is a work of fine art" and also "Don't you have your own sitting room? Must you co-opt mine in this way?" The truth is I don't have my own sitting room, though technically there must be one specified for my use somewhere in the palace. It's just that I rarely receive people in a formal capacity. I suppose I can't be trusted not to spill a pot of tea on some dignitary or make some other sort of gaffe that would no doubt threaten affairs of state.)

(Luckily, the two of us are not involved in affairs of state, so hopefully I do not make a mess of things here. And though I must admit I regret the distance between us, at least I cannot spill a pot of tea on you from afar.)

The courier who delivered this letter will call again to see if you have a reply. He will ask for a day-old bun. Don't feel any pressure to write back, of course. But I would dearly enjoy hearing from you and hearing of your return journey with Iliana and Quad. I must admit, I feel a little envious to have missed it.

Most sincerely,

Hapless

(Or shall I say Prince Hapless, Duke of the Northern Realm, Peer of the Scholar's City, to be fully proper? An absurd mouthful, to be sure. I proposed an acronym once—PHDotNRPotSC—but it was soundly rejected. Fathomless. I think if one is to be burdened by titles, one ought to have a say in how they're conveyed.)

Dear Hapless (or would dear PHDotNRPotSC be preferred?),

Thank you for your letter, and for the discretion of your courier, who was indeed very stealthy in his delivery. (It really was like a Court of Intrigue novel!) I hope he won't have too much trouble traveling so far back with my reply. I heard from several patrons at the bakery that travel through the Underwood has now been prohibited. I've been wondering whether there's been any resolution regarding the ambush. I do hope you'll be safe on your journey back to school.

Our trip from the Capital was uneventful, all told. It's a return to daily life for me now. Things have been a bit somber in the bakery lately, as our journeyman, Jonas, was unable to sit for mastery during his trip to the Capital. Truthfully, I don't believe Mrs. Basil really intended to let him try for it when she brought him along with her. He's gloomy, which makes me feel gloomy. But at the same time, a small part of me is selfishly glad that he's still here. Maybe that's awful to admit.

Thank you for starting a volley. I've never played grass ball before, so this is a volley I'm much more assured of returning properly. I was never very good at sports in school.

Kind regards,

Aurelie

Dear Aurelie,

Sports were just about the only thing I was good at in my lessons! I also enjoyed music, though admittedly, I was terrible at it. When we were children, Honoria studied string instruments and I studied percussion. Imagine, if you will, the Kingdom's worst cello and drum duet.

No need to worry about the couriers.

There is a network spanning north and south, so no one rider bears the burden of traveling too far—only far enough to deliver to the next courier. Gallant prefers this system, as efficiency is his ideal. Perhaps our parents should have named him accordingly. King Efficiency does have a certain ring to it, don't you think?

Our King Efficiency has indeed banned travel through the Underwood, at least until the Court meets to discuss what might be done about the safety of the woods. Regarding the ambush, Steward assures me that Gallant is investigating and insists that I will be safe at school and should focus on my studies. But I must admit, it was such a strange business that it's been difficult to put out of my mind entirely.

I wouldn't feel guilty for being glad that your journeyman is still with you if it eases your burden or brings you comfort to have his company. I'm sure it cannot compare with how happy you would have been for him had he been able to achieve mastery.

What is this Jonas like, by the way? Is he quite tall?

Dear Hapless,

Jonas is fairly tall, I suppose? His wife is very short, though. The top of her head

comes up right to the center of his chest.
I've always wondered—well, it's a bit silly.
But I suppose it's less embarrassing to write
it down than to say it out loud . . . I imagine
that the first time Jonas and Katriane ever
embraced, her head must have fit in just the
right spot on his chest. I've always wondered
how they felt at that moment. Maybe they
thought to themselves that this was how
people were meant to fit together.

I take back what I said. It looks even
more embarrassing written down. . . .

Dear Aurelie,

Jonas's wife sounds lovely. A wife! Lovely
indeed. I don't think your thoughts are silly
in the least. Though I must admit I didn't
take you for such a romantic. . . .

Dear Hapless,

I'm not a romantic.

Dear Aurelie,

Are you quite certain?

Twenty-Two

Dear Aurelie,

     I'm happy to report that I have made it safely to the Scholar's City. Thankfully, the journey north featured nothing more threatening than an undercooked stew at an inn in Greenshire. (The indigestion it invoked was inconvenient but survivable.)

     Though I'm very glad that we are now both in the Northern Realm, I must admit that my return to school has not been as refreshing as I had hoped. My general lectures this semester are terribly dull. Why the study of magic necessitates a course in mathematics, I have no idea. Far worse, in that particular class I am forced to sit behind Lord Defiance, who (as you may recall) is aggressively unpleasant.

     I don't think I ever got the chance to formally thank you for what you said to him

at the palace, by the way. It truly was most
satisfying. . . .

Dear Hapless,

    I suppose you could make the case that
an understanding of the natural world
facilitates the study of magic and that
mathematics is part of the natural world?
Whatever the justification, I hope that Lord
Defiance's massive head doesn't eclipse your
view of the front of the classroom. He and
I had only a brief interaction, but I'm sure
that what I said to him was entirely justified.

    This made me wonder—you must have
met with Iliana and Lord Defiance often
over the years. Why didn't you ever mention
anything about Iliana's rank when we were
adventuring together?

Dear Aurelie,

    I suppose I didn't feel it was my place
to say anything if Iliana didn't want it to be
known. I can understand the desire to cast a
title off. To be someone else, even if just for
a little while. If Iliana found that, I wouldn't
want to be the one to take it from her. . . .

Dear Hapless,

    Who would you be, if you were someone
else?

Dear Aurelie,

I would be Bastian Sinclair.

I fear you might laugh at me for that. But there is no fiction I love so much as *The Pauper's Play*. Bastian Sinclair is a singular inspiration of mine. He has nothing at all at the start and then becomes more successful than anyone could have possibly imagined. And everyone who had ever doubted him— proven completely wrong!

My dear Steward played the role once, to great acclaim. He was actually understudying me, to tell the truth. I believe the production was all the better for his stepping in, as admittedly an eleven-year-old Bastian would have been a bit jarring. The scene in the alehouse with Madame Vermillion certainly would've played differently.

To play Bastian Sinclair though—to live that story! I must admit, it has its appeal.

(The alehouse scene notwithstanding.)

Who would you be, Aurelie? What would you do?

Dear Hapless,

I can assure you, I have no idea. I'm not sure what that says about me, except that I have very little imagination. . . .

Dear Aurelie,

On the contrary, I think you have a
prodigious imagination! I believe one
must in order to do magic, don't you? My
mentor, Professor Frison, laments my lack
of imagination. I thought maybe after our
adventure—after that strange bit of magic
I did—that I might have more success with
my magic this year. But I'm sorry to say thus
far my studies are not progressing any better
than before. And it's not just magic. I've
had a run of essays recently with record-low
marks. I'm not only a poor magician but a
dreadful writer as well. Truly a double threat!

Dear Hapless,

I have to disagree with you—you write
these letters, don't you? And nothing about
them is dreadful. You express your thoughts
quite well. . . .

Dear Aurelie,

This is different! Writing letters is . . .
or should I say, writing to you is . . . It's just
different.

Dear Hapless,

Imagine your essays as letters to me, then.
Imagine you're telling me all about what
you're learning. (I will be very eager to listen.)

Twenty-Three

Dear Aurelie,

What is your earliest memory? We've been discussing this topic recently in my independent study, and Professor Frison seemed somewhat less than amused that my earliest recollection is of the time I threw one of Honoria's dolls down the grand staircase. I think he hoped for something that we could interpret a bit more, like a mural over my bed in the nursery that transformed itself to me, or a large, cryptic hound that I saw through the window on some foggy night. Maybe I should have made something up. . . .

Dear Hapless,

My first memory . . . I suppose it must be of the rug in the sitting room at my parents' house. It was patterned with flowers of different shapes and sizes. I remember lying on the rug by my mother's feet and tracing each of the flowers in turn. Certain ones looked friendly, almost as if they were smiling up at me.

I don't know what your professor would make of this, or if it has any bearing at all on my magic. I haven't thought of that rug in a long time. I did always have a fondness for it.

Dear Aurelie,

What became of the rug? Did your mother redecorate? Mine had little patience for interior design. I suppose all the inclination for it got pushed into Honoria, who would redecorate the inside of a teacup if she could.

Dear Hapless,

I couldn't say what happened to it. I haven't been home in . . . nearly five years, I think? I imagine it was sold long ago. . . .

Dear Aurelie,

Do you miss your home? Five years is an awfully long time.

Dear Hapless,

I can't say I really miss it. But . . .

sometimes I do miss my old school. It was somewhat close to the Scholar's City, just south of the Northern Mountains. The winters there were dreadful. I think of it occasionally at this time of year, when the weather begins to turn. I liked the order of the school year, and my classes, and my teacher—Miss Ember. I miss studying magic with her. And also . . . well, she was just always someone who I liked talking to. She was easy to talk to. I miss that as well.

Dear Aurelie,

I hope you have others in your life that you can talk to now. I hope that I may be one of them.

Dear Hapless,

Thank you for that. It's very kind of you to say.

Dear Aurelie,

I really do mean it, though.

Dear Hapless,

I know. That's what makes it especially kind.

Twenty-Four

Dear Aurelie,
        I miss my mother at this time of year. When winter is just on the horizon. Before I started at the university, this is when my family and I would visit her tombstone at the Royal Chapel and leave flowers. Could I be terribly honest with you? It always struck me as odd—my mother never cared much for flowers. She cared for walks along the river and good piano concertos and lemon meringue. It's foolish, but I wish I could bring her something she actually enjoyed. Not that she could even enjoy it.

Dear Hapless,
        I don't know how well this lemon meringue tart will travel to you, or what sort of state it will be in when it arrives. But if

possible, please enjoy it on your mother's behalf. I imagine she would like that very much.

Dear Aurelie,

It was only a little bit squished and entirely delicious.

Thank you, thank you, and thank you.

Twenty-Five

Dear Aurelie, Hapless wrote, and then stared at the words on the page.

He had wanted to write *Dearest Aurelie* for some time, but it didn't feel like the right moment yet. If only there were some subtler transition. *Dearer Aurelie*, perhaps?

He turned his view to the window of his dormitory, overlooking the campus. The sky was a slate gray that told of snow, though none had fallen yet. The winter holidays were almost upon them, and Hapless would be returning to the Capital in a matter of days. Final exams were nearly over, and Hapless was ready to focus fully on his next big undertaking.

Namely, his second quest.

His original quest had been unsuccessful, of course. At least on paper. He hadn't found the Sun Stone. And there was the ambush in the Underwood, which still prickled at the back of his mind now and then when he recalled it. But the rest of the quest had been delightful, and he had met Aurelie, and that was success in itself.

It had been at the very start of the semester when Hapless was unpacking his trunks in his dormitory that he came upon his bound edition of the Sworn Scrolls. (They weren't actually available for the masses in scroll form, which was a little disappointing, though the Royal Library on campus did have most of the original documents.)

He had flipped through it on a whim and landed on a page titled "The Stone of Circumspection." Something in the passage caught his eye. He read through it.

Then he sat down on his bed and read it again, closer this time.

It was written in that convoluted language (of course, these sorts of things always were), but what it seemed to boil down to was this: the Stone of Circumspection saw through enchantments. So if one acquired the stone, one could use it to demonstrate that no magic had been used on them.

Say, for example, in the case of a kiss. An excellent, unforgettable, life-altering kiss.

It seemed like just the thing. And so Hapless's second quest had begun.

He had to proceed with the semester, of course, quest or no. But in spare moments that fall—between classes and lessons with Professor Frison and letters to Aurelie—Hapless had gone to the library. He looked at the original Scrolls, compared them to his edition, scoured for any mention of the stone. Cross-referenced other documents, letters, old leather-bound tomes.

And now the semester was all but over, and on his way back to the Capital for the winter holidays, Hapless planned to propose a detour.

"Just half a day's ride out of the way!" he assured Steward as his party prepared to depart from campus. "Only the briefest of diversions!"

Steward looked exasperated—probably par for the course, with Hapless as a charge—but eventually he relented.

And so they traveled west, farther afield than the road around the Underwood called for, and maybe it took slightly longer than half a day, but it fell out just so: Hapless successfully guided them to Lantern Bay. A small outcropping of rock above the sea, a narrow cave, several torches, and a precarious rock climb later—there was the unearthing of a stone. (And without a single ambush all the while, Hapless was pleased to note.)

The Scrolls described it as *dark as midnight*, and maybe his was a little lighter than midnight—more of an indigo maybe?—but Hapless was certain it was the Stone of Circumspection.

After the winter holidays, he brought it to Professor Frison for evaluation, and the professor was interested enough. Initially. He was less interested after several dozen attempts to elicit some kind of effect from the stone. It couldn't undo the simplest of spells.

"It's not meant to *undo*, though," Hapless insisted, "but to *see through*."

"To see through an enchantment, you must break the enchantment," Professor Frison said. He was a dignified-looking man, the sort you'd expect to become a foremost magic scholar, with a piercing gaze and hair that was snow white. He considered the stone one last time and then placed it in front of Hapless on the large wooden desk that stretched between them. "I'm afraid what you've found for yourself, my boy, is a lovely-looking rock. Nothing more."

"This is it, though!" Hapless hadn't scaled that cave wall for nothing. "I know it is."

He couldn't explain it, but he just knew. Maybe it was like the way Aurelie described magic—*you just reach inside yourself and it's there.* Hapless reached inside himself and found nothing but certainty that this was indeed the stone.

And so he had it set into a ring. Not a betrothal ring. The band was too big, for one thing—he had sized it for himself, after all. And anyway, betrothal was something that came later. Betrothal was something for people Honoria's age at least, or Gallant's to be sure, though Hapless wondered if Gallant would ever marry. (There stood a very real chance that there was no one residing in the Kingdom whom Gallant could love nearly as much as he loved the Kingdom itself).

But the ring—the stone—was meant to show Aurelie, to prove to her, that Hapless was genuine. He intended to tell her all about it.

Just as soon as he could prove that the stone was as real as his feelings.

Twenty-Six

A rotating series of couriers brought Hapless's letters to Aurelie. Among them was a youngish man with close-cropped hair and a faint mustache who was as skilled at stealthily delivering and retrieving the letters as any Court of Intrigue spy. By early spring, Aurelie and Hapless's correspondence had progressed with such frequency that he had tried everything on offer at the bakery. He preferred the morning buns, same as Iliana, which Aurelie baked herself each day.

"Reminds me of being small," he said one afternoon, as Aurelie passed him a bun across the counter and he discreetly passed her a letter back. "My nan baked ones just like these for special occasions. A bit more cinnamon in hers, though."

"I'll take that under advisement," Aurelie said.

"No, no, don't change a thing! Yours are quite good." He dropped his voice. "Maybe even better. Don't tell Nan."

Aurelie smiled.

The bell over the shop door chimed as the courier left.

Aurelie began wiping down the counter, the letter safely stowed in her apron pocket. An instant bright spot to the day.

Whenever one of the couriers arrived bearing Hapless's wit and observations, his complaints, his jokes, his thoughts on whatever Aurelie had written, his questions for her, his little asides (*I saw a painting today that I thought you might appreciate—I think it's from that same crazed sheep artist that Honoria commissioned at the palace*), Aurelie couldn't help but feel . . . warm from the inside out. A bit like magic, but at the same time, it wasn't like magic as she knew it at all, coming only from within. This was outside of Aurelie, a spell that in its very nature couldn't be cast alone.

"Whatever you have in mind, it will never come to pass," Mrs. Basil said.

Aurelie turned. She hadn't known Mrs. Basil was nearby, but there she stood in the doorway to the kitchen, her gaze narrowed on Aurelie. Jonas was out, hunting down ingredients for a special order. There were no other customers at the moment, the typical afternoon lull.

"Pardon?" Aurelie said.

"Do you think I haven't noticed your *repeat customer*?" She nodded in the direction of the front door.

Aurelie blinked. "I thought repeat customers were good for business."

She wouldn't have dreamed of saying something like that to Mrs. Basil long ago as a new apprentice. At fourteen, when everything was new and different and seemed to hang solely on Mrs. Basil's generosity. But now Aurelie was nearly eighteen. She was still committed to her apprenticeship—of course she was—but there was something that chafed about it that hadn't before. Something that made it harder to hold back sometimes.

Mrs. Basil just stared.

"You are of an age where you think you may have something of an appeal," she said. "But I can assure you, no one will offer for an apprentice. Certainly that man won't, no matter how many smiles you ply him with—he knows just what you are."

Aurelie glanced toward the door, though the courier was long gone. Mrs. Basil thought—but that was ridiculous—

Mrs. Basil approached Aurelie, stopping just in front of her. They were nearly of a height. Aurelie could see every line on Mrs. Basil's face.

"With some great degree of assistance, you may be considered tolerably pretty. But you have no education, no family, no money, no support. You have nothing. You *are* nothing."

Aurelie's cheeks flamed, awash in resentment, anger, shame.

Mrs. Basil continued. "I recognized this, and I took you in regardless. I am offering you something that no one else will. I'm offering you independence. It's what I myself achieved. It's not Mr. Basil who built this bakery, you know. Mr. Basil had the nerve to die long ago. *I* achieved mastery. I built this. And one day, perhaps, if you are exceedingly lucky, if you work tirelessly and obey my orders and keep your flirtatious smiles to yourself, you may have something of your own as well."

Mrs. Basil's gaze lingered on Aurelie for one more moment. Then she retreated. Just before she passed through the door to the kitchen, she paused and turned back to Aurelie.

"You may think that I'm being harsh with you. But I assure

you, it's entirely for your own good. One day you'll realize the impact I've had on your life, and you'll be truly grateful."

Aurelie didn't speak. She couldn't have, even if she wanted to, with the tightness in her throat.

Mrs. Basil left the room.

As soon as the bakery closed for the day, Aurelie went into the back alley. She told Jonas she was going to eat, but she stuffed the unwanted scone into her pocket and pulled out Hapless's letter instead.

She broke the seal. She began to read.

Dearest Aurelie,

I have been thinking of you. In fact, I feel these days that I am always thinking of you. School is dreadful. Writing to you makes it more bearable. I wish I could remember any single bit of wisdom my professors are trying to impart even a fraction as well as I remember kissing you. I know you said it was an enchantment, accidentally done—I know you said I would hate you twofold—but you must know by now that it's not happened, and never could. It never will.

Please write back as soon as you can, so I may have the chance to write again. I'm stupid and sick with missing you.

Yours,

H

"Aurelie?"

The back door opened, and Jonas poked his head into the alley.

It had grown dark. Aurelie's hands were stiff and cold. She still held the letter.

Dearest Aurelie, it said.

"Aurelie," Jonas repeated, and Aurelie heard him as if from far away.

"Hm?"

"Are you all right?"

I'll write to you, if you'd like, the prince had said, and what was the harm in that, in a simple exchange of letters, except that it was the prince who had said it? And it was Aurelie that he had said it to?

There was a hollow feeling in Aurelie's chest.

You have nothing. You are nothing.

"Yes," she said.

Jonas stepped into the alley. "What's that?" He gestured toward the letter. "Is it from your parents? Did something happen?"

"No." She shoved the letter into her apron pocket. "It's nothing."

"All right . . ." Jonas looked uncertain. "I've just about finished up inside. I'll be heading out soon." He paused. "Why don't you have dinner with Katriane and me? It's been a long while, hasn't it?"

Aurelie shook her head, then forced the words out. "I have more work to do. But thank you."

"Sometime soon, then?"

She tried her best to smile. "Maybe."

Jonas looked unconvinced, but he nodded nonetheless and headed inside.

Aurelie pulled the letter back out. One letter, of many. Of so many. Too many. She had let it go too far, hadn't she, for too long. She had found comfort—and joy and delight and amusement and happiness, a whole host of feelings that she never entirely had access to before, certainly never as potently—in something that she had no right to. And it hadn't just been foolish of her—it had been selfish.

You can stomp out embers but not a flame, Mrs. Basil was fond of saying.

Aurelie let magic pool in the palm of her hand and called forth a bit of heat.

She touched the corner of the letter. It caught and curled into flame, falling to the ground as it blackened and turned to ash.

Twenty-Seven

Your Highness,

Thank you for your kind attentions. I'm afraid I've been misunderstood in my acceptance of them. I didn't mean to convey anything more than friendship after our travels together last summer. Please refrain from writing further.

Sincerely,

Aurelie

PART TWO

In Which Nothing Goes as Planned

Twenty-Eight

Hapless found himself once again in a carriage. His mind was burdened. Chiefly among his thoughts that afternoon: the matter of school. The spring semester had ended rather unsatisfactorily.

"How were your exams, Your Highness?" Steward had asked as the coachmen loaded Hapless's trunks onto the carriage.

"They certainly happened!" Hapless had replied with a laugh.

"And your marks?"

"Recorded for posterity!"

If one said anything pleasantly enough, people would recognize one's enthusiasm first and the content second, and maybe they would laugh, and maybe then they would forget their original question.

The truth was, Hapless was a failure. A joke of a scholar at best. Certainly the only one among his current party to have absolutely obliterated his course of study.

At least, as far as Hapless knew. Sitting and stewing in the back of the carriage, he wondered if any of the guards accompanying him had ever had a course of study outside of . . . guardsmanship, or however it was they came to their posts. (He had wondered, after the ambush last summer, how easy it was to come by a guard position, but Steward assured him that the process was "most rigorous.") Maybe one of them had taken a pottery course to expand their horizons and done quite poorly at it. Maybe their mother still treasured their misshapen vases.

Hapless had no vases—at least, none of his own craftsmanship. Certainly there were vases in his chambers in the palace (probably? There were fresh flowers, occasionally. They had to be contained somehow). He had nothing to show for the past nine months of study.

It would be all right—it always was. His father would nod with understanding. Gallant would glance up from his papers and say, *Better luck, old chap.* (He probably wouldn't glance up—that was Hapless's embellishment, but if one is going to daydream, one might as well daydream being paid some mind for once.) Honoria would cup his cheek and smile a downturned kind of smile and tell him he had done his best, hadn't he, that was what counted. And that was the worst part—they truly believed it. That it was the absolute best he was capable of.

If only he weren't so stupid . . . If only he could just learn to pay attention . . .

His fingers itched. He wanted to get out of the carriage. He wanted to run a mile or more. He wanted to pen a letter he wouldn't send. He wanted to send it anyway.

That was the other issue—the other burden on Hapless's thoughts, the one that threatened to overtake all the others, if he allowed it.

His correspondence with Aurelie had ended.

It had been over for almost two months now, and yet he couldn't stop thinking about her, and her bright eyes, and her very polite rejection.

> Please refrain from writing further.
> Sincerely,
> Aurelie

It was the 'Sincerely' that had done it. Before, her letters were simply signed 'Aurelie' (in a very even script, measured and straightforward—no unnecessary flourishes. Hapless loved an unnecessary flourish himself, but he also loved the simplicity of Aurelie's hand. He loved everyth—but it was no use, was it?). She must have wanted him to know how sincerely she meant what she had written, that she thought only of their friendship, that his feelings were misplaced.

Sometimes Hapless felt like Aurelie's letters were the only thing getting him through the weeks and months at school. It could turn his entire day around, returning to his rooms and seeing a letter from her waiting for him on the mantelpiece. Knowing that he would get to share in a bit of her thoughts, her feelings, knowing as he held the letter in his hands that she had so very recently held it in her own. Was it all purely out of friendship? Had he misinterpreted? Was he truly so inept?

He glared down at the lace edging on his sleeves. It spilled out from the tight cuffs of his jacket, which was a deep purple. It was a hideous color. He looked like a bruise. What had he been thinking when he chose this? Or did he ever really think at all, about anything?

Hapless felt wretched.

It was in this general mood that Hapless's carriage pulled up at last in front of Winsome House. A small group of servants and footmen stood out front, along with Honoria. It touched his heart a bit, seeing her there to receive him. It wasn't the sort of thing they usually did.

"There's so much to do" was her opening greeting as he stepped down from the carriage, his legs stiff from hours of sitting.

"It's lovely to see you too," Hapless replied.

Honoria's eyes were bright as she gave him a quick glance and then pressed a kiss to his cheek. "You look like an eggplant."

"Thank you."

"What happened to silks and stripes?"

"That was ages ago."

"Midnight blue?"

Hapless still felt wretched. "I'll never wear blue again."

"Well, you're in blue and white for the wedding, so you shouldn't commit yourself to that oath until after the vows."

"Blue and white?"

"Naturally. Colors of the Kingdom."

"It's a bit traditional, is all."

"Well, I *am* the crown princess." She frowned. "What did you see yourself wearing?"

"Nothing. I was planning to cause an incredible scene."

Honoria managed to look both annoyed and amused. "We have so much to do."

"You mentioned that just a moment ago."

"And it hasn't stopped being true."

Hapless held out a hand. "Lead the way. Show me what needs doing."

Honoria squeezed his fingers as they made their way up the grand front stairs of Winsome House. "I'm glad you're here."

It made Hapless feel marginally better.

Twenty-Nine

Aurelie had no shortage of washing up to do.

She stood at the sink with one half-cleaned pan in hand and paused to make a quick gesture over the water, which was a little hotter than comfortable. She didn't turn around when someone entered the room (which they did with a great deal of stealth and likely no small amount of self-satisfaction). There was no reason to stop cleaning, despite suddenly having a visitor. In fact, the visitor was more of an impetus to continue, if anything.

Finally, a throat cleared. "I know you know I'm here."

"I know nothing." Bits of sugar caked the bottom of the pan, remnants of an exceptionally good batch of buns, and Aurelie gave them a particularly vigorous scrub.

"Truly humble of you to finally admit that."

There was nothing for Aurelie to do but sigh and turn to regard Iliana, who was now leaning casually against the massive worktable in the center of the bakery's kitchen. "What do you want?"

"To be one hand's length taller," replied Iliana conversationally. "Or a team from Ardent Fields. I'd take either, or both, if you're in the mood for granting wishes."

"Iliana."

"Yes?" She inspected her nails as if they meant anything more to her than a means with which to gouge.

"Why are you here?"

"A consultation," she said. "Of a sort."

Aurelie hadn't "consulted" for Iliana for some time now. Iliana had been in and out of the village over the last several months, and the few times she had come by, Aurelie had been too busy, or too tired, or too disinclined to seek.

Right now the idea of dredging up any more magic than it took to heat the water was unappealing. "You know I can't—"

"Yes, of course. You've been terribly dull these last two months and more committed than ever to the production of baked goods." Iliana's gaze pinned Aurelie's at last. "It's about the prince."

Aurelie's heart squeezed. "What is it? What's happened?"

"Nothing. Yet."

"Don't be cryptic."

"But that's my specialty."

"*Iliana.*"

"If name repetition is key to invoking your particular brand of magic, by all means, please make me one hand's length taller."

"I'm going to take this pan and—"

"Princess Honoria is getting married," Iliana said. "At Winsome House, the royal family's western estate. I imagine that's a fact you're already aware of."

The palace simply won't do for Honoria's wedding, Hapless

had written some months back. *She prefers our summer home, Winsome House, which boasts lovely gardens and greenhouses and a lake and a hedge maze. It will also be a massive pain for everyone in the Capital to travel to, and as Honoria put it, will therefore "prune the guest list to only the most dedicated."*

"I'll be attending the wedding," Iliana continued. "I was hoping you would be my guest."

Aurelie gave an empty breath of laughter. "Seriously?"

"Why not?"

"I can think of several reasons."

"Such as?"

Aurelie gestured to the kitchen at large. "I'm a bit occupied, for one thing."

"Oh yes. Those pans certainly won't wash themselves."

Aurelie couldn't help but snap: "I know you think that my work is inconsequential, but we don't all have the luxury of doing whatever we please, *Your Ladyship.*"

Iliana straightened up. "I believe that something unsavory may happen at the wedding," she said, her tone suddenly clipped. "That Hapless may be in jeopardy again. I thought you might want to assist me."

"In jeopardy," Aurelie repeated. "How?"

"I've been circling it for a while now. Something about the ambush in the Underwood wasn't right."

"Yes, maybe it being an *ambush* has something to do with that."

"Why would they use Impossible weapons and not strike Hapless? Unless the intention was never to strike him at all. If they aimed and missed, it means they *meant* to miss. What if they wanted to take him instead?"

The thought made Aurelie's stomach clench. "Take him? Where? Why?"

"And Elias Allred," Iliana continued, as if Aurelie hadn't spoken. "Everything surrounding his disappearance—the very nature of it, vanishing from Copperend's party in the Underwood . . . I think . . ." She shook her head. "I think that what happened to him could happen to Hapless. No one could touch the prince while he was at school—he's constantly surrounded at the university. But now that he's at Winsome House, which is certainly remote, and with the cover of a large event like the wedding—"

"What proof do you have?" Aurelie said. "That he could really be in danger?"

"I don't," Iliana said. "I just . . . I have a feeling."

Aurelie cast a look around a bit helplessly. "I can't drop everything for a *feeling*."

There was something uncharacteristically pleading in Iliana's expression. "I'm not magic. At all. You know that. But maybe *this* . . . maybe it's a kind of magic too? I just . . . know we have to be there. *You* have to be there. If we need to find Hapless, you can seek him. If something goes awry, he'll listen to you. You have magic. You're smart. You're my partner in this."

"Your partner? Really? Your partner who makes twenty percent? Your partner who receives a *fraction* of information at any given time, about any given thing that you deign to concern me with—"

"You care about him," Iliana interrupted. "I know you do. You can't truly think I never caught the comings and goings of those couriers."

"Iliana—"

"I need you to come with me."

Aurelie's voice broke, just slightly. "I can't."

For a moment, Iliana regarded Aurelie the same way she had the very first time they met, that first visit to the bakery when Aurelie had refused the seeking stones. *I'm sorry, I think you must be mistaken.* A moment of evaluation. A mind being made up.

"Fine," Iliana said, and then she turned and left.

Everything had been far less complicated before the adventure.

Early the next morning after Iliana's visit, Aurelie lay on her straw mattress, staring up at the ceiling of her tiny room. A fly circled overhead, lazily buzzing, the only sound in the dark of pre-sunrise.

Aurelie tried not to think about Iliana—blast Iliana, truly—or Hapless, but it was difficult to stop once she started. One thought gave way to another, to that time spent together, to last summer, to the kiss, to everything that happened afterward—

It didn't bear reflection.

Aurelie forced herself to think of other things. Any day now, she would be promoted to journeyman. Mrs. Basil had even spoken directly of it—"It was during Jonas's fourth year, I believe, that he advanced to journeyman," she'd said.

Aurelie had been too afraid to speak, lest she scare the idea from Mrs. Basil's mind.

"I suppose I'll have to find a new apprentice eventually,"

Mrs. Basil had continued with a frown, and then mused, "Two journeymen," as if she was considering the idea.

Aurelie couldn't go haring off after Iliana again. She just couldn't. It wasn't only a promotion that was on the line—it was her future. She couldn't risk it just because Iliana had a *feeling*.

At least, that's what she told herself, lying there on her mattress.

She had to get up. Heat the ovens. Put in last night's dough. Start the fresh dough for buns and cinnamon rolls. Prepare ingredients for Jonas. There were many things to focus on. None of them were Hapless or the possibility that he could be in peril. Or Hapless's smile. Or the peril.

And certainly none of them were his final letter.

She had burned all the ones that came before it. If Mrs. Basil ever found any of them, she'd undoubtedly try to sell them to whichever publication paid the highest. Aurelie could just see the headlines:

PRINCE'S POOR PARAMOUR PREPARES PASTRIES FOR PITTANCE!

Or worse:

PRINCE SEDUCED BY MAGICIAN BAKER: ONE BITE IS ALL IT TOOK!

Aurelie had never paid much attention to royal gossip, but ever since their adventure, her ears caught every mention of the royal family made by customers in the shop. She heard of King Gallant's victory in Court as his road through the Underwood was finally approved. She heard of Princess Honoria's wedding preparations and the debate over whether she should invite Sylvain Copperend to the affair (for if he really was her uncle, one villager asserted, it would be rather rude not to). And she heard of Prince Hapless, the hopeless student, beloved but benighted. It was evident that he was widely thought to be a fool. Every royal family had one, apparently—handsome and guileless, like a big yellow dog that tracks mud through your kitchen but wags his tail and cocks his head and is instantly forgiven. You just couldn't help yourself.

Aurelie knew the truth of it—the prince's smile was indomitable, his manners impeccable, he cared too much about things that didn't really matter and not enough about things that did. Whenever she thought of him these days— and she tried desperately not to—it was with an infuriating mix of warmth and longing and despair.

She sat up abruptly, scooted off the mattress, lifted it up, and pulled out the letter.

She ran a finger over the broken wax seal—a deep scarlet, with the impression of a sunflower set into it. *I can't use the royal seal, can I?* one early letter read. *Trying to maintain a bit of stealth and all that. Besides, I always liked this one. Sunflowers were my mother's favorite, and I am nothing if not mawkishly sentimental.*

Aurelie unfolded the parchment. The letter began *Dearest Aurelie,* but there was a line drawn through the last three letters of *Dearest.* The prince's penmanship was elegant but careless. Too many unnecessary loops. Ink splatters abounded.

Dearest Aurelie,

The flourishes on the *D* and the *A* were simply unreasonable.

I've just received your letter. I want
only to tell you that it was received and
that I don't wish to cause you any further
discomfort. I must apologize. I've been too
forward. Please forgive me.

I wish you all the best, in everything.
I wish you the world, in fact, for you deserve
no less.

Yours most sincerely,
Hapless

There was no point in rereading it—Aurelie had long
since committed it to memory. She knew the curve of every
letter, every stray speck of ink. Every time she looked at it, she
felt the urge to set fire to it, like she had done to all the other
letters. Each of them signed *Prince Hapless*, and then *Hapless*,
and then simply *Yours, H.* Until this last one.

She shouldn't have saved it. It was like pressing on a
bruise. But she just couldn't help herself.

She brought forth a bit of magic now, letting the warmth
pool in the palm of her hand, but she didn't set a spark.

Instead, she slid the letter back beneath the mattress.

Got up, washed, got dressed, scraped her hair back into
a plait.

Then she knelt and took the letter back out, pressed it
flat, and slipped it into her apron pocket.

She went to the kitchen and set about heating the ovens,
preparing ingredients, starting the dough. Jonas arrived,
nodded to her, and wordlessly began to work. There was
oftentimes too much to do for any real conversation to take

place between them. But sometimes the two of them worked silently side by side in the kitchen, and it was by choice. It was peaceful—more relaxing than any conversation, somehow. They could be quiet together, and there was a familiarity to it, a comfort that Aurelie dearly appreciated.

It certainly allowed her to be alone with her thoughts, which was sometimes good. Sometimes not.

Yours, H! she thought, cutting through a sack of flour and emptying it into one of the largest mixing bowls.

Yours sincerely was one thing. Even *Yours most humbly*. They were polite. Nearly impersonal, really. But *Yours*! Stripped of a modifier, it meant just what it said. And *H*! Not only his name, sans title, but his name, sans all other letters but the first. Stripped to its most basic form, its most intimate.

The prince didn't know what he was doing. Maybe he really was a fool.

All the more reason to meet Iliana. What if she was right? What if he really was in danger and something terrible happened, and Aurelie could have prevented it somehow? She would never forgive herself.

Jonas spoke eventually. "What happens to the dough if you stare at it hard enough?"

"Pardon?"

He shook his head, amusement in his eyes. "You seem preoccupied."

"No, it's just . . ."

Aurelie watched as Jonas measured out one cup of sugar and then another into his own mixing bowl.

I wish you the world, she thought. And, *Yours, H.*

"My . . . friend . . . is in trouble," she began haltingly. "I think. I don't know." A pause. "Well. I guess it's not the kind of trouble you really *know* until it's too late. . . ."

Jonas looked up, eyes widening. "Ah." His tone was delicate: "Maybe . . . you could speak to Katriane—"

Katriane was pregnant. Jonas had practically glowed with the news when he had told Aurelie, several months ago.

"Not like that!" Aurelie exclaimed. "Not . . . that. My actual friend." Though that wasn't quite the truth, either. "Something is wrong—maybe—I don't know for sure—"

"Then you should help them," Jonas said. "If it's in your power to."

"It's . . . a bit . . . time-sensitive. I think."

Jonas raised his eyebrows. "And the time is now?"

Aurelie nodded, eyes darting toward the staircase. Mrs. Basil roomed above the bakery. She wouldn't stir until mid-morning at least.

"Is it your finder friend?" Jonas asked.

"No." Aurelie bit her lip. "No, it's . . . it's someone else."

"Ah." Jonas observed Aurelie for a long moment and then said, "Don't worry. I'll manage Mrs. Basil."

"But—"

"Go and help your friend." He smiled a little. "Maybe you could take a walk in the park with them afterward."

Aurelie felt the outline of the letter in her apron pocket. There was no doubt what she needed to do. It was probably a done deal before she even rose that morning.

She was kidding herself—it was a done deal as soon as Iliana had turned up. Or to be quite truthful, it was a done deal the day they had rescued Prince Hapless from the ambush, even more completely hopeless the moment he brushed himself off and then looked at them all with a sheep-ish grin that had barreled through Aurelie like half a dozen sporting horses from Ardent Fields.

"Thank you," Aurelie told Jonas. She wanted to clasp his hand—something—but she held back. She dropped a quick curtsy instead, which teased the corners of his lips up, and then she darted into her room to grab a few things. She wasn't sure how long she would be gone—she wasn't even sure how she was going to find Iliana, or find Winsome House without her—but she was resolute.

She reached for an empty flour sack on her way out the door, and as she pulled it from the pile, a small square of folded paper fell to the floor.

Aurelie picked it up and unfolded it.

I'll depart at 7 in the morning from the Marquis flats, it read. *If you should change your mind.*

(I know you will.)

(I know everything, remember?)

Thirty

The Marquis flats stood several stories tall in red stone, with large arched windows and an imposing black door. Aurelie stood motionless in front of this door as the bell tower in the town square began a series of chimes: one, two . . .

This was a terrible idea.

Three . . .

Aurelie turned and started back in the direction of the bakery.

Four, five . . .

But Hapless—

Six . . .

I wish you the world . . .

Seven.

Aurelie turned back.

The door suddenly swung open, and a very fashionable lady stepped through it. She was holding a leather traveling case and wore a fine dress of coral-colored silk, with turquoise trim at the elbows and neck. Her hair was pinned up and adorned with a headband that had an almost comically large white feather extending from it.

She glared daggers. "Not a single word, Baker."

"Why in the world—"

"That's four words. Here." Iliana swung the traveling case at Aurelie. "You can change in the carriage."

"What—"

The steady clop of hooves against cobblestone sounded in the distance. Aurelie looked over her shoulder as a grand carriage, pulled by a team of large chestnut horses, appeared at the end of the street. Heads turned to follow its progress as it made its way down the street and pulled to a stop in front of Aurelie and Iliana.

"I had to give my mother my address to arrange this," Iliana said as a groom jumped down from the carriage to open its door. "Heaven knows I'll have to move now."

Aurelie watched as the groom handed Iliana into the carriage. Then he turned to Aurelie, and after just a moment's hesitation, extended a gloved hand to help her in as well.

"Thank you," Aurelie said, sliding into the seat across from Iliana. The interior of the carriage was just as fancy as the exterior, the seats done in velvet, the trim in dark wood. The door shut, and Aurelie looked at Iliana in the seat opposite her. "Am I allowed to ask what's happening right now?"

"We're attending a wedding, remember? A *royal* wedding. We can't exactly pull up in a hackney coach, can we?" Iliana reached up suddenly as if to fuss with the feather and then just as quickly dropped her hands back onto her lap. "It's best to get used to these horrid clothes now. We'll be stuck in the likes of them for a week or more anyway."

"*A week*?" Aurelie repeated as the carriage sprang into motion.

"Of course. There's the travel, and then there's all the folderol that comes with these sorts of affairs—a wedding isn't just the ceremony, you know—"

"I'll be fired the moment I get back."

Iliana waved a hand. "It'll be fine. Hapless will send along a royal missive or visit your bakery himself, and your heinous patron will be so out of her gourd about it that she'll forget you slipped off at all."

Aurelie had reservations. Lots of them. She could still turn back—jump down from the carriage now, hurry back to the bakery, and Mrs. Basil would likely never be the wiser.

But after a moment's thought, Aurelie realized . . . she didn't want to.

"Fine," she said.

There was still the future to think of, of course. There was still being a journeyman. So she added, "But then that's it."

"What do you mean?"

"I'm going with you, but then it's over. It's over as soon as we're done."

"What is?"

"This." Aurelie waved a hand between them. "This thing where you call on me and I drop everything and I *risk* everything and something inevitably goes horribly wrong!"

"Nothing will go wrong."

"Why would you say that? Why would you tempt fate?"

"Fate has no power over me," Iliana said, and blast her, she probably believed it.

The dress Iliana brought for Aurelie was far more expensive than anything Aurelie had ever worn in her life. It was also far too long, which became apparent the moment they stopped for lunch at an inn. Aurelie stepped out of the carriage and promptly tripped on her hem and fell over.

Iliana looked much too amused as she pulled Aurelie to her feet. "Have you never gathered your skirts before?"

"In case you haven't noticed, I'm not nearly as tall as you."

"That's quite all right. We all have our shortcomings."

"Well, you're certainly not getting me into one of those," someone said from behind them. Aurelie turned and was greeted by the sight of—

"Quad!"

Aurelie had seen Quad more often than she had expected to since their adventure last summer. The first time, Aurelie had been standing in the back alley hurriedly eating her supper when a voice emerged, seemingly from the stone wall of the building next door. Aurelie had nearly jumped out of her skin.

"You eat quite quickly," the voice had said, and then a pair of eyes blinked out at her, and a figure stepped away from the wall. It was Quad, who shook as if to dry off, losing the color of the stone and transforming into her usual self. "Is it because you have no one to talk to?"

"I . . ." Aurelie knew the truth—she ate quickly so she could get back to work. But for some reason that wasn't what she replied that day. "I suppose so. Yes."

Quad had nodded, and then after a long pause, said, "I've seen better alleys."

When it became clear that Quad wasn't going to continue, Aurelie spoke. "Oh?"

"Mortal invention, alleys. We don't need them. You don't have alleys if you don't have buildings."

"No buildings? Where do you live?"

"I live wherever I am. I'm living right now."

Aurelie smiled.

She had offered Quad part of her meal that evening. Quad had tried it and deemed it "acceptable," stood with Aurelie while she finished her food, and then left with no stated intent to return. However, several weeks later, it happened again—Quad appeared, shared a bit of food, left with little fanfare. Then she returned another night. And returned again. Sometimes days apart, sometimes weeks. Aurelie began to bring out different baked goods for Quad to try—whatever leftovers from the day she could sneak with little notice. Quad had an opinion on everything. The hard rolls were a bit too salty. The lemon tart was delicately flavored. The scones were just what they should be.

"You could be a food critic," Aurelie said once.

"What's a critic?"

"Someone who gives their opinion on things."

"Oh, I'd be quite good at that."

Aurelie grew accustomed to meals with Quad every now and then. She had no idea what Quad got up to in the meantime. She never saw both her and Iliana together. But she came to appreciate Quad's quiet company, her occasional questions, and her plentiful critiques of the bakery's offerings.

"You both look terrible," Quad said now, standing outside the inn with Iliana and Aurelie, amusement alight in her eyes.

"Hello to you too," Iliana said. "I thought I told you there's a dress code."

"Mortal invention," Quad replied. "Are we going to eat?"

They dined at the inn and then set out again together. Quad occupied the seat next to Iliana in the carriage, since as Quad put it, "I can't afford to look at you straight on for so many hours. I'll laugh myself to death."

The carriage ride stretched into the afternoon. Aurelie watched the scenery gradually alter, the trees changing shape and configuration, the land flattening out. She had never been westward before.

After several hours spent peering out the window, she looked across at Iliana. That ridiculous feather bobbed up and down as the carriage passed over uneven terrain.

Aurelie recalled suddenly the memory of the feather on the desk in Headmistress's office, that childhood day. Iliana's feather was much showier. It would return to a fancier bird, no doubt, somewhere it could stand out against vibrant colors.

"Hey!" Iliana squawked suddenly, reaching for the feather as it separated from the headband.

Aurelie startled. "Sorry!"

Quad made a grab for the feather as it levitated its way toward the window. She managed to catch hold of it.

"Sorry," Aurelie repeated, sheepish. "I was just thinking."

"About what?"

"The feather test," she said. Quad gave her a questioning look. "It's a way to assess magic in children."

"How does it work?"

"You look at a feather and imagine it being different."

Quad considered this for a moment. "Feathers are quite malleable," she said. "I suppose it's as good a place to start as any." She handed the feather to Aurelie. "I'd like to take this test."

"Why?" Iliana said. "You already know you've got magic."

"Not much else to do, is there?"

"Not true. We could play a round of cards."

"Do you have a set of cards?" asked Aurelie.

Iliana's face did something that was perilously close to a pout. "No."

"You can take the test too," Quad said graciously.

"I already took it as a child! And to the surprise of no one, I failed spectacularly."

"There's no way to fail spectacularly," Aurelie said. "Either something happens or it doesn't." She scooted over and placed the feather on the seat beside her. "Give it a try, Quad."

Quad considered the feather as Aurelie watched with interest. She had never seen anyone take the test before. She looked over at Quad and then back down at the feather—

Only the feather was gone.

"What did you do with it?" Iliana asked.

Aurelie reached out onto the seat next to her, feeling only cushion until her fingers brushed against—

The feather reappeared.

Quad smiled briefly.

"You made it disappear," Aurelie said. "That's the same thing that—" She swallowed. "That's what Hapless said happened to his. He wanted to make it disappear."

"Makes sense," Quad replied. "He's got old magic in him."

"What do you mean?"

"The charm he did on the guards in the village, for one. The disguise at the inn in the Meadowlands, for another."

Aurelie frowned. "But you disguised him at the inn."

Quad shook her head. "He disguised himself first."

Something pulled at the edge of Aurelie's mind. Something Hapless had said that morning in the Meadowlands, several times in fact: "'I'm quite sure no one will recognize me,'" Aurelie murmured.

"Since we already knew him, we were immune to the enchantment," Quad said.

"And since you know old magic, you could tell it was there in the first place."

Quad nodded.

"Well, that's a fine feather in his cap," Iliana said. "And speaking of feathers . . ."

Aurelie handed the feather over. "Why do you even care about it?" she asked, watching as Iliana fixed it back into the headband.

"My mother says that headpieces suit me. They add *visual interest*."

"Good heavens, now you sound like Hapless."

"The real answer is, I *don't* care, but I'm of the opinion that if one is going to do something, they should do it right."

Aurelie couldn't argue with that.

Thirty-One

The problem with weddings, in Hapless's opinion, was that they weren't just the vows. They were an entire multiday affair. There was the lovers' ball. The family breakfast. The ceremony itself, the wedding feast, the promenade, the reception . . . It went on and on and inexorably on. Honoria even wanted some of the truly old and archaic rituals—the pouring of sand and lighting of candles, the ancestral wreath, the fox run. . . .

It would be nearly a week spent in festivities. And Hapless didn't feel the slightest bit festive.

He would simply have to fake it.

"Smashing!" he called, peering into Honoria's chambers. She was standing in front of a full-length mirror while Noelle and Felizia darted around, straightening her hem and smoothing invisible wrinkles in her train. "Stunning! The very height of fashion and elegance!"

Honoria met his gaze in the mirror. "What's wrong with you?"

Maybe faking it required a subtler approach. "I hardly know," Hapless said.

Noelle gave a poorly concealed snicker as another one of Honoria's ladies-in-waiting appeared.

"Duchess Swift has arrived with your cousins," she announced. "And Duchess Bright, with her children and two guests."

Hapless's heart rose suddenly in his chest. "Iliana is here?"

"Yes."

"And the guests. Who are they?"

There was no reason to ever imagine that Iliana would bring—Hapless could scarcely dare to hope—

And yet—

"Undisclosed," Honoria said, meeting Hapless's eyes in the mirror. "Just who one wants at their wedding. Unidentified strangers. The uncertainty, the unpredictability, it really adds a particular thrill to an already stressful affair, doesn't it?"

"I'm sure they'll be delightful," Hapless said quickly.

"Don't give me that."

"What?"

"That pacifying tone, just like Gallant. The both of you sometimes, I swear—"

"I'm not like Gallant."

"You're more alike than you think."

"I don't know why you would say something so cruel."

Honoria smiled, seemingly in spite of herself. "We shouldn't tease our brother."

"But it's such fun." Hapless turned to the lady-in-waiting. "Do you know where Duchess Bright and her family are staying?"

"In the east wing," she said. "They'll be overlooking the courtyard, I believe."

"Thank you," Hapless said, and saluted Honoria. "Looking tip-top! Glowing and all that!" And then he hurried off.

The east wing, regrettably, was rather large.

Winsome House in general was large, but the family chambers, where Hapless spent most of his time when in residence, were at least manageable. One didn't need a map and a compass to navigate them.

But the east wing was a maze of hallways and doors and staircases and verandas, and one could get properly turned around. Hapless peered into every open room and knocked on the doors of the closed ones. (He accidentally entangled himself in a fifteen-minute conversation with Lord Price, who Hapless had interrupted in the middle of shaving and who didn't seem to mind at all holding a conversation with a face half-full of lather.) And then he remembered that the Brights would be facing the courtyard, but then he got turned around as to which side faced the courtyard. . . .

It was a while spent searching.

It was worth it.

Because at last, he happened upon a drawing room with its door half-ajar and heard a very familiar voice—

"Honestly, Baker, yours are far better."

Hapless didn't stop to consider that he should knock, or announce himself, or do anything rational or practical of the sort—he simply pushed through the door and burst into the room, as if the people inside would disappear if he weren't fast enough.

It was a relatively small room, with an intricate gold-wrought ceiling and a cluster of pink-and-white upholstered furniture. An array of sandwiches and cakes was spread across a low table at the center of the seating arrangement. Quad and Iliana sat on a sofa, sipping tea. And there by the mantel, examining a ceramic figurine, was Aurelie.

All three of them looked up when Hapless appeared. Iliana looked surprised. Quad looked entirely placid. And Aurelie startled, knocking the figurine off the mantel. It fell to the ground and smashed into pieces.

"Oh, hell," she said, and then clapped a palm over her mouth.

On the one hand, Hapless wasn't exactly sure what kind of reception he had been hoping for. On the other hand, he was just so purely happy to see the three of them.

"Prince," Iliana said, rising to her feet. She was not dressed for adventuring as she usually was, but was outfitted quite finely nonetheless. "We weren't expecting you."

"No, I was . . . that is to say, I thought that I'd—" Hapless crossed suddenly over to Aurelie as she stooped to pick up the pieces of the figurine. "There's no need to bother with that," he said.

She shook her head. "I can try to fix it—"

"It's nothing. Honoria puts these sorts of things every-where. I've got about two dozen different ceramic farm animals in my room, I have no idea what I'm meant to do with them."

He gently took the pieces from Aurelie's hands. (*Aurelie's* hands—*Aurelie,* here!) It was a ceramic coach driver and a pumpkin-shaped vehicle, now split into several fragments.

Hapless desperately wanted to say something . . . effortlessly charming. Yet something that still managed to evince an air of indifference. He wanted to be charismatic but aloof.

But all he said was "I wouldn't much like riding around inside a pumpkin."

He grimaced.

But then Aurelie met his eyes for just a moment. "No?"

"No. The seeds alone would make for close quarters. And I look dreadful in orange."

For a second, Aurelie looked as if she might smile.

Then Quad cleared her throat loudly. Hapless looked over.

"Sorry," Quad said. "This cake is rather dry."

Iliana grinned. "Are you happy to see us, then, Prince?"

"Yes." Too eager? "I suppose." He looked back at Aurelie, but she had moved away, toward one of the chairs. Hapless set the pieces of the broken figurine on an end table. "Yes," he repeated. "I didn't know you were planning to attend."

"Yes, well, I've always been fond of your sister," Iliana replied.

"Have you?"

"I suppose. In an abstract sort of way." Iliana took a quick sip of tea. "Anyway, we're all here to wish her well."

"Will you be attending the lovers' ball this evening?"

"Of course."

Hapless's gaze slid toward Aurelie. She was staring in the direction of the windows.

"And will you . . . *all* be attending?"

"I wouldn't miss it for the world," Quad said, and then took another teacake.

"I thought you said they were dry," Iliana said.

Quad shrugged. "It wasn't an indictment."

Hapless smiled a little.

Thirty-Two

I feel . . . overdressed," Aurelie said, standing side by side with Iliana and peering into the full-length mirror of their dressing room. Both the dress that Iliana wore and the one she had lent to Aurelie were . . . aggressively adorned. Trimmed to the skies and back with ribbons, lace, bows, pearlescent beads, all manner of decoration.

"The lovers' ball is essentially an ode to the couple's courtship," Iliana explained. "The guests are meant to reflect the . . . how should I put it . . . the *ardor* of that courtship through their fashions. A simple gown would be an insult."

Quad—seated at the vanity on a tufted pouf—gave a snicker. "I'd rather be insulted."

"You'll have to do something about your clothes as well," Iliana said. Quad sighed and then came and stood between Iliana and Aurelie in front of the mirror. She reached out and grabbed the fabric of each of their skirts.

Aurelie watched, enraptured, as color from each of their dresses leached up Quad's hands and onto her tunic and pants, transforming the fabric into a swirling pattern. Beads and bits of sparkle followed in its path, dotting her collar and cuffs.

"Sufficient?" she said, and Iliana nodded, looking impressed.

Aurelie considered her own reflection again for a moment. She looked entirely absurd. She couldn't help but wonder what Hapless would be wearing, and from there, she couldn't help but think of his expression as he burst into the sitting room earlier, of his hands as they had gently prized the pieces of the broken figurine from her fingers. There was so much she wanted to say to him and yet nothing at all that could be said. She wasn't here to find out how he had been these last months, how his classes had turned out, what looks he had settled on for his new spring wardrobe. If he was all right. If he was happy. None of it was her purview.

There was only the possibility that he was in danger. She couldn't lose sight of that, of why she was even there in the first place.

"What are we supposed to do when we get to the ball?" Aurelie asked Iliana.

"We enjoy ourselves," Iliana said simply. "We act like guests."

"That's it?"

"And we keep our eyes and ears open," Iliana added. "Naturally."

Eventually, they made their way downstairs—a longer process than Aurelie could have imagined. Calling it Winsome *House* was a bit of a misnomer. It was larger than the entire high street in Aurelie's village.

They joined the crowd streaming toward the ballroom,

and Aurelie fell slightly behind Quad and Iliana as she struggled to manage her hems. (The dress was far too long for her.)

It was then that someone called out to her.

"Aurelie? Is it really you?"

Aurelie turned and was greeted by the unexpected sight of a familiar face—a face from years ago, once round and rosy, now somewhat matured. The smile was just the same, though, delighted and genuine.

"It *is* you!" Marthe cried, and grasped Aurelie's hands. "Oh, look at you! Look at us both!"

Aurelie was transported instantly back to childhood, to school, to nights in the dormitory as Marthe's bunkmate. Marthe had been kind and sunny, as generous with smiles and laughter as she was with hair ribbons and the sweets sent by her parents.

Aurelie blinked in surprise. "Marthe! What are you doing here?"

"I'm accompanying my great-aunt," Marthe replied proudly. "I'm her companion now, isn't that wonderful? Auntie's quite rich, and it just so happened we called on her at the midsummer holidays two years ago, and she and I got along quite well, very well indeed, and so she's decided to settle on me!"

If any one of Aurelie's school friends was to unexpectedly become an heiress, Aurelie was glad that it was Marthe. Aurelie had no doubt she would do very well living in comfort, being pleasant and hospitable and wearing beautiful clothes.

"That's wonderful," Aurelie said.

"But what about you? We were all so sad when you left school, but I was always certain you would accomplish something incredible."

"Hardly."

"I should say so! You're here, after all! At the *royal wedding*! Oh, I'd just love to hear all about—"

"Marthe!"

Up ahead, an older woman in an impossibly elaborate gown beckoned to Marthe.

"I need to attend to Auntie, but let's talk more inside, all right? I want to hear everything." Marthe squeezed Aurelie's hand once more and then hurried off to join her aunt.

It was before the first dance that everyone was called to attention, and Gallant brought Honoria and Lord Adamant up to the dais to introduce them as a couple. "A marriage bound for felicity and prosperity," Gallant proclaimed, really making a meal of it. Honoria glowed nonetheless, and Adam looked well pleased.

Hapless was happy for them, truly, but he couldn't ignore the feeling that had been brewing inside him all evening—the desire to seek out Aurelie, to talk with her, to sort out what had happened, to explain about the Stone of Circumspection . . .

But Hapless had *duties* to attend to. He entertained several duchesses (friends of his mother, awfully kind but prone to tilted heads and sad eyes, as if he were still a young boy in mourning) and talked to Viscount Ably about the crops this season (the viscount had the most impressive mustache

Hapless had ever seen and a pleasant countenance under-neath, which helped soften how truly dull his chosen topics of conversation usually were), and he prayed for the music to start so he would have an excuse to slip away and finally find his friends.

The first dance began at last. Hapless scanned the room once more for Aurelie, Iliana, and Quad but saw no sign of them. The crowd was massive. He ended up cheerfully wrangled into a dance with Viscount Ably's daughter, who was several years younger than him and a much livelier conversationalist than her father. In the span of one dance, Hapless heard about every one of her particular friends at school, who was in whose confidence, and why everyone was in love with Lady Manner's younger son but not the older, who had received an open-top carriage for his birthday—but not a very nice one—and was far too boastful about it, all things considered.

"I see," Hapless said, and, "Truly?" and also, "Did he?" and, "You don't say!"

Miss Ably clasped his hand at the end of the dance and said breathlessly, "You're far more appealing than your brother, no matter what anyone says about you being dim-witted," and then dashed off, leaving Hapless both confounded and flat-tered.

There was hardly a break in the music after that. Before Hapless could peel off and search for Aurelie, the next dance began and he found himself standing across from Lady Pith. Iliana's paramour.

Lady Pith was very beautiful, in a way that Honoria would probably consider "too conventional." Honoria often said that true beauty necessitated one or more dissonant features to *truly captivate*. There was nothing at all dissonant about Lady Pith. She had deep brown eyes and long dark hair that was pinned elaborately, with several curls escaping and framing her face.

Hapless knew her, but only a little—same as he knew many of the members of the nobility. Thrown together at functions like this over the years, sharing a dance or a bit of conversation but never delving much beyond the surface. He knew Lady Pith was pleasant but not demonstrative; she had a habit of assessing someone with a single look that would make Honoria proud. Pith would have been in Hapless's year at the university, but she elected to stay in the Capital and continue her studies with a music master there. She was a skilled violinist and hoped for a career in the Royal Symphony.

Hapless wondered what she thought of the orchestra this evening. He noticed a twitch of her lips as the strings section took over the melody, and he was uncertain whether that indicated a positive or a negative reception.

"Have you seen Iliana this evening?" Hapless asked eventually, as they danced their way through the set.

Pith nodded. "She's here. With a friend in tow."

"Aurelie."

Pith inclined her head.

"She's a good sort, Aurelie," Hapless said. "Very . . . she's very . . ."

There were so many things about Aurelie that were captivating. Hapless wasn't sure which ones fell under Honoria's rubric of true beauty—the angle of her jaw, maybe, or the particular curve of her bottom lip—but all together, Aurelie wasn't just beautiful. She was the most interesting person Hapless had ever known.

Pith's expression didn't change much, but there was amusement in her eyes. "Oh, very." She glanced back over Hapless's shoulder. "Iliana seems particularly fond of her."

"They're not . . . I mean, that is to say . . . I don't think that Iliana . . . though Aurelie is . . . very—"

"So you've said," replied Pith with a small smile. She shook her head. "I'm not jealous."

"I would never presume."

Pith's eyes shone. "Of course not."

Across the ballroom, Aurelie stood watching.

"Here," Iliana said, returning to their stretch of wall with two fluted glasses.

A pair of girls paused nearby, and Aurelie could just overhear one of them murmuring: "Duchess Bright's daughter. The one who runs wild."

Iliana handed Aurelie a glass and then clinked hers against it. "To running wild." Then she took a long drink.

Aurelie glared at the two girls, neither of whom seemed to notice.

"Don't trouble yourself," Iliana said. "My mother always says that to be talked of is to be thought of, and to be thought of is the greatest compliment that one can pay you. Whether they intend it as such or not." She finished off her drink and then eyed Aurelie's.

Aurelie rolled her eyes and exchanged her full glass for Iliana's empty one.

Then she turned her attention back to the center of the room.

She could just barely glimpse Hapless dancing with the girl who was no doubt the infamous Lady Pith. The same Lady Pith who Aurelie had seen so long ago, in her very first seek for Iliana. *Camille.* She looked just as Aurelie had seen her then, though somehow impossibly more elegant in person, her movements graceful and assured. The picture of nobility.

The set ended, and Hapless bowed over Lady Pith's hand.

"He's fond of you, you know," Iliana said, following Aurelie's gaze. "In case it wasn't painfully obvious."

"He's fond of you, too. And Quad and his steward and his coachman, I'm sure, and every chambermaid and groom, every member of the peerage, those pastries, that statue. He likes everyone and everything; it's exhausting."

Iliana eyed her. "You're fond of him, too."

Lady Pith had retrieved her hand and stood in conversation with Hapless as the next set began.

"And what about you?" Aurelie asked. It seemed only fair.

"Oh, please. Hapless is like a cousin to me."

"I meant Lady Pith."

Iliana shook her head. "That's nothing."

"Oh really. Why do you carry her glove?"

"In case one of my hands gets cold."

"You're remarkably thickheaded."

"From you, that's nearly a compliment. You're the most thickheaded person I've ever met in my entire life."

"I thought there was something between the two of you."

Aurelie and Iliana both watched as Lady Pith dropped

a curtsy to Hapless and then turned and cut through the crowd behind her.

"Maybe," Iliana murmured. "But nothing of substance. We're too different."

"You're a hypocrite."

"What?"

"*Hypocrite*," Aurelie repeated. "You're the one—you keep saying Hapless and I—"

When Iliana looked over, there was unexpected sadness in her eyes. "Pith is not Hapless. He's . . . kind and earnest, he doesn't care about certain things the way he's supposed to. But Pith is . . . practical." Her gaze returned to the crowd. "Don't mistake me—that's part of her charm. She knows . . ."

"Knows what?"

"That I could never be this." A shake of her head. "I could never go back."

"You're back right now."

"This is different. This is . . . tourism. A trip to the Marshes of Avila in midwinter. Three days are lovely, two more are tolerable, and by the sixth, you're sick of the bugs and you smell like swamp and all you want is to return to the life you know. Forfeit the one you've borrowed." She shook her head. "Everything here is borrowed. Nothing fits right."

"I've never been on holiday," Aurelie said after a pause. "Let alone often enough to become sick of it."

"It was an insufferable metaphor, I'll admit," Iliana replied with a wry smile. "My apologies, Baker. I hate being back here. It brings out the worst in me."

"I'll forgive you if you tell me your Court name," Aurelie said.

Iliana's eyes went heavenward. She heaved a sigh.

"Iliana," Aurelie pressed.

"You know, I can never tell if you're blessing me or cursing me when you do that."

"*Iliana.*"

"It really is charming, you know, with that Northland accent of yours. The tones are so much more *rounded*—"

"Your name."

She shook her head. Heaved another sigh, bigger this time. It could launch a fleet of ships. "Fine. It's . . . Lovely."

"Undoubtedly. Let's hear it."

"No, that's it. Lovely. Lady Lovely."

"Oh," Aurelie said, and then, "*Oh.*"

"I don't want to hear one word."

"But that may be the best thing I've ever heard in my entire life."

"Then we need to engineer a *vast* improvement to your life, don't we?"

"Truly, how could your parents be so totally removed from who you actually are as a person?" Aurelie said, and it was meant to be a joke, but Iliana's smile went brittle at the edges.

"I've often asked myself the same thing," she said, and after a pause, "Well, they certainly couldn't have named me Lady Thorough Disappointment Who Eschewed a Life at Court to Hunt Bounties."

"Lady Annoying would be much more to the point."

"Hilarious."

"Lady Full of Herself. Lady Nearly Intolerable. Lady Thoroughly Average-Looking Except for Her Eyes."

"My eyes?" Iliana looked pleased.

"Lady Inflated Ego. Lady Insufferably Confident. Lady Far-Too-Self-Satisfied."

"I'm only hearing positives now." Iliana tipped back the last of her second drink and then glanced over at Aurelie. "You should get to thinking of your own Court name. Just in case things work out with the prince."

Aurelie shook her head. "I really do despise you."

"And speaking of . . ."

Aurelie looked up, and there was Hapless, making his way through the crowd.

Heading right toward them.

Thirty-Three

Aurelie and Hapless stood on the terrace together in silence.

It had been the prince's suggestion, after he had approached Aurelie and Iliana and said all the things that you expected someone to say in a ballroom (or at least, the things Aurelie imagined that people said). He complimented their dresses (Iliana's answering look was murderous), commented on the number of guests, and noted that his sister had never looked happier.

"Lord Adamant is a very agreeable fellow," Hapless had said, and Aurelie was certain that anyone would say the same about Hapless.

It was only after several moments of standing together in the ballroom that Hapless leaned toward Aurelie and said, "What do you say, shall we take in a bit of night air?"

"Is it so different from the daytime air?" was the only thing that Aurelie could think to respond, and she instantly cursed herself for it.

"It absolutely is," Iliana cut in quickly. "You should see for yourself. I'm off to find Quad."

And then Iliana had conveniently melted away into the crowd, despite the fact that Quad had been standing fairly close by the whole time, "keeping watch," as she put it, and blending quite well into the paneled wall of the ballroom.

As it turned out, the night air was indeed beautiful. It was the perfect temperature outside. There was a sweet scent on the breeze—

"Heartfruit," Hapless said, when Aurelie remarked on it (after a long enough pause of not remarking on anything that someone had to say something, just for the sake of it). "The pink varietal only grows in the Capital. Something about the water from the river, coming from the mountains as it does, and the quality of rock in the riverbeds . . ."

It was quiet again.

"I meant to tell you—" Hapless cleared his throat. "I've been meaning to say that you look very nice."

"You said so inside," Aurelie said, and couldn't help but smile a little.

Hapless smiled back. "I said your dress was very nice. But I mean to say that *you*—"

"It's too long. The dress," Aurelie interrupted. Stating the obvious. "It's Iliana's. She told me to chop the bottom off, but I think it would've sent the duchess into hysterics."

"Iliana doesn't appreciate couture," Hapless said.

"She does—it just has to be something you could kill a bear in."

"Oh yes, things with spikes, and chains, and . . ."

"Pockets. Don't forget pockets."

"She does love a pocket."

Silence.

"And how are you finding the ball?" Hapless asked eventually.

"Crowded." It was the first thing that came to mind, and Aurelie blanched. "It's nice, as well. Of course. It's . . . like something out of a story." She had taken her gloves off, and she twisted them together now. They would be wrinkled beyond recognition before the evening was out. "I suppose to you, it's just another evening."

"Well, one's sister only gets married once," Hapless said, and then considered it. "Or, so one hopes."

Aurelie smiled. "What's the best ball you've ever attended?"

"Hmm." Hapless threw his head back, considering. The sky above them was inky black, speckled with stars. "Lady Frankly threw an excellent midsummer party a few years ago. Gallant and Honoria drank too much wine, and Gallant challenged one of Frankly's sons to a duel."

"Did it proceed?"

"It might have, but then Gallant threw up and was good for nothing after that."

Aurelie huffed a laugh.

"It's . . ." Hapless's smile faded a notch. "It's rare to see him cut loose. After my mother—after he became king, he became . . . Well, he was always serious. But so much more serious than before. Even Honoria . . . both of them have this sense of duty that I . . . can't understand, I guess. That I just narrowly managed to escape by being born third. And by being born as myself, I suppose. No one really takes me seriously." It was quiet for a moment. "Nor should they." Hapless smiled again, sort of—more of a grimace, really. "Tell me, is there anything you'd like to see in the Westlands while you're here?"

There had been a moment there—an opportunity—that passed too quickly. Hapless swept right through it, didn't allow it to land, didn't allow Aurelie the chance to consider saying something to the contrary. She couldn't call it back—she didn't have the courage or the skill. But she wished she did.

"I haven't given it much thought," she said instead.

"I must admit, I was . . . very surprised to see you here." It suddenly seemed like Hapless was closer than before—when did that happen? They were side by side at the balustrade. Aurelie could feel his sleeve brushing against her arm. "And pleased. Of course."

"Well, I . . . wanted to see Winsome House." Aurelie's voice stuck in her throat. "Another . . . pinnacle of mortal architecture and all that."

"Could I ask you something?" Hapless's gaze was intent.

"Yes."

He was fumbling with a ring on his left hand, twisting it absently. "Did I . . . ruin things by . . . Was it too much? Was I too much? Was that why you wanted to stop writing?"

It was the address, to start: *Dearest Aurelie.*

It was *I have been thinking of you.*

And *Writing to you makes it more bearable.*

And *I wish I could remember any single bit of wisdom my professors are trying to impart even a fraction as well as I remember kissing you. . . .*

Aurelie had read those words, and read them again, and then again. She had stared at the parchment for so long, the letters dissociated into nothing but meaningless curves and angles.

Hapless swallowed. "Because I can . . . be less, you know. I can . . . match you, however you'd like."

"I don't want that."

"Because you don't want me?"

"Because you shouldn't have to be less." Aurelie's voice was hoarse. "It's not . . . That's not it."

"Then what is it?"

She thought of the day they met. After they saved Hapless, Iliana advised him to leave his party—and he had agreed without a second thought. He was always *quite sure*. He was always unruffled, entirely unconcerned, and that's probably how he ended up in an ambush in the first place, by not being troubled by the fact that the forest was dangerous, not caring enough that the trip was risky, or even aware that there were risks at all.

So maybe the prince could think that he cared about her, and maybe he did at the moment, at this second, maybe he truly did. But he didn't care enough to think beyond the moment. The consequence of growing up royal was that he never had to think of consequences at all.

All Aurelie had were consequences. And one consequence of being a poor baker's apprentice was that you'd have nowhere to go if you threw your position over for a prince, and the prince threw you over in kind.

And it would happen, inevitably. Not with malice. Not intentionally. Hapless was joyous and exuberant and enthusiastic, but he was also careless. He just was. It would happen because he would get excited about something else, some new adventure.

Hapless's question hung between them, and Aurelie shook her head.

"I'm needed at the bakery," she said, her voice strangely wooden to her own ears.

"Do you even like being an apprentice?"

Aurelie spoke before she could think. "It's not about liking. I'm working toward something. Liking it is a luxury."

Hapless shook his head. "I don't understand why you toil away for mastery when you could be doing so many other things. You could be in school. You could be studying magic." There was an earnestness to it, something imploring in his eyes. But the ultimate feeling that settled in Aurelie's chest was one of indignation, of . . . disgust.

"You really don't know how anything works, do you?" she replied, and Hapless just blinked. He should have been named Guileless. He should have been locked in a tower for his own safekeeping. "How else would I live? What else would I be doing?"

"Working somewhere else if you have to! Somewhere better!"

"Where are my options?" Aurelie flung her hands up. "I had to leave school—my parents certainly couldn't afford to take me back. Where do I go from there? What do I do? Search for fairy gold in the woods? Make tree bark soup and sleep in a hollowed-out log and *hope for the best*? Can you really be that naive? Truly, is your life so apart from reality? Do you understand how many people there are in this Kingdom who have even fewer options than I do?"

Hapless looked confused, chastened. He began tentatively, "My brother says that . . . that people have only to work hard, and then they'll reap the bounty—"

In a flash, Aurelie recalled another one of Hapless's letters:

Bastian Sinclair is a singular inspiration of mine. He had nothing at all at the start and then becomes more successful than anyone could have possibly imagined. . . .

"Oh, so that's the solution," Aurelie said. "I see. I understand now. It's that I'm simply not *working hard enough*—"

"That's not what I meant! I meant that—"

"That what? I'm reaping the life that I deserve?"

"That you're brilliant!" he burst out. "You do work hard—you work so hard—and you should be rewarded for it. You should have everything you want, and if you're not happy there, then you should . . . you should just leave, Aurelie. You shouldn't go back—"

"And where would I go?"

"To the Capital." Decision was alight in his eyes. "With me. Please."

Silence.

"It doesn't have to be—*we* don't have to be—anything at all. But you could stay there, at the palace, or—or you could go to the university instead. You could do anything you wanted—"

Aurelie sputtered.

"I could buy you a house somewhere," Hapless said. "And a rug with flowers on it. I would do that if you let me. So please, just . . . let me."

He meant it. He did. It was plain as day across his face. But Aurelie just shook her head.

Hapless swallowed. "Why not?"

"It would be the same, wouldn't it? Owing everything to someone else. The work I'm doing now is so that one day I won't have to be in that position anymore."

"It wouldn't be the same at all—"

"At least Mrs. Basil understands what it is that she's doing," Aurelie said. "You don't know how anything works! You say your steward is like family to you, and yet you call him Steward—I bet you don't even know his real name! You don't know how much a loaf of bread costs or how many *years* it takes to achieve mastery or why someone would even want to in the first place! I can't leave any chance I might have at a future to stay and keep you company until you get tired of me."

Hapless blinked, looking stunned. Hurt. A breeze ruffled his hair slightly, the air still just as sweet as it was before.

"What can I do, then?" he said after a long pause. "How can I help? Just . . . tell me what to do, and I'll do it."

Aurelie ignored the painful squeeze in her chest and said, "Send a rider to my village, to the bakery, with a royal missive saying I was absent in aid of you."

"Done."

"I can't bring the note myself. Mrs. Basil will think I forged it with magic—"

"You don't have to explain," he said. "What else?"

"That's all." It was the most uncomfortable feeling—the press behind Aurelie's eyes, the sting of it. "Thank you," she said.

Then she left.

Thirty-Four

Hapless had no desire to return to the ball.

He stood on the terrace for some time, looking out over the gardens. When the gardens became tiresome, he turned around, leaned against the balustrade, and looked through the windows of the ballroom instead. It was brightly lit and glittering with the motion of the dancers, the crowds milling around, the sweep of dresses and capes. He spotted Honoria dancing with Adam, her face flushed and beaming. He watched Gallant in conversation with several peers from the Eastern Realm, Gallant's posture stiff and unyielding.

Hapless could track Steward's approach and was therefore not surprised when Steward slipped through the doors and joined him on the terrace.

"Are you all right, Your Highness?"

"Quite well, thank you." It was an outright lie, but one that propriety dictated. "Just wanted a bit of air."

Steward inclined his head. "Please let me know if there's anything you need."

Hapless tried to muster a smile. "I've got plenty of air at the moment. But thank you, I will."

Steward moved to leave.

"Wait." Hapless straightened. "Could I . . . ? Would it be all right if I asked you something?"

"Of course."

He hardly knew what it was he meant to express, but it came out all the same: "Your son, Elias . . . he was meant to be my steward."

If Steward was surprised by the subject, his face didn't show it. It never did—the man was unflappable. "That's correct."

"But he chose an apprenticeship instead."

Steward inclined his head.

"Why would he—do you know why?"

Hapless remembered Elias—or at least, the childhood impression he had of Elias. A time when anyone older than Hapless seemed smart and important and capable, but Elias seemed especially so. He was always reading. He had a quick wit. Hapless sometimes wondered if Elias had considered Hapless to be a burden, if he would've stayed in service to the royal family if he had been set down for Honoria or Gallant instead.

"He wanted to choose," Steward replied after a moment. "He wanted to forge his own path, I suppose, instead of having it . . . prescribed."

"What's so wrong with things being prescribed? My whole life is prescribed. I didn't choose it, and yet I don't—" He cut off abruptly.

Steward gave a slight smile. "I believe my son would point out the inherent difference in life prescribed as a prince and a life prescribed in service to one." He looked away. "But Elias has always been a free thinker, with his own notions of how the world should work, his own ambitions that I tried to understand, I did, but we argued often, I must admit. . . ." He shook his head. "I believe there is honor in service. I wished that he had felt the same way. I still wish it. If he had stayed, if he had followed course . . ." He swallowed. "He may even have been standing here with you now."

"And you could be enjoying your retirement."

"It was my own choice to stay on. As I said, I consider it an honor. I only mean that had Elias stayed, he would never have been lost to us."

"He may still be found."

"Few who disappear in the Underwood ever return."

"We returned."

"We did." Steward straightened. "And thanks to the king, the woods may be safer yet for travel."

Hapless's eyes went to the ballroom windows again, to where Gallant stood. "He's quite glad to have that road approved, isn't he?"

"Indeed. It's a victory, to be sure. You played your own small part in it, and for that I'm truly grateful."

"What part was that?"

Steward blinked. "Well. The ambush. I believe it was a tipping point for many members of Court."

"Gallant never said what happened to the attackers," Hapless murmured. "Or what they wanted in the first place. I suppose he thought I'd forget about it." He frowned. "I suppose he was not wholly wrong on that count."

"I'm certain it was taken care of."

"What does that mean, though?" Hapless asked. "Taken care of how?"

Steward paused for just a moment. "I couldn't say."

Hapless looked at Steward and then peered again through the glass to where Gallant stood in the ballroom.

"Will you excuse me?" Hapless said, and moved past Steward and into the ballroom.

The air was warm and stuffy, too many candles, too many bodies. Hapless's collar felt too tight all of a sudden, his waist-coat too snug.

Gallant held a wineglass in one hand as he talked with a dignitary.

Hapless strode up. "Could I interrupt?"

"Hapless. What are you—"

"Quickly now, thank you," Hapless said, pulling Gallant away and out onto the terrace.

"What has gotten into you—"

"Was it you?" As the pieces of it slotted into place in his mind, Hapless's heart began to beat faster, his blood pounding in his ears. Heat rose in his face. He felt like a pot about to boil over. "Did you order an attack on me?"

"What?" Gallant looked completely baffled.

Steward reappeared then, a brief burst of noise coming from the ballroom as the door opened and closed and he stepped back out onto the terrace. Hapless only spared him a glance before focusing again on his brother.

"In the Underwood. The ambush. Was it you?"

"Don't be absurd."

"Tell me the truth," Hapless said, and somehow it felt like whatever Gallant said or did next would be the most important thing that had ever happened between them.

Gallant tried smiling. "Honestly, Hapless, the notions you get sometimes—"

"Don't! Don't you dare!"

Steward stepped forward. "Your Highness, why don't we—"

"If someone doesn't tell me the truth this instant, I'll leave right now and never return. Ever. I swear it."

Pain flashed across Steward's face. "You must understand," he said haltingly. "You were never in any harm. We were assured—we had the *utmost* assurance—that it was . . . it was to be staged only. It was to make a point that the Underwood isn't safe, because it *isn't*, and His Majesty felt that an event such as that would persuade the Court—for the safety of the people—"

Hapless didn't know whether to laugh or cry. Gallant had turned away to face the gardens.

"You didn't even bother to have them *change their uniforms*," Hapless said. It felt as if his words were coming from very far off. "You think so little of me. Of my intelligence. You didn't even bother to dress them up like ruffians! You thought that I would cower in my carriage with my head down while your guards playacted an ambush around me. You truly think that of me."

"Hapless—"

"You think I'm that stupid. And maybe I am, honestly, for refusing to see something so obvious simply because I never considered that my own brother would ever, *could* ever—"

"Your Highness—" Steward began, but Hapless couldn't tear his eyes away from Gallant, from the rigid line of his shoulders.

"You would use me like that." Hapless's voice sounded far more pitiful than he wanted. He wanted to be strong, to be *righteous*, but suddenly all he could feel was a painful lump in his throat and a deep sense of grief, though he couldn't even explain what it was that he had just lost.

"Hapless . . ." Gallant sounded tired. He didn't turn around.

"Don't." Hapless shook his head. "Don't even try."

He left the terrace.

Hapless walked the paths among the carefully cultivated flower beds on the grounds of Winsome House with more purpose than a moonlit stroll usually warranted. He couldn't help but stride through as if he were urgently intent on some destination, though without any such destination in mind. He just wanted distance. Distance from Steward, from Gallant, from everything—how many people knew that the ambush was entirely fake? He was never in any danger at all, until he was, at least to their eyes—until Iliana, Quad, and Aurelie came and ruined the grand plan.

Hapless marched through the rose garden, underneath the trellises of wisteria, through to the grove of heartfruit trees, blossoming in pink and white.

It was there that he heard footsteps.

He stopped, and they stopped. He looked around but saw no one.

And so Hapless continued, the moonlight dappling through the leaves of the trees above him.

He heard a twig snap.

He whipped around. "Who's there?"

Lord Defiance stepped out from behind a tree.

It was no secret that Hapless had never particularly cared for him. Hapless didn't know the Brights very well, but he had seen Iliana and Defiance at enough events over the years to gain something of a sense of them (though Iliana went by her Court name back then, which suited her spectacularly poorly. Not that Iliana wasn't lovely, but it certainly wasn't one of the first adjectives that sprang to mind when one thought of her).

Defiance was always listening in on people's conversations, saving bits of gossip or opinions he thought were particularly foolish so he could bring them back up later. He gained entrée into various circles well enough—half off his title, half from his looks, which were admittedly *symmetrical*. But one only had to spend a short while with him to realize how slippery he was.

"What are you doing out here?" Hapless asked.

Defiance shrugged. "If you must know, I'm waiting for a lady friend."

"All the way out here?"

"I'm the soul of discretion."

"Hm."

Defiance smiled. "You're funny when you're suspicious. It's like watching a great big dog trying to do complex mathematics."

"Could you go somewhere else, please?" Hapless asked. He didn't intend to stay in this particular part of the grove, but now that Defiance was here, Hapless had no desire to cede it to him.

"I think not. I have no wish to give up my rendezvous, and certainly not on your account."

The tone of voice—the words themselves—

Hapless's head snapped up.

The young guard in the Underwood. *I've no wish to die today, and certainly not on your account.*

It couldn't be. Absolutely not. There was no chance—no way—

Hapless looked at Defiance. And then his gaze dropped to the ground. There, etched into the path just behind Defiance, was a seeking circle.

Hapless frowned. Could it be—

It was his last thought before everything went black.

Thirty-Five

urelie was leaving. Of course she was. She had to. But first she had to fix the ceramic statue she had broken, the one of the man and the pumpkin coach.

It mattered very little in the grand scheme of things, and she knew that quite well. But she couldn't leave Winsome House having ruined absolutely everything. She had to fix *something* if it was in her power to do so.

If she remembered correctly, the sitting room was through the long, windowed gallery, three doors down from the painting of the severe-looking man in satin pantaloons . . .

She arrived at the door and pushed it open, and there was the pink and gold sitting room. It had several lamps lit. An unimaginable luxury, lighting rooms that no one would probably even use this evening.

Hapless's hero Bastian Sinclair would never be so wasteful.

Bastian Sinclair is fictional, Aurelie told herself, stepping into the soft glow of the room. *And I am a fool.*

While Aurelie berated herself, she hunted for the pieces

of the ceramic statue, but they were nowhere to be seen. A search of the room yielded nothing whatsoever.

It was for no reason, then, that she had come here. Foolishly, embarrassingly, tears sprang into her eyes. Even worse, before she could attempt to push them back, they fell.

This may be the stupidest moment of my entire life, Aurelie thought. *The most irrational reaction to the most absurd thing.*

Everything would've been all right if you could've just fixed something, another treacherous part of her said.

And then suddenly there were voices in the hallway.

"There, on the left, that one's open."

Footsteps approached, and in another completely nonsensical move, Aurelie dashed behind one of the curtains.

"See, it's empty. I told you no one would be up here." The voice was all too recognizable. It was Iliana.

"There are no instruments in here. I can't play for you if we're not in the music room."

Aurelie wasn't familiar with the other voice. It was pleasant sounding, smoother and softer than Iliana's.

"Maybe we can think of something else to do," Iliana said lightly.

"Lovely—"

"Pith. You're the only one allowed to call me that, you know. But even then I must admit I hate it."

"Iliana," Lady Pith corrected.

"Camille," Iliana replied.

"You're the only one allowed to call me that," Lady Pith murmured.

I am in the wrong place at this very moment, Aurelie thought, and it was true on so many levels.

It was too late to say anything. To step out from behind the curtains. But Aurelie also didn't want to be witness to anything so undeniably . . . personal.

It had gone very quiet, and then came the sort of soft sounds that could only mean someone was kissing someone else and the someone else was enjoying it.

After a moment of Aurelie's mounting panic, Lady Pith spoke, somewhat breathlessly. "This is not—"

"Hmm?"

The sounds continued.

"This is not a good idea," Lady Pith said, and then there was the rustle of fabric brushing across the floor, the train of a dress sliding over carpet as Lady Pith retreated.

"Why not?" Iliana had never sounded so off-kilter.

"Why not?" Lady Pith repeated. "I can give you ten reasons."

"By all means, enlighten me."

"*One*, we're in Winsome House, with *two*, both of our families, and *three*, the entire royal family, not to mention nearly every member of Court just downstairs—"

"That seems like one reason to me. It's rather cheating to split it up like that."

"*Four*, you treated me abominably the last time I saw you—"

"I thought we had a perfectly nice time."

"Yes," Lady Pith said after a pause, and Aurelie thought of what Iliana had said earlier that evening: *Nothing of substance. We're too different.* "Yes, we did. But I have no desire to continue in that manner—"

"Then why did you come here with me? If you had no desire?"

There was a charged silence.

Another rustle of fabric. Then the sounds started again.

Iliana broke off this time. "Awfully conflicting signals, my darling."

"You drive me mad," Lady Pith replied.

There was movement. Settling on furniture.

Aurelie looked frantically over her shoulder at the window behind her. Could she open it without drawing any attention?

But then: "Last time I said it was the last time," Lady Pith said, and there was the sound of movement again, shifting and standing and putting space in between. "I meant it."

"It's just a bit of fun."

"I know. But I want something more than fun."

"What's more than fun?"

"Love."

It was quiet.

When Iliana spoke, her tone was light, but Aurelie could hear the fragile quality to it. "I can't say I know much about that."

"Believe me, I'm aware."

Another moment of silence.

"I should get back," Lady Pith said at last.

"I really would like to hear that sonata sometime."

Lady Pith didn't reply. The opening and closing of a door followed.

When Iliana spoke, her voice came from much closer than Aurelie expected. "Quad, if you're in that curtain right now, I'm going to be very angry."

Aurelie dutifully pulled the curtain back.

Iliana's hair was a mess. "Oh, even worse." Her expression was dark.

"I'm sorry, I didn't mean to overhear—"

"You didn't mean to overhear from behind this curtain where you hid yourself so as not to be seen?"

"I panicked."

"Why?" Iliana narrowed her eyes. "Where's Hapless? What happened? Why are you even in here?"

"I wanted to fix the ceramic pumpkin."

"What?"

"The coach, and the coachman, the one that got broken." Aurelie sidestepped Iliana and crossed into the room.

"What are you talking about?"

"I have to go back."

"Pardon?"

"To Basil's."

Iliana moved to face the gilded mirror on the wall and began fixing her hair. In this room, in this light, with the luxurious gown and the jewels winking at her throat, Iliana looked like a completely different person. An otherworldly version of herself, one who attended balls and cared about the state of her hair.

"All in good time, Baker," she said.

"Iliana, I need to go *now*. I can't stay here another day."

"It won't make much of a difference at this point, will it? Either your mentor will fire you or she won't."

Aurelie's voice stuck in her throat. "You said it would be all right."

"And I'm sure it will be. I don't imagine she'd cast off your free labor so cavalierly. Most apprentices these days have more self-respect than to work for room and board alone. You're a rare find."

"What's wrong with you?"

"Nothing." Iliana turned to face Aurelie. Her hair was only marginally better. "I'm the same unpleasant person I've always been. And I'll help you get back, I will, but not right now."

"Why not? There's clearly nothing for you here."

Iliana's expression turned stony. "The prince may still be in danger. There's more going on than you know—"

"Of course there is, because you never *tell me anything*! And yet you expect me to follow you here and there, at your every beck and call. No wonder Lady Pith is tired of you, it's *exhausting*—"

It was then that the door swung open, and as if summoned, Lady Pith appeared. She stopped short at the sight of Aurelie and Iliana.

"I—"

"This isn't—" Iliana took two large steps away from Aurelie, despite the fact that they weren't standing particularly close to each other in the first place.

"It's . . . That's not . . ." Pith shook her head. "It's your brother, Iliana. You must come quickly."

Iliana crossed over to Pith but then turned back to Aurelie when she reached the doorway. "Stay here, Baker. Don't do anything rash. Just . . . wait for my return."

Thirty-Six

Aurelie didn't wait. She didn't stay to see what mishap had befallen Iliana's brother. Instead, she fled as soon as Iliana and Pith had disappeared down the hallway.

It sounded dramatic that way, to be *fleeing*, but really, it wasn't nearly as expedient as she'd like—slow progress in Iliana's too-big dress, making her way back to their rooms. Figuring her way out of the dress, hastily removing the fancy hairpins Iliana had lent her. Changing back into her regular clothes. Tying up her apron strings once more.

Then there was the matter of finding her way out of Winsome House.

And then, finally, standing under a portico in the warm night air, there was the matter of figuring out exactly how she should do the actual fleeing. She was in the middle of a vast estate. She had no notion of the surrounding territory. No idea where she could even find transportation.

Panic was beginning to well up inside her when suddenly she heard a voice. "Aurelie?"

She turned, and there stood Marthe in the large arched doorway, along with the older woman who had beckoned Marthe earlier. She was leaning on Marthe's arm for support.

"Are you quite all right?" Marthe asked.

"I, uh. Yes. Yes, I am."

"Auntie wanted to smoke her pipe," Marthe said, and Aurelie caught sight of the elaborately carved pipe in the older woman's hand. "I thought it best to do so in privacy. But it seems you wanted a bit of privacy yourself?" She turned suddenly to the woman. "Auntie, this is my school friend, Aurelie. Aurelie, this is my great-aunt, Baroness Plumb." Baroness Plumb gave Aurelie the slightest nod as Marthe went on. "You've changed your clothes, Aurelie. Are you sure you're all right?"

"I am. I just . . . I need to leave. Now."

"But the festivities have only just begun! I've heard they're even going to do the fox run, which I've only read about—"

Aurelie shook her head. "I can't. I need to get back to my village. But I don't—" It took a great deal of effort to say it out loud. "I don't know how."

Marthe considered this for a moment, while Baroness Plumb—clearly deeming the conversation to be of little interest—lit her pipe.

"I suppose if you must leave . . . ," Marthe began tentatively. "There's a village several miles off. I'm sure you could find further passage there. You could borrow our carriage to get that far, if you'd like."

Aurelie didn't understand why, but she felt like bursting into tears again.

She didn't, though. She just nodded, and her voice came out tight. "That would be lovely. Thank you."

"Of course. Let me find a groom to make the arrangements. Keep Auntie company, won't you?"

Marthe disappeared back inside, and Aurelie was left with Baroness Plumb.

Baroness Plumb took a long pull on the pipe, and when she spoke, smoke poured from her lips. "You look like a servant. What sort of standards did they keep at that school of Marthe's?"

"I'm an apprentice."

"Hm." The smoke smelled oddly sweet. "My mother was a bookbinder. She wanted me to follow in the trade, but I refused, so she took an apprentice instead. And much to my chagrin, I fell in love with him."

Aurelie didn't know how to reply, but the baroness continued.

"We had some very happy years together before he passed and I married the baron. Some unhappy ones as well." She took another draw and then tilted her head, considering. "It's the average of it that really matters in the end. More so than the highs and lows."

She smoked the rest of her pipe in silence, and just as she was tilting out the ashes, Marthe returned, looking a bit breathless.

"They'll bring the carriage 'round for you here when it's ready," she said. "It shouldn't take too long at all."

"Thank you."

"Think nothing of it." Marthe crossed over and took one of Aurelie's hands, gave it a squeeze. "You were always so patient with me when we were in school."

Then she crossed back to Baroness Plumb, who looped her arm through Marthe's.

"Back to the ball," Baroness Plumb commanded.

"Of course." Marthe cast a look back at Aurelie. "Please, if you need anything else . . ."

"I'll be all right," Aurelie said, though she wasn't certain of that in the slightest. Marthe gave her a nod and a small smile before she and the baroness returned inside.

Aurelie never should have left the village.

It was so much easier, looking back, to see every wrong step along the way. Don't agree to attend the wedding. Don't accept Iliana's request to go into the Underwood. Don't start a working relationship with Iliana in the first place. Keep your head down. Do your work. Achieve baking mastery.

(Have no fun, no adventures, meet no one, see nothing of the world. . . .)

As Baroness Plumb's carriage passed through the gates of Winsome House, Aurelie tore a seam out of a small section of her apron and removed several bills—enough, she hoped, to buy passage north.

When she reached the village that Marthe had spoken of, she located a hackney coach that was departing in the morning and bought a ticket. It was more expensive than she'd imagined—she had to rip out more seams and retrieve more bills.

The trip felt endless. Aurelie's stomach growled when they stopped to change horses in a western town. She bought some food—as cheaply as she could get it—but ultimately she could barely eat. Her stomach was in knots. This whole endeavor had been a terrible mistake. She knew it, and though she hoped for the best throughout the journey, it was painfully obvious the instant she slipped through the back door of Basil's Bakery and saw Mrs. Basil standing there that only the worst would come to pass.

Mrs. Basil was a small woman, rather thin but partial to voluminous silhouettes. Her dress wasn't nearly as fine as anything Aurelie had seen at the ball but still featured many ruffles, a cinched waist, and gathered sleeves that went tight at the elbows. Aurelie was certain it would devastate her to know that the style had shifted at Court and her look would now be considered déclassé.

Aurelie was also certain from the look on Mrs. Basil's face that the royal missive from Hapless hadn't arrived. The one that was supposed to assure Mrs. Basil that Aurelie was absent in aid of the prince. The one that was meant to smooth everything over.

Maybe a courier will arrive just in time, she thought wildly. But she couldn't deny the much more likely scenario: maybe it was never sent in the first place.

She should have felt a sinking feeling, as if her insides were plunging to the floor. Instead, she was numb—and yet, at the same time, she felt strangely, terribly vindicated. Because she *knew* this was going to happen. She had no one to blame but herself, really.

It made it easier, somehow. It made it an inevitability, when Mrs. Basil looked at her and said, "Decided to show your face, have you? How blessed I am that my apprentice *deigns* to appear for work, after *days* away, leaving us completely in the lurch—"

Was there even any use? But still, Aurelie couldn't stop herself. She had to try.

"I'm sorry, Mrs. Basil. There was an emergency—"

"An emergency? Concerning whom? Your loving family? Your many acquaintances?"

"I had to help a friend."

Mrs. Basil's lip curled. "A *friend*. I see. You consider me quite dim, don't you? I don't know what else I'd expect. You didn't think I'd notice your pathetic attempts to reel in an admirer. And it's clear that you certainly didn't think I'd notice you associating yourself with that other . . . *person*. Debasing yourself with magic to assist *unseemly* sorts like that."

"My magic benefits you, too."

"I'd hardly say so. Your magic is broken, like everyone else's. A waste of time! An insult to propriety!"

"My magic heats your baths, it keeps your dough cool, it starts your ovens—"

"Corrupted!" she continued.

"And all that aside, I bake your goods, I sell them, I do everything I can as best as I can, as fast as I can, and yet you treat me as if I'm some sort of *criminal*—"

"I took you in! I took you from nothing, and despite all your efforts to thwart me, I have tried my very hardest to make you into something!"

"Yes, hungry, and exhausted, and bitter, that's what you've made me!"

Mrs. Basil just looked at her for a moment, her face gone carefully blank. Then she approached Aurelie, the fabric of her skirts sliding across the floor.

She leaned in toward Aurelie, face close. "Everything you have is because of me," she said, voice frightfully quiet. "Because of *my* kindness. Just remember that when you're on the streets. Remember that when you're begging for scraps and people look away in shame at the sight of you." She turned away. "You're dismissed, utterly and forever. You've done nothing but steal time from me, and I'll make sure everyone knows the unrepentant thief that you are."

Aurelie sputtered. Magic burned her palms with nowhere to go.

She left.

Jonas followed Aurelie outside.

"Aurelie!" he called, and her footsteps slowed. She looked back at him—his brow furrowed, his eyes full of regret. He must have overheard everything—there was no way he couldn't have.

"Go to my house," he said. "On the south side of Chapel Street. Go and wait there, and we'll . . . we'll sort everything out."

"It's all right." Aurelie's voice stuck in her throat. "This was my fault. I never should have left."

"What about your friend? Were you able to help them?"

Aurelie nodded, even though it was a lie. She hadn't helped anyone at all. She had only succeeded in making things worse.

"Go to my house," Jonas insisted, almost as if he knew she wouldn't.

"I will," she replied, and she knew it too. Jonas wasn't her brother. He wasn't responsible for her. She was the reason for this. She had no one but herself to blame. Jonas was overworked already, worked thin, and the baby—even with

Katriane's savings from Chapdelaine's, they would barely be able to manage until she returned to work—and both of them still trying for mastery. . . .

Aurelie nodded. "Thank you. I will."

It felt like the last time she would ever see him. Her eyes stung.

She told herself it was the dust.

Thirty-Seven

Where do you go when you have nowhere to go?

Aurelie walked around the central square a dozen times or more and wondered how soon Mrs. Basil would take a new apprentice. She wished she could warn them off—*spare yourself, truly*—but then, what right did she have? She'd take the position back herself in a heartbeat.

Four years of work wasted.

Maybe she could get a position at Chapdelaine's. Maybe Jonas and Katriane really could help her—

But positions there were scarce, or else Jonas would have gotten one himself. And they would never take on someone that Mrs. Basil would so surely badmouth around town. Aurelie could just imagine it: *Poison to your business! You'd be better off burning your money in the streets than hiring her!*

Aurelie felt a flare of indignation. She would never have to see Mrs. Basil again. That was the main positive in this situation. The only positive.

She decided to rent a room for the evening, like Iliana

had done for them on the journey to the Capital. It had seemed easy enough.

There was an inn on the north side of the village called the Armbruster. Aurelie knew of it only because of a patron who came by every now and then—he was a clerk there.

He was the one seated at the front desk when she arrived. When he told Aurelie the price of the room, she nearly turned right around and left.

"That's for . . . one night?" She hoped it was a mistake. Maybe he thought she meant to rent for the week, or even the month.

"Best prices this side of the Underwood," the clerk told her. "If you go to the Lansdowne across town, they'll right gouge you."

Aurelie wasn't sure if he was telling the truth or not. She had no way to know. First the cost of the coach, now this—it was alarming how fast money could go.

She swallowed. "I . . . I could barter."

"We're not really in the business of that."

"I know magic. If you need . . . some task or something done, I could do it."

He let out a guffaw. "And have to redo it myself double? Hardly, thank you."

"I can seek, if you . . . if you have a set of stones."

He raised an eyebrow. "You don't even have your own equipment?"

Aurelie didn't speak.

"Never really understood what use seeking was to anybody, anyway."

"Just . . . if you need someone found."

"Could you find my wife's good humor?" the clerk said.

Aurelie didn't laugh.

He softened a little. "Sorry, miss. But it's a lost art, ain't it? Fairly useless in this modern economy."

Aurelie nodded.

"Do you want the room or not?"

She looked outside. The sky was darkening.

She could walk to the outskirts of town and try to find a barn to sleep in. That's the sort of thing people did in stories, wasn't it? But she was hardly sure if there would be any barns out there to sleep in. She knew shockingly little about the village, despite having been there for four years—only what she overheard from customers at the bakery or what she could glean when running out to get ingredients if they failed to be delivered.

"Yes," she said, and took the room key.

That night Aurelie took the remainder of the money out of her apron and counted it. She needed a plan. Her stomach growled too.

She had a piece of bread in her pocket, leftover from the journey.

She could double it with magic. She expanded it and ate half, saving the other half to expand again in the morning. It would lose flavor each time, and she risked exponentially growing her hunger if she continued in that vein, but maybe it was just something people said, and anyway, she didn't have much to lose. The money sewn into her hem was all she had. She needed to make it last as long as possible—who knew where or when she would be able to find work again.

As Aurelie lay in bed that night—a real bed, raised up off the floor—a memory came to her, unbidden. A soft-spoken voice, a pair of hands earnestly clasped.

If you need anything, Aurelie, please—don't hesitate to reach out. You have my address here.

Thank you, Miss Ember.

I do hope you'll be happy in your new position. There was something in Miss Ember's eyes that hinted that she may have doubted that.

I'm sure I will be, Aurelie had replied, because she only ever wanted to be a good student, to please Miss Ember. There must have been some fantasyland where Miss Ember was her older sister and Jonas was her brother, and she was loved and cared for and confident in that. Where everyone was fed and employed, everyone was happy.

You can stand under that roof if you'd like, Mrs. Basil liked to say of such lines of thinking, *but it won't keep rain off your head.*

Aurelie considered the wooden boards of the ceiling overhead. She could go to the school—to Miss Ember—and ask her for . . . if not help, then advice at the very least. What to do next. Where to go when you don't know where to go, when you've been dismissed from your job summarily with no recommendation.

She decided on it before her eyes eventually drifted shut. She would set out for school in the morning.

Thirty-Eight

Hapless woke to find himself locked in a tower.

At least, he assumed it was a tower. It was a round room, walled in stone, with one narrow window very high up that showed nothing but a sliver of blue sky.

He felt as if he'd awoken from a deep sleep. His mouth tasted strange. He ran a hand through his hair. He was still in his clothes from the lovers' ball. He should've fought for an outfit in charcoal or black when he had the chance. The blue jacket might fare well enough, but the white pants and waistcoat would show every speck of dirt from the stone floor where he currently found himself laid out.

These were the thoughts that came to him first, blearily, as he woke—the window, the stones, the dirt, his clothes. Then there was the realization that he had actually been kidnapped, and there was absolutely no one around to appreciate the irony.

And then, with a heartrending jolt, he sat up, realizing that he had very much not fulfilled his duty to Aurelie. He hadn't sent the rider to her bakery.

A wave of nausea hit him—half from sitting up too fast, half from crushing guilt. How long had it been? Where was she? She couldn't possibly be back in the village yet, could she? Would she be fired? Would she hate Hapless irrevocably?

Although the recollection of his brother—of his betrayal—stung, Hapless couldn't help but hear Gallant's voice in his head: *Assess the situation.* It was Gallant's first move, his opening salvo, ten times out of ten. *The river is flooding, Your Majesty.*

Assess the situation.

A door stood to Hapless's left—locked, of course. The ceiling of the chamber must've gone up twenty feet, the window probably twice as high up as Hapless was tall. The walls were too smooth to climb. Hapless's head pounded.

Before he could assess anything further, the door opened, and a man entered the room.

Hapless had seen him before. Across the dining room at an inn. The man had been much flashier then. Now he was dressed in an understated but undeniably fine fashion.

"Ah," Sylvain Copperend said. "You're up. Excellent."

He held a large book, which he set down on the ground. He then stepped out of the room, returning a moment later with a second person, who was bent and leaning heavily on his arm.

It was Professor Frison. Hapless's mentor for magical studies.

Professor Frison was old, certainly, but he looked as if he had aged ten years or more since Hapless last saw him, less than a week ago. (Was that even possible? Less than one week since he had regarded Hapless across his wide wooden desk with disappointment in his eyes. *I'm sorry, my boy—I simply cannot in good conscience award passing marks for your work.*) He looked at Hapless now with only the barest flicker of recognition in his eyes. He seemed . . . worn thin. Translucent around the edges.

"Here, Professor," Copperend said. "I've brought you your student. Here is the prince."

"The prince?" Professor Frison said weakly.

"It's me." Hapless moved forward as Professor Frison swayed on his feet. Copperend steadied him. "What have you done to him?"

"I assure you, it was self-inflicted," Copperend replied. "If he were more skilled in magic, it would cost him less."

Copperend gestured with one hand, as if pulling something out of the air, and a chair appeared in the middle of the room. For a moment Hapless could only stare. It was the sort of magic he had only read about.

"You're a magician," Hapless said.

Amusement flickered across Copperend's face. "And they say you're slow-witted." He led Professor Frison over to the chair. "Sit, Professor. Regain some of your strength before we begin again."

Professor Frison shook his head. "No. No, please. No more."

"Come, now," Copperend wheedled. "I've gone to all the trouble to get the prince here."

"I can't," Professor Frison wheezed.

"Then let's have Hapless do the honors." Copperend reached into the pocket of his jacket and pulled out a small leather pouch. "Go on." He extended it toward Hapless. "Take it."

Hapless would have given anything at that moment for one of Quad's charms. For Quad herself, or Iliana, or Aurelie—better yet, for all three of them to swoop in and sweep away the threat with a flick of the wrist. To laugh about it afterward, safe and at a remove.

Copperend smiled, teeth shiny and straight. "I insist."

Hapless glanced toward the door. It was the only way out of the tower. He could fight, but Professor Frison certainly couldn't. Could Hapless get them both out? Could he risk trying? Copperend had no weapons. He hadn't attempted to lay a finger on Hapless yet. But Hapless got the distinct impression that it was because he didn't need to. The absence of a weapon was somehow more concerning than the presence of one would've been.

Hapless took the pouch from Copperend's outstretched hand. He cautiously opened it and peered inside. "Seeking stones."

"Another astute observation. Very well done."

"What am I meant to do with these?" Hapless asked.

"I want you to seek," Copperend replied. "For me. For your dear uncle Valiant."

"Valiant is dead."

"Are you quite certain?"

"Yes," Hapless said, his jaw set. "My uncle is buried in the Royal Chapel. I've seen the tomb myself."

"Were you present on the day of his death?"

"Obviously not."

"Have you seen inside the tomb with your own two eyes? Have you seen your uncle's bones?"

"No."

"Even if you had, could you be entirely confident whose bones they are? Could you say, without a shadow of a doubt, that they belong to the former heir to the throne? Or is there a chance—even the slightest possibility—that they are the bones of a decoy?"

"A decoy," Hapless repeated dryly.

"Don't sound so incredulous, Prince! Give it a good thought. How would anyone know for certain? How could they prove it?"

"How could *you* prove it?"

"That's exactly what I intend to do," he replied. "And you and the professor are going to help. We're going to seek Valiant. We'll seek him as many times as it takes to find him. We'll seek him until we find me." He picked up the large book and flipped it open. "And here's the best part—do you know what I discovered?"

"I can't say that I do."

"With two circles overlapping—with a second seeker—it's possible to create a window into the first seeker's sight. In that way, we can *all* see what they see. It'll be irrefutable. I'll show the Court that a search for Valiant leads to Sylvain Copperend."

"And will you tell them how you got that irrefutable evidence? Or will you make us disappear, like Elias Allred?"

Copperend looked up from the book and regarded Hapless. "What do you know of Elias Allred?"

"I know he was your apprentice. And I know his father. I know how desperately he wants news of his son."

Copperend turned back to the book. "I'm afraid he was of little use to me."

Hapless swallowed. "Well, I don't think I'll be of much use, either. Did Professor Frison mention that I'm a failure? I can't do magic. I certainly can't seek."

Copperend just stared. "That's a pity. But, fortunately, I have someone else who can."

Hapless's heart leapt into his throat as Copperend flicked one hand and the door swung open.

Thirty-Nine

Aurelie journeyed to the Mercier School for Girls. It was nestled in a valley alongside the Northern River. The campus was undeniably picturesque—Aurelie had felt like she was walking into a storybook when she first arrived there as a child. The school buildings were stately and well-kept, and the grounds were lush and green, dotted with tall trees.

The gates were open, but the door to the main building was locked when Aurelie arrived. A young girl—a first or second year probably, no doubt serving page duty—answered. Her expression was curious as Aurelie explained that she—travel worn, in magic-cleaned clothes, nearly three days on expanding and eating that same piece of bread—was a former student.

"I'd like to see Miss Ember," Aurelie said, and then shook her head. "I need to see her."

The page frowned. "Sorry. Miss Ember isn't here."

"Where is she?"

The page looked off to the side and then leaned in, eyes wide. "No one knows."

Aurelie's stomach lurched. "Is she all right?"

"She's been missing half a week now."

"Missing?"

"Gone. Vanished. Quite suddenly." She dropped her voice. "Some upper years think she ran off to get married. There was a man in the village she was seen with—"

Miss Ember wouldn't run off. She was the most responsible person Aurelie had ever known, even and measured and levelheaded.

"Has anyone looked for her?"

The page shrugged. "Headmistress said it was managed. She's quite livid, I heard."

There was a voice in the hall then, and the page glanced back.

"Sorry, miss," she said to Aurelie. "I'll tell Miss Ember you called. If she ever returns." Then she shut the door.

Aurelie headed away, walking entirely without purpose or direction. Where was she to go? What could she do now? And most troubling of all—what had happened to Miss Ember?

She was missing. And no one knew where she was, but maybe no one knew how to find her the way Aurelie did. The way Miss Ember had taught her.

In an instant Aurelie had a purpose. She turned back toward the main building and then broke off to the left, toward the dormitories.

If Miss Ember had left suddenly, maybe her belongings were still here. Aurelie found the window she thought was

Miss Ember's—three floors up, where the lower-year girls lived—and stood underneath it.

She thought of her feather test. Thought of that sensation. She hadn't meant to open the window back then, but maybe that's why it happened, without conscious effort. Aurelie focused on the bag of seeking stones—a soft, tan leather pouch, a pattern of interlocking diamond shapes stamped into the center of it. She thought of the sound of the drawstring being pulled. The feel of each stone.

Above her, the paned glass of the window swung open, and in a moment, the bag descended and hovered in front of her.

She snatched it from the air and took off.

Aurelie made her way to the woods on the outskirts of the school's campus and searched for a stand of trees—*birchwood amplifies seeking*—and hoped it wouldn't be inhabited by earth-dwellers.

She found a copse of birches. It was a sunny day, and the late-afternoon sky was a deep blue. There was a small stream running adjacent to the trees. A gentle wind rustled through the branches overhead, and for a moment Aurelie considered simply lying down and resting. She was tired, and it wasn't the exhaustion of hard work. Tired in a different, visceral kind of way. Drained from within.

She found a small patch of dirt exposed at the base of one tree and set about drawing the circle and marking the symbols.

It's a lost art, ain't it? the clerk at the inn had said. But Miss Ember had seen fit to teach it to Aurelie anyway.

One evening, shortly before Aurelie had left school, she

and Miss Ember had shared a pot of tea after their lesson. They often did. That particular evening, Miss Ember had peered over her chipped cup and told Aurelie that she knew Aurelie could seek as soon as she saw her feather test.

"You drew from within," Miss Ember had said, eyes alight. "Other children . . . they pull heat from the fire and light the feather aflame. They leach color from the surface the feather rests on and transform it superficially. But you . . . you *willed* it to move, and you willed the window to open. That sort of magic has to come from somewhere. It comes from within." She paused. "I knew then that you could learn to seek, because you were willing to give. And I knew that you could master it because you were willing to let the magic take."

Kneeling before the circle on the forest floor, Aurelie thought of Miss Ember's face, her hands upon the teapot as she carefully poured tea, her eyes as she looked at Aurelie—kind and observant.

And there it appeared, behind Aurelie's eyelids—an image taking shape. Uneven rectangles of stone, stacked and mortared. A tall, narrow window with diamond-paned glass. And a figure . . . two figures . . . four . . . Miss Ember was one of them, unmistakably, but also—there, bursting through like a beacon—

It was Hapless.

It didn't make any sense. But before Aurelie could ponder it further, another of the figures turned toward her. He wore a simple but elegant jacket and held a large book. His face—Aurelie had seen him before. At an inn in the Meadowlands, clasping hands with the innkeeper. Surveying the room and settling on Hapless, for just the briefest moment.

Sylvain Copperend. The man who claimed to be the lost king Valiant.

Right now he looked in Aurelie's direction. He looked . . . *at* Aurelie. And smiled a little.

"Who do we have here?" he said. His voice rang out with perfect clarity, as if he stood directly before her.

Aurelie wrenched back, and the image shattered. A wave of exhaustion swept over her suddenly, irrepressible and all-consuming.

She collapsed and knew no more.

Forty

The woman was a schoolteacher. At least, that was Hapless's assessment. She was maybe Gallant's age and wore a pale gray dress that was embroidered around the cuffs with a design of interlocking circles. That meant she had studied education in the Scholar's City.

"Your Highness," she said, dropping into a curtsy upon seeing Hapless.

Annoyance flashed across Copperend's face. "None of that," he said. "When I'm king, we're doing away with honorifics. It's all meaningless anyway."

He instructed Hapless and the teacher to draw two seeking circles. Hapless had never drawn one in his life, so he took the chalk the teacher offered him and knelt next to her, trying to copy what she drew upon the stone floor.

"What's your name?" he whispered.

"Ember," she said quietly. "Evangeline Ember."

Hapless blinked. Aurelie's favorite teacher was named Ember. The one who taught her seeking. "Do you teach at a school for girls?"

"Yes," she replied.

"There's no need for conversation," Copperend said, and Hapless looked up at him.

"I don't understand why you're doing this."

"I told you—"

Hapless was suddenly struck with an idea. "I'm not the prince," he said, his mind racing. "You're mistaken. I don't know why you've kidnapped me and my father and sister, but we're not who you think we are. We have nothing at all to offer you. I've been told I resemble the prince—it's the hair, I think; I've heard his is a similar color—but surely you must see how different we are up close. *Surely* you must see that."

Copperend didn't speak.

"I'm a clerk at my father's gallery in the arts district," Hapless continued. "My sister works in a dressmaker's shop. We cannot help you. We know nothing of magic. Please let us go." He looked right into Copperend's eyes. "Please. You are mistaken."

Copperend blinked, and then slowly a smile teased the corners of his lips. "It's a decent attempt, I'll give you that." He considered Hapless with interest. "If I were less proficient myself—*far* less proficient—I might be inclined to such deception. But you don't understand how it works, do you? How there are layers to it. No one has taught you properly. He certainly hasn't, has he?" He gestured to Professor Frison, who sat motionless in his chair. "I might have myself, in a different—well, it doesn't matter now. You cannot simply conjure. You must *make* me believe you. Illusion is nothing without persuasion. Persuasion is nothing without intent.

You need all three, perfectly balanced, working in concert. You're unbalanced. Do you know why?"

"I told you, you're mistaken—"

"It's because you're desperate," Copperend said. "And this isn't an invitation to practice. I have things to accomplish, after all. Shall we begin?"

Forty-One

A urelie awoke to something nudging her shoulder. Not sharply, but insistently.

She opened her eyes, though doing so felt like pushing up an enormous set of weights. The forest had grown dim. Above her stood a figure, holding a stick and poking her in the arm.

"Quad?"

Quad stopped poking.

"What are you doing?" Aurelie asked blearily.

"I was going to ask you the same thing."

Aurelie tried to stand but stumbled upon doing so and nearly fell back down. She had the most peculiar feeling— more than being hungry or tired, it was as if she had worn thin at the seams, near to ripping apart.

Quad heaved a sigh, dropped the stick, and went to Aurelie's side. "You're very foolish."

"Well, we mortal children are rather stupid," Aurelie said

with as much of a smile as she could muster. It was a bit pathetic—more of a grimace than anything.

"You're no child. You're older than me."

Aurelie couldn't remember if she and Quad had ever touched—had they hugged? Shaken hands? If they hadn't, surely they should have—but her arm was currently slung across Quad's shoulders as she stumbled alongside her. She couldn't remember ever feeling this exhausted—not after three straight days of baking, preparing for a visit to the village from that viscount, not after spending an entire night seeking for a particularly tricky bounty with Iliana, not after four years with Mrs. Basil. She had no idea where they were going, but Quad seemed directed enough, leading them through the forest.

"That can't be right," Aurelie replied. "I can't think of any rocks that I'm older than."

They came upon a small thatch-roof shack, almost camouflaged among the trees.

"Older in an intellectual sense," Quad said as she navigated Aurelie through the door. "Though clearly you lack any." She led Aurelie to a pallet in one corner of the shack.

"How can you tell?" Aurelie asked, collapsing onto the pallet. It was much softer than she expected. Leafy green—was it made of actual leaves?—and plush.

"You've fallen in love, for one thing," replied Quad.

"Does that make me older, or does that mean I lack sense?"

"Both," Quad said, and then, "Go to sleep," and Aurelie did.

When Aurelie woke, there was a second person in the shack—the sweep of a coat, the sound of boots pacing across the hard-packed floor. It was Iliana.

She turned abruptly when Aurelie moved to sit up. "You're awake."

Aurelie's voice came out in a croak. "I am."

Iliana crossed the room and knelt in front of her.

Aurelie had never seen Iliana in such a state. She had never really seen her in a state at all—Iliana was always cool and collected, completely in control. Now she clasped Aurelie's shoulders harder than was comfortable, with a mingled look of relief and desperation and exasperation in her eyes.

"I went to Basil's to find you and she said that you'd stolen from her and fled. She said I should track you down and turn you in."

"I didn't steal from her."

"Of course you didn't. That woman is a crook! She's a . . . a *ne'er-do-well*! I'm going to go back there and raze that place to the ground! I'll bake her heart into a pie and eat that pie and then tell everyone how disgusting it is!"

Aurelie couldn't decide whether to be touched or horrified. She settled on a mix of both.

"You'd be insulting yourself," Quad said evenly. "If you'd baked the pie."

Iliana squeezed Aurelie once, hard, and then stood up and walked away. "You're a complete idiot."

"Pardon?" Quad said.

"I meant Aurelie."

"Oh. Yes, that's fair."

"Hey!"

Iliana turned back around, and her expression was even worse somehow. Hurt.

"We could've helped you," she said. "*I* could've helped you. I know I was terrible to you at the wedding—I know that, and I'm sorry, I was in an abominable mood—but you didn't have to run off like that. And you never had to let yourself get to this state—magic sick to the point of collapse! I bet you were eating expanded food too, weren't you?"

Aurelie looked away. Iliana's voice had a strangely fragile quality to it when she next spoke. "Why do you think you have to do everything on your own? We're your friends." She shook her head. "Don't you understand that? We're your *friends.*"

Colleague died on Aurelie's tongue, along with *associate.* She looked at them both—Iliana, color high in her cheeks, and Quad, arms folded, expression grim—and let the words sink in. *We're your friends.*

Aurelie didn't trust herself to speak. Instead, she swallowed and looked toward the window. It was dark outside—she had no notion of what time it was.

She broke the silence eventually. "Is this your house, Quad?"

Quad shrugged. "It's *a* house."

"How did you find me?"

"We tracked you," Iliana said.

"Why?"

Iliana looked away. Something about her expression made Aurelie sit up straighter.

"Why?" she repeated.

"Hapless has disappeared."

Ice shot through Aurelie's veins.

"It happened during the lovers' ball," Iliana continued. "My brother was with him just before he vanished. Defiance came tearing in from the orchards, saying that someone had attacked them. Defiance was knocked unconscious, and when he awoke, the prince was gone—"

"I saw him," Aurelie said.

"Sorry?"

"I searched for Miss—for my teacher. She's missing too. Hapless was with her. And so was Sylvain Copperend."

"Copperend," Iliana repeated.

Aurelie nodded. "He must've taken him." She swallowed. "He must have done something to Elias Allred, too, don't you think?"

And now Elias was gone completely. Vanished. What if the same thing happened to Hapless and Miss Ember? What if soon no amount of seeking could find them?

Aurelie's voice hitched. "You were right."

Iliana's expression was grim. "What else did you see? Where were they?"

"In a round room made of stone. . . . There was a window, high up . . ."

"What else?" Iliana's gaze sharpened.

"It had diamond-paned glass."

"More."

"I don't know. . . . It was—the room was . . . empty. There wasn't anything else that . . ." She paused. "In the window . . . in the spot where each diamond met, there was a circle."

Iliana's eyes lit up. "Thank you. *Thank you!* This is why

you're the best, and other seekers are useless! This is why we're the perfect team—"

"Do you know where he is?"

"The Scholar's City," Iliana said. "He's back where he came from. He's at the university."

Forty-Two

The buildings of the Scholar's City stood tall and imposing. Most were made of gray stone, some moss covered, some weathered and crumbling. It felt storied. *Proper academic*, as Hapless had once described it to Aurelie.

The university's campus lay on the east side of the city. Aurelie, Iliana, and Quad passed through an arched gateway onto the grounds. The verdant green lawns were lined with more stone buildings. All of them had windows set with diamond-paned glass, each bearing the same circle pattern Aurelie had seen—the crest of the university.

It was a sunny day, with a bright, cloudless sky, but there was an eerie stillness to the campus.

"The term has ended," Iliana explained as they headed across a wide lawn toward a row of buildings. "And that means the Festival of Wisdom has begun."

"What's that?" Quad asked.

"Rather a big holiday for a city dedicated to scholars. I

imagine most everyone is at the celebration in the city center at the moment."

Just then, movement up ahead caught Aurelie's eye. A hooded figure dashed out from one of the buildings.

Iliana spotted it too. In an instant, she took off at a run.

Aurelie and Quad followed, Aurelie doing her best to keep up despite her exhaustion. They caught up just in time to see Iliana overtake the hooded figure in front of a building labeled HUMANITIES in large wrought-iron letters. She seamlessly pulled a sword from her coat as she slammed the hooded figure against the wall of the building.

With the sword pressed to the figure's throat, she ripped back their hood.

It was Lord Defiance.

"What are you doing here?" Iliana snapped.

"Well." Lord Defiance's voice came out strange, his head pressed back against the stones to keep his throat as far from the blade as possible. "Isn't this a pleasant surprise?"

Iliana pushed closer. "You took the prince."

"I didn't."

"You were the last person to see him. Conveniently. And now you're here. Also conveniently."

"I told you, I was knocked out. I wouldn't call it particularly convenient. When I awoke, he was gone." There was an unexpected earnestness in his voice. "I have no reason to lie."

Iliana considered him for a moment. Then, to Aurelie's surprise, she stepped away. She still gripped her sword. Defiance made a show of rubbing his neck.

"As for why I'm here, I could ask the same of you."

"Why were you in the Underwood during the ambush?"

Iliana demanded, and Aurelie frowned. Lord Defiance was part of the ambush?

"The same reason you were, ultimately," Defiance replied. "To protect the prince. I would've told you earlier if you had asked me, but that's not something you'd think to do, is it? Actually communicate with anyone?"

As much as she hated to agree with Lord Defiance on anything, Aurelie understood the sentiment.

"So you're not involved with the kidnapping." Iliana's tone was as serious as Aurelie had ever heard it. "You're not working for Copperend."

"No," Defiance said. "Of course not. Are you?"

"On my honor."

"I don't know how reassuring I find that, considering you have none."

"That's ironic, coming from you." Iliana leveled her sword at his chest. "Lord Defiance, loyal to no one but himself, blind to anything that won't line his purse or advance his standing—"

There was a crack in Defiance's cool exterior—anger flashed across his face. "As if you're any different! As if you're not a *blistering* hypocrite!"

"I'm nothing like you."

"You are, *Lovely*, and what's worse is that you're deluded enough to not even realize it. At least I know what I am." He shook his head. "You can run away and play at being ordinary. You can wear leathers and sleep in wayside inns and eat *crusty bread and cheese*, you can pretend to have *suffered*, but it won't change who you are and where you came from—"

Iliana's eyes glinted. "Sword. Now."

"I haven't got one."

"Perfectly fine. I've got two," Iliana said, and drew a second sword from her coat and tossed it to Defiance.

What followed was the clank of metal on metal, swift and bright. Iliana spun to the left, Defiance danced right, both of them whizzing past where Aurelie and Quad stood.

"I'm not sure what crusty bread and cheese have to do with it," Quad remarked.

"I think it's symbolic," Aurelie replied, as they watched the pair advance and retreat, attack and parry.

"Do you think they solve all their arguments this way?"

"Probably," Aurelie said, as Iliana feinted to the left and caught Defiance off-balance. She checked him in the side and he toppled to the ground, the sword clattering from his hand.

Iliana snatched it up and stood over him, both swords pointed at his chest. "You're rusty."

"I've been at school."

"Doing your little experiments."

"Protecting the prince," Defiance said. "Just as the king asked me to."

Iliana blinked. "What?"

"Isn't that what we're here to do?" Aurelie stepped in. "Protect Hapless? Don't we have to find him and save him first? Maybe we should . . . get to doing that?"

"The baker's right," Defiance said.

"The baker has a name," Iliana replied, voice acidic.

"To be fair, you never use it," Aurelie said, and Defiance smiled. It changed his face entirely.

"You know what—I might actually like her."

"You will do no such thing," Iliana said.

"I can like whoever I please."

"You're all being quite aggravating at the moment," Quad said loudly, and Aurelie spun around to face her.

"*I'm* trying to get us back to the task at hand!"

Quad looked unimpressed. "Ineffectually."

Aurelie threw her hands in the air. "I'm going to go cast the stones. You all can stay here and argue if you'd like."

"Wait." Iliana lowered her swords. "You need birchwood, don't you?"

"The benches in the lecture halls for literature are made of birchwood," Defiance said.

"How would you know that?" Iliana asked.

"I know things." Defiance climbed to his feet. "I thought we'd established that. Baker, I'd be honored to direct you to the hall." He extended an arm toward Aurelie.

Aurelie ignored it. "Lead the way, then."

Defiance grinned at Iliana. "I might definitely like her."

The lecture hall was filled with rows of raked benches and tables that led down to a massive set of chalkboards at the front of the room.

Defiance ran down and grabbed a piece of chalk, dashing back and presenting it to Aurelie with more flourish than was necessary. Aurelie knelt on the floor at the base of one of the benches and drew the circle. The others stayed back as she closed her eyes, cast the stones, and reached out.

She could see it, or flashes of it—the same stone-walled

room, the window, high and narrow. There was only one person in the room at the moment, and it was undeniably Hapless. Miss Ember wasn't there.

She focused harder, trying to glean more about the room, the walls, something to distinguish it, but the more she reached out, the more the image flickered, until it sputtered and disappeared.

Aurelie leaned back against the bench behind her. "I can't tell anything more than before. It's a circular room, made of stone, with one window."

"That's useful enough," Defiance said. "It must be a tower room. Only a handful of buildings on campus have them—we'll search them all."

"Hapless is alone now," Aurelie said. "I don't know about Miss Ember—"

Iliana stood. "We'll find Hapless first and then look for the teacher. Baker, you stay here and we'll—"

"I'm not staying behind." Aurelie struggled to her feet.

"You can barely stand. Cast the stones again when you can and look for your teacher. In the meantime, rest."

"But—"

"Aurelie," Iliana said. "Please."

No one should be allowed to weaponize a name in that way, but Iliana wielded it effectively.

Aurelie slumped back down. "Fine."

"Good." Iliana patted the top of her head. "Don't do anything stupid."

"Don't treat me like a child!" Aurelie said as Iliana checked the daggers at her sides.

"Do you really want those to be your parting words to me?"

"It would be fitting," Defiance said. "They're very frequently your parting words to Mother."

"Was Iliana a disagreeable child?" Quad asked Defiance.

"Dreadfully."

"I hate that you're here," Iliana told Defiance, and then she turned to Quad. "And I hate that you're encouraging him."

Forty-Three

When Hapless opened his eyes, he was still in the tower. Alone this time.

He sat up slowly, his head pounding. If he felt like this—and he had almost no magic to begin with—what would happen to Professor Frison? How much pain must the professor be in, having spent so much magic seeking? Miss Ember had told Hapless, quietly, between attempts, that because Hapless drew the circle, he helped power the search. What would have happened to Professor Frison without Hapless there to draw magic from? How much longer could Miss Ember hold out, burning her own magic?

He had no idea how much time had passed. Copperend's attempts to prove his birthright all melded together.

"Again," Copperend had said, when they failed to locate Valiant once more, Frison seeking from one circle and Miss Ember casting the image of Frison's search above them, eerie and colorless, an empty void.

"We cannot find what does not live," Frison had wheezed, his voice high and thin.

"I live and breathe before you, Professor," Copperend had said. "Try again."

And again, and again. At one point Copperend had cut a line across Hapless's hand and pressed the blood to his own forehead. They tried again. Nothing.

"Not through bloodlines, then," he said, and then sighed and pulled out a handkerchief. Hapless thought Copperend might offer it to him to wrap his hand, but instead, he used it to wipe the blood from his face.

"There's something to it, though. I know there is," Copperend said. "Something of the bond between you and me, dear nephew."

Right now, alone in the tower, Hapless closed his uninjured hand into a fist. He couldn't let Copperend continue. He had to free Professor Frison and Miss Ember. He had to fight back, no matter what.

When the door next opened, Hapless sprang to his feet as quickly as he could.

But it wasn't Copperend who appeared in the doorway. It was Quad.

"All right, Prince?" she said.

Hapless's heart leapt. "What are you doing here?"

"Liberating you. Gather your things."

"I don't have any things."

She smiled, or something like it. "Then we're all set."

Hapless couldn't say definitively that Lord Defiance was the last person he expected to see upon leaving the tower room—seeing his great-uncle Sprightly probably would've been more jarring, for one—but he certainly didn't expect to see him leaning coolly against the stone wall of the passageway, a sword dangling casually from one hand.

"What are you doing here?"

"Fancied a trip north," Defiance said.

"You were there in the orchard that night. And in the woods during the ambush. You're the reason I'm here!"

"I'm the reason you're walking out of that room right now."

Quad glared at Defiance.

"One of the reasons," Defiance amended. "And if you want to walk out of the building, too, we'd better get moving."

Hapless complied, following them both down the curving staircase, but he wasn't satisfied. "You were the last person I saw before I was attacked."

"I was attacked too," Defiance replied. "I woke up and you were gone. And I can't say I appreciate the accusatory tone. I've done a great deal in service of you."

"Oh really? Such as?"

"Off the top of my head, I took Intro to Composition *and* Problematic Mathematics because of you, not to mention I had to sit through Poets and Playwrights of the Age of Indifference. What were you even thinking, enrolling in that as a first-year course?"

"What are you saying?"

"I've been your shadow," Defiance said. "Ever since you went away to school."

Hapless blinked. "That's not—you haven't—you don't even—"

"Sentences make a great deal more sense when you actually finish them, Prince."

"That's impossible," Hapless finally settled on.

"Why?"

"Because you're terrible, and you hate me."

"The first point is arguable, and the second is inconsequential. I was called into service by the king."

Gallant. Of course. "He sent you to school with me," Hapless said. "To look after me, like a child."

"He sent me to protect you. And rest assured, I would've gone to school anyway. His Majesty knew I was smart enough to pursue my own course of study as well as yours."

"You're not even studying magic."

"Neither are you, the way you're going about it."

"Hey!" Hapless pulled on the hood of Defiance's cloak, and Defiance stopped short on the stairs. Hapless nearly crashed into him and sent them both stumbling.

"This mortal small talk is awfully unnecessary," Quad said from ahead of them.

"This isn't small talk."

Quad turned, eyes narrowed. "It's medium talk at the most. Regardless. The others will wonder what's taking so long."

Hapless frowned. "The others?"

"My sister and the baker," Defiance said, and Hapless's heart rose.

Forty-Four

Aurelie waited in the empty lecture hall. When she felt strong enough to stand, she paced slowly up one row of benches and down another, winding all the way around to the front of the room, the bag of seeking stones held loosely in one hand.

Iliana returned first, alone.

"We agreed to meet back here after an hour," she told Aurelie. "I searched the northern half of the campus. Quad and Defiance went south."

"Together?"

Iliana nodded. "I thought that would be best."

"Why?"

"Well, for one, if I went with Defiance, I'd probably kill him."

"Why didn't you all split up?"

Iliana hesitated for a moment. "Defiance has always been . . . unpredictable. I thought it best that he remain supervised." Before Aurelie could reply, she continued. "How are you, then?"

"I'm fine."

"I find that hard to believe." Iliana crossed over to peer out one of the windows lining the left side of the hall. Then she turned abruptly back to Aurelie.

Aurelie couldn't make out her face, silhouetted as she was in the light from outside. "Why didn't you tell me?" Iliana asked. "How bad it really was with Basil?"

"Why is that important right now? There are way bigger—"

"I knew she was abominable. But I never thought she would actually . . . turn you out onto the street like that. Maybe I'm . . ." Iliana's voice was uncharacteristically small. "You must think I'm quite naive. You out of everyone must see the truth about me."

"What's that?"

"That I don't know anything."

It was quiet.

"That's how it works, though, isn't it?" Aurelie said eventually. "Someone asks you how you are, and you say fine; you say very well. You don't say how you really are because they don't really care, do they?"

"I care," Iliana said. "If I ask, I care. If I ask, tell me the truth." She paused. "So. How are you? How do you feel?"

"Tired," Aurelie said, her voice breaking.

"Magic sick?"

"No. Yes. Both. I'm just tired."

"Rest, then," Iliana said. "I'll keep watch for the others."

Aurelie was about to reply, but just then the doors in the back of the hall burst open, and there was Hapless.

He was whole, entirely in one piece, only a fair bit scruffier and dirtier than before and a little pinched around the eyes. He still grinned upon seeing them, striding down the center aisle to the front of the room and looking for a moment like he was going to grab both of them up into an enormous hug.

He pulled back at the last moment, though, and clasped hands with Iliana heartily, before turning to Aurelie.

Aurelie wanted to throw her arms around him, but she held back, instead looking him over, inspecting him for damage. For as rough as he appeared, his smile was still as powerful as ever.

"You're here," he said.

"So are you."

"Yes, we're all here," Iliana said, and from the back of the lecture hall, someone gave a particularly loud cough. Aurelie blinked and looked to the back, where Quad and Lord Defiance were standing. "What a reunion," Iliana continued. "Shall we be on our way?"

Hapless shook his head, at the same time Aurelie said, "No."

"We can't leave Professor Frison and Miss Ember," Hapless said. "We have to find them too."

"Yes, of course," Iliana replied. "But please, for the love of all that is good and holy, let's be strategic about this. The last thing we need is to get ourselves captured."

Forty-Five

They got themselves captured.

The group had made their way through the building where Hapless had been kept. They searched each room, Aurelie sparing a bit of magic to unlock the doors that wouldn't readily open.

They were entering a small classroom on an upper floor when Aurelie felt a strong shove to her back, which caused her to stumble into Hapless in front of her, both of them toppling over. Two more thuds sounded next to her in quick succession.

Then the door to the classroom swung abruptly shut.

Aurelie rolled off Hapless—"I'm sorry!" "That's quite all right."—and saw Iliana and Quad sprawled out next to them.

Iliana was on her feet in a flash.

"Damn it." She ran to the door and tried the handle. "Damn it, damn him—" She pounded on the door. "Let us out!"

Defiance's voice on the other side of the door was muffled. "This is for the best, I swear to you."

"Let us out!" Iliana pounded harder, each fist falling heavier, until suddenly she wrenched back with a wince, clutching one hand to her chest.

Aurelie hurried over and grabbed Iliana's hand, quickly inspecting it. It was raw and red along the side.

"He's done something to the door," Iliana choked.

Aurelie stepped up to it and hovered one palm along the wood paneling, feeling nothing. "Maybe I could—" she began, reaching for the doorknob.

"Don't." Quad sidled up next to them and picked up a discarded quill off the ground. She held it to the surface of the door. The feather glowed orange and then caught.

Quad pulled it away and blew out the flame.

"Defiance!" Iliana called, and then, "*Defiance!*" But there was no response.

"It'll be all right." Hapless stood, surveying the room. "We'll find a way out of here."

They couldn't find a way out.

The room held six rows of tables, six sets of benches. It was walled in stone and had three tall windows that were too narrow to fit through.

It was hard to mark the passage of time, but hours must have passed. The small slivers of sky that Aurelie could see through the windows had turned pink, then purple, and were now fading into a deep blue. There were no candles or lamps in the room, so she brought a glow to her fingertips, even though she knew she couldn't sustain it for long. The magic would burn fast, like a fire made only of tinder.

But it lit up the space for now, made it feel a little less foreboding.

"Don't you have anything for this?" Iliana asked Quad, for probably the tenth time. "Something that helps you walk through walls or . . . dissolve stone or something?"

"Don't be absurd," Quad replied, and then it was quiet again, though she could be heard muttering *Dissolve stone!* disparagingly every so often.

"He should've been here by now," Hapless said eventually. "If Defiance is working for Copperend, then Copperend should've already turned up."

But no one came. The sky grew black. There were no stars out. Aurelie pushed a little more into the glow of her hands, let it shine a little brighter.

"You know," Iliana said after a while, casting a look at the prince. "If you had been named something besides Hapless, maybe we wouldn't be in this mess."

It was meant to be a joke, Aurelie knew, but Hapless's expression was stricken.

He was sitting on the ground with his back up against the wall, one leg stretched out in front of him, the other drawn up, his arm wrapped around it. When he spoke, his voice was quiet.

"It's not my real name."

"Really?"

He nodded. "I know everybody treats it as such. And I've read the headlines, of course. 'Prince Hapless the Helpless.' 'Prince Hapless the Hopeless.' Kind of writes itself, I must admit."

Aurelie opened her mouth to speak, to refute it, but before she could, he went on.

"As soon as it was uttered—I don't know by whom; I was too little at the time to remember—it was impossible to undo. People took to it too much."

"What were you called originally?" Aurelie asked.

"Dauntless," he replied, and it was quiet for a moment before he continued. "I think my parents wanted me to be . . . fearless, and determined, they wanted me to be . . . capable." He swallowed. "It was a nice thought, if not quite fitting."

Aurelie thought suddenly of the phantom voice in the Underwood:

When the time comes, speak his true name.

"Dauntless," she said.

Nothing happened, except that Hapless looked over at her. "Evokes a different kind of feeling, doesn't it? You'd expect someone a lot more . . . " He waved a hand. "And a lot less . . ." He gestured to himself. "You'd just expect someone . . . better."

Quad got up and crossed the room to where Hapless sat. She crouched down next to him and cupped her hands around his ear, leaned in, and said something that was too quiet to be heard.

Hapless's brow eased immediately. A look of contentment came over his face.

Quad leaned back on her heels.

"What was that?" Hapless asked.

"My name," replied Quad. "A fair trade, I'd say." She stood. "I'll continue to call you Hapless, with your permission. I've grown rather fond of it."

"So have I, in a way," he said.

"You may continue to call me Quad," she said, and gave a small smile. "I'm rather fond of it as well."

Forty-Six

So Hapless had traded his tower cell for an empty class-room. Though the empty classroom had the firm advantage of also including his friends, however much he regretted their situation.

Hapless cast a look over to where Aurelie lay sleeping across the room. She looked uneasy, curled up atop Iliana's coat. Her fingertips still glowed faintly, a soft orange, like the embers of a dying fire.

Quad was standing nearby, motionless—the Quad equivalent of sleep.

Iliana was still awake. She had settled a few feet away from Hapless, her back against the wall, mirroring Hapless's position. It had been quiet between them for some time, but Iliana spoke eventually.

"I have to tell you something."

"All right."

"It's . . . not pleasant."

"Let's have it quickly, then."

Iliana took a breath and then said, "The ambush in the

Underwood . . . It came from the palace." A beat. "It came from your brother."

Hapless swallowed. "I know."

He could barely see Iliana's face through the darkness, but he could hear the movement, her head turning sharply to look at him.

"You do?"

"Yes. I found out the night of the lovers' ball."

Iliana let out a puff of air. "I'm sorry."

It pained him to ask—maybe it would be better not knowing. But he couldn't help it, not after what Defiance had claimed, supposedly assigned by Gallant to watch over him. Iliana had just appeared in the Underwood, after all, right in the nick of time—she had a habit of doing that.

"Did you know all along? Were you in on it?"

"I wasn't. I only discovered the truth after you were taken from the ball. I swear on my life."

"Swear on something less valuable," Hapless said. "At least swear on mine."

"Prince—"

He cut her off. "I understand."

"What?"

"Why you'd leave Court. Why you would choose another life. I would probably do the same if I could."

"It's not like you to sound so defeated."

He gave an unhappy breath of laughter. "Maybe you don't know me very well."

"Nonsense." Iliana tipped her head back, resting it against the wall behind her. "I'd say I know you well enough. Certainly better than I know my own brother."

"I don't understand what he's about," Hapless said. "He said he was sent to school to look after me. And yet . . ."

"And yet."

It was quiet for a little while after that.

"If you left Court, what would you do?" Iliana asked suddenly. "Where would you go?"

"I don't know," Hapless said. "I wouldn't really want to leave my family. I wish . . . I wish I could keep them and trade the rest."

"Even the king? You'd keep him, too?"

The hurt flared up inside him but shrank back down just as quickly. "Even him." He paused. "And anyway, running away . . . I just like the idea of it, I guess. I don't know how it'd really feel in practice."

When Iliana spoke again, it was measured. "Is that . . . why you like Aurelie?"

"What do you mean? The idea of her?"

"Yes. Or . . . I don't know. Does she represent . . . choosing another life?"

"No," Hapless said. "And you of all people shouldn't have to ask why I love her."

"What makes you say that?"

He gave her a look, despite the relative darkness. He couldn't tell if Iliana was really getting it, though, so he decided to say it aloud as well.

"Because you love her too."

A breath of laughter followed. "I don't feel that way for Baker. Not that she's not . . . smart. Headstrong. Incorrigible. Qualities I certainly look for in a girl—I'll admit that."

"There's more than one kind of love, you know," Hapless

said. "We don't have to love her the same way in order to both love her."

Iliana didn't reply.

"She deserves all kinds, really," Hapless continued. "I don't think anyone's ever looked after her in the whole of her life."

"That teacher," Iliana said. "Ember."

Hapless hummed in agreement. "I should have Miss Ember knighted when this is all over."

"You know, you can't just go around bestowing knight-hoods at the drop of a hat. This is why you're not allowed to judge mastery. Everything would be the best thing you've ever seen. *Egad, this cake is divine! That dress is divine! That painting—*"

"Divine?"

Hapless couldn't be certain, but he thought maybe Iliana was smiling. "See?"

So Hapless smiled back, through the darkness. But it faded after a moment.

"He scares me," he said. "Copperend. He's not . . . There's something not right about him."

"Well, his predilection for kidnapping is definitely concerning."

"He's not Valiant."

"Of course he's not."

"He's powerful, to be sure, but it's not just that. He thinks he can just . . . decide something and make it true."

It was his single-mindedness, Hapless thought. His absolute faith in something absolutely false. And knowing it was false and not caring—trying to make it true nonetheless.

Iliana scooted a little closer, reached out, and punched Hapless's arm lightly.

"We'll be all right."

"He needs seekers." Hapless looked back toward Aurelie. "We can't let him have her."

"We won't."

"You're very confident."

"I know," Iliana replied. "It's one of my best qualities."

Hapless smiled.

They sank into a thoughtful silence. When Iliana spoke again, there was an uncertain note in her voice.

"Can I confess something to you, Prince?"

"Of course. Though technically it's Gallant's job to pardon."

There was a pause before Iliana spoke. "I saw the boat."

"Sorry?"

"The one you tried to conjure for us when we were on the river last summer. White and gold sails?"

Hapless frowned. "You saw it? Why didn't you say?"

"Because Aurelie and Quad didn't see it. And I didn't want you all to think that I'm . . . I don't know . . ." She swallowed. "*Susceptible.* That I can be fooled, just because I'm not magic like the rest of you."

"Why are you telling me now?"

"Because you deserve to know. You have magic. And you *are* capable."

Hapless shook his head. "I tried it on Copperend. It didn't work. He saw right through it."

"Maybe you just need more practice." It was quiet for a moment. "You could show me something now if you wanted."

"What would you like to see?"

Iliana's voice was barely a whisper. "Pith."

Hapless glanced over at her. She seemed to be looking out into the room.

Hapless looked out in that direction as well. "Lady Pith and I danced together at the lovers' ball."

"I know."

"She dances quite well. Very light on her feet. She keeps time like a clock. The music just . . . flows through her."

Hapless imagined Lady Pith as she appeared in the ballroom—dipping into a curtsy from across the set, stepping forward with one hand raised to complete the figure, turning in a slow circle while a measured minuet played in the background. The white gloves, the jewels in her hair—

Iliana's breath caught.

—the sweep of her neck, the poise in her expression. Lady Pith was the type who was meant to be royal. She was someone whom Gallant and Honoria would be all too happy for Hapless to make a life with. But Lady Pith's eyes never quite settled on Hapless whenever they danced together. She was always discreetly scanning the crowd for someone else. Someone who was unlikely to appear. Someone Pith surely wished would appear nonetheless.

Hapless wasn't sure how much of this he had spoken out loud. All he knew was that Iliana had scooted closer than before. She threaded one of her arms through his and rested her head on his shoulder.

The minuet played in his mind. Lady Pith turned and turned again, looking back with a small smile. She retreated to her line as the music drew to a close, dropping into a curtsy, head bowed.

The music faded.

"Are you all right?" Hapless murmured.

"Mm."

"I won't think less of you, you know."

"For falling prey to your conjuring?"

"For being in love."

"I'm not."

"There's no need to lie."

"There is." Iliana's voice was hoarse. "For me, there is."

"Why?"

"The fact that you have to ask means that you won't understand," Iliana said, and then she squeezed his arm. "You have an open heart."

"And yours is closed?"

Iliana didn't reply.

Forty-Seven

It was early morning when the door to the classroom swung open.

Aurelie had been awake for some time, watching the sky lighten to a pale gray. Hapless and Iliana were still asleep, but they sprang up at the sound of the door hitting the wall behind it, and Quad melted away from the classroom wall, taking on her usual appearance.

The doorway was empty.

"Is this a trap?" Aurelie asked.

Iliana frowned. "If it is, it's a strange one."

"I'll check," Hapless said, moving to the door, but Iliana grabbed his arm.

"Let me."

She moved toward the doorway, stuck her head through. "Nothing," she said, looking back. "No one."

"Should we—" Aurelie began.

"Not question it?" Quad interjected. "I agree. Let's get out of here."

"We can't leave without—"

"The professor and the teacher, yes," Iliana said. "Let no one say we don't value our Kingdom's educators. You should seek them if you're able, Baker, but not here. Let's find somewhere else to regroup."

Hapless led the group to a large park that bordered one side of the campus. It was, for the most part, carefully cultivated, with manicured flower beds and straight, even lines of trees. But it gave way to a thick forest, and that was where they found a stand of birch trees.

It had rained sometime in the night, and the ground was damp. Aurelie knelt in front of one of the birches and drew a circle at its base.

She had only just closed her eyes when a great burst of energy threw her backward.

There in the center of the circle stood a man.

Hapless was at Aurelie's side in an instant. She grasped his arms as he helped her to her feet. She didn't want to let go.

"I've only come to talk," the man said. It was Sylvain Copperend.

He looked right at Aurelie. There was something about his appearance, some look about his eyes that made Aurelie's skin prickle.

"Remarkable, isn't it?" he said. "Transportation through the circle. I've pioneered it myself. Are introductions necessary? I imagine Hapless has spoken of me."

"We know who you are," Iliana said. She had drawn her sword from her coat. Copperend didn't appear to have any weapons.

His lips curved briefly into a smile. "Then you know what I want."

"The prince," Iliana replied.

He shook his head. "The throne."

Next to Aurelie, Quad had her hand on her belt. Very slowly, almost imperceptibly, she flicked up the flap on one of the pouches attached to it.

Copperend's gaze snapped to her. "I wouldn't," he said. "I want only to talk. And besides, I brought you all something."

He bent and reached through the circle—into the earth—and heaved another person out of it, head and shoulders appearing first, then the rest of him.

Lord Defiance.

Copperend dragged him to his feet and kept one hand on his shoulder, clasped tightly. Defiance's expression was blank, almost as if it were frozen, though his eyes darted around wildly.

"I thought we might trade," Copperend said. "That's the sort of thing we royals deal with, isn't it? Trade negotiations?"

"Where is Miss Ember?" Aurelie asked.

Copperend looked at her, his gaze piercing. "She's quite well. But I'm afraid the professor isn't in the best condition."

Hapless's voice was choked. "Where is he?"

"Fortunately, I've learned what I need to do," Copperend continued, as if Hapless hadn't spoken. "He was useful, in that way. But it's left me in a bit of a predicament." His eyes hadn't left Aurelie. "I saw you before. I felt you reach out."

"I wasn't reaching for you," Aurelie said.

"We found each other regardless. And I'd like your help. As Hapless may have told you, I have something I need to prove, and in order to do so, I need him, myself, and two seekers. I'll give you this young man in return. He's a delight—like a hero straight out of the old stories. Swooping in and declaring my arrest. It was boldly done, if ineffective."

Aurelie's eyes darted to Iliana, whose grip tightened on the hilt of her sword.

"What do you say?" said Copperend.

No one spoke.

And then Quad moved suddenly, pulling a charm from her belt and crushing it in her hand in one smooth motion. But before she could deploy it, Copperend made a gesture in the air and the powder exploded in Quad's face. Aurelie grabbed hold of Quad as her body went limp, and lowered her to the ground.

"I advised you not to, didn't I? There's always fair warning with me. Now." Copperend pulled Defiance closer. "Would you care to motivate your friends?" He squeezed Defiance's shoulder.

Defiance's knees buckled and his face contorted in pain, his mouth open on a silent cry.

"Perhaps he's out of words for the time being," Copperend said. "Pity."

Aurelie couldn't see Hapless's face, kneeling as she was on the ground next to Quad, but she saw his shoulders straighten, his hands clench into fists at his sides.

"I'll help you," Hapless said. "Bring him forth."

Copperend smiled, all teeth. "Meet us in the middle."

Hapless glanced back at Aurelie. She tried to condense everything she could into a single look—*don't do it! Don't help him! Don't trust him!* But if Hapless saw it written across her face, he ignored it and stepped forward anyway.

Copperend pushed Defiance along in front of him to meet Hapless partway between the circle and where the others stood.

Aurelie knew they couldn't let this happen. She looked frantically at Iliana, only to find her standing frozen, her eyes locked on Defiance.

Aurelie looked down at Quad, lying motionless in her arms. How long would the charm last? And if it didn't wear off, how would they break it without Quad's help?

And then Aurelie realized with a jolt that Quad was looking back at her.

Quad winked.

Aurelie's heart leapt.

"Your word," Hapless said, "that no harm will come to anyone else here. Or Professor and Miss Ember." He extended a hand toward Copperend.

"You won't bargain for yourself?"

"No. I imagine you mean to do me harm."

"You're more pragmatic than I expected."

"Your word," Hapless repeated.

Copperend observed Hapless for a moment and then took his hand from Defiance's shoulder and clasped Hapless's own.

Several things happened at once: Defiance fell to his knees just as Hapless pressed suddenly toward Copperend, their hands still clasped, forcing him backward. Aurelie and Quad sprang into action as Hapless drove Copperend back toward the circle.

Aurelie threw her arms around Hapless's waist and yanked hard, setting him off-balance, while Quad slammed her arm down on their clasped hands, disrupting the grip. Copperend stumbled backward and disappeared cleanly into the earth, as if falling into a hole.

Quad bent down, quickly wiping the circle away.

"Well done," Hapless said, a bit breathlessly.

Quad looked pleased. "Good thing we don't make charms that work on ourselves."

Relief coursed through Aurelie. She felt weak with it. "Good thing he didn't know that."

Iliana crossed to Defiance and pulled him to his feet. He clutched his throat, eyes wild.

"We'll sort you out," Iliana told him. "But not here. We need to—"

"That was an exquisite move!" a voice called. Aurelie whipped her head around. Some fifty paces away stood Copperend.

No, thought Aurelie, and, "Damn it," Iliana swore aloud.

"Run," Hapless said.

And so they ran, as fast as they could, all five of them, Iliana and Quad breaking one way with Defiance struggling along between them, his arms slung across their shoulders, Aurelie and Hapless tearing off in the other direction.

They ran, and suddenly Copperend was thirty paces ahead of them.

"I appreciate the amplification properties of birchwood myself," he called. "You'll find I've drawn circles all throughout these woods."

Hapless grabbed Aurelie's hand and pulled her in a different direction. Copperend was gone again and then reappeared, fifteen paces to their right now.

They changed directions yet again, heading to the center of the woods, where the trees were thickest.

Hapless threw himself down behind a large fallen tree, pulling Aurelie with him.

"There's no sense in running," he said. "We don't know where he might appear next."

They could hear footsteps in the distance.

Hapless looked at Aurelie, eyes ablaze. "Bread costs five copper," he said.

"What?"

"At least, it did at the bakery by campus," he continued, quiet and fast. "I used to walk down there to buy a loaf every morning that I could—it made me think of you. Steward's name is Hubert Allred. He has four grandchildren, and they call him Papa. The length of mastery is dependent on the discipline, but baking should take no less than three years and no more than five."

"What are you—"

Hapless clasped Aurelie's shoulders, leaned in, and for a split second she thought he meant to kiss her, but instead, he looked her right in the eyes. "He needs you. And he needs me, too, so let's not let him have us both." He gripped her shoulders tighter, leaning in closer, their foreheads nearly touching. "He cannot see you." His eyes were bright. "He cannot see you. *He cannot see you.*"

And then Hapless stood.

"Here," he called, striding out from behind the fallen tree.

"Ah," Copperend said.

"Hapless—" Aurelie stood too.

"I finally figured it out," Copperend said. "I've been going about it all wrong, you see. I've been trying to forge something anew when what I need to do is *connect* to what already exists. I've figured out how to do that. Through you."

Aurelie realized with a sickening lurch that there was now a dagger in his hand. It had a jet-black handle and a blade etched with loops and spirals.

This, Baker, is an Impossible knife.

"You'll be arrested," Hapless said.

"Who will ever know?" Copperend replied. "Who is here to bear witness but the trees?" He smiled a little, and Aurelie realized—*he cannot see you.* "Maybe you were always meant to play this role in my life. Poetic justice, I suppose, as I was meant to play one in yours, whether I wanted to or not."

Aurelie cast a look around wildly, her gaze landing on a tree branch lying to Copperend's left. She could pick it up and swing it at him—

But before she could move or even think, Copperend sprang into motion, throwing the dagger at Hapless.

It was too fast, aimed too true. There was nothing to be done. Aurelie watched in horror as Hapless fell to his knees and then collapsed to the ground.

She dropped down beside him. It was terrible, the hilt of the knife sticking out of him, the bloom of red across his shirt, his eyes gazing up at her, his lips parted.

"Why would you do that?" Aurelie's voice broke on it. They should've kept running. He should've used his magic on himself instead. None of this was right. She traced her fingertips over Hapless's face, and his cheek dimpled slightly with a smile. How was it he could still do that? How was it possible that his goodness could still surface, even now in the face of everything, even as his grip on Aurelie's arms slackened and blood colored his lips?

"You know why," he whispered, and managed one more labored breath before his eyes rolled back.

Forty-Eight

The thing Hapless thought as he lay dying—because surely he was dying, surely this was it—was not actually one thing but a rush of things all at once. He thought of a chasing game Gallant used to play with him when they were children, how he would humor Hapless, letting him catch up and throw his arms around him and hang on. He thought of his mother's favorite jam, jarred in the kitchens at the palace, a little too sour for his taste, but she loved it, so he loved it too. He thought of his father's beard, scratchy as he dropped a kiss to Hapless's forehead, of his sister's dog, the littlest one, trying to carry a too-big stick through a gateway and Honoria laughing, laughing, doubled over with it, of Steward turning a circle in his Bastian Sinclair costume: *How do I look, Your Highness?* He thought of Quad, stooping and gently cradling a blossom, pointing out the tree from which it fell—of Iliana, extending a hand, pulling Hapless to his feet with a grin.

He thought of Aurelie and the fierce look in her eyes on

the balcony, the night of the lovers' ball: *You shouldn't have to be less.*

When you put it all together, the sum of it was that he was loved, and that he had loved, and that he was so much more fortunate than most, but most of all, he was fortunate in that.

He thought of his lament in the Underwood, long ago: *I might be the worst magic scholar who ever existed.*

And Aurelie's reply: *Well. At least you exist.*

He thought, *I would do whatever it takes, so long as she keeps existing.*

Then he thought no more.

Forty-Nine

It was the moment Aurelie needed magic the most. What was the point of it if there wasn't something that could fix this? Reverse it? Her mind raced—*spell it warm to double cold, spell it clean to double grime*—if she spelled Hapless dead, would he return alive twofold? *Dead*, she thought, and *Hapless*, and *half a dozen horses*. She felt cold fury, and desperation, more hopeless than she'd ever imagined was possible, all at once, concentrated to the head of a pin, a single bolt of lightning.

All this in an instant. She would have to kill Copperend, she supposed.

Hapless was still breathing, faintly.

Maybe Iliana would do it? Could Iliana? Had she ever killed anyone before?

None of them could do it. None of them would. But Hapless was still—

Hapless—

Aurelie clutched his hand as blood blossomed steadily across his shirt.

She looked up at the man across from them.

And . . . it wasn't Sylvain Copperend at all. This man wore Copperend's clothes, but he was far younger. He was slightly turned away from Aurelie as he carved the seeking symbols into a birch tree. When he looked back in their direction, it was with keen, light blue eyes—

It was a face that had peered out at her from a bounty: *30,000 gold, living or dead.*

He crossed over to them, his eyes alight. Aurelie knew that he still couldn't see her. He focused only on Hapless.

"You will be useful to me, even in death," he murmured. "Even more so, I believe."

When the time comes, speak his true name.

"Elias Allred," Aurelie said.

Copperend—Elias—*lost in the Underwood*—a trick within a trick within a trick—straightened, his body suddenly stricken, his expression frozen, eyebrows arched in surprise.

The ground shook, and in an instant he was gone— swallowed whole by the earth beneath his feet.

Fifty

I *can't stay in the dormitories like everyone else,* Hapless once wrote to Aurelie.

> I have to stay at Crimson House, where those of the royal lineage—peers of Scholar's City— reside while in school. The rooms are always prepared to receive royals. My aunt stayed in this particular apartment, and my great-uncle, and great-great aunt, so on and so forth. It's a bit odd sometimes, lying in bed and imagining that they slept in the exact same spot. Literally. All the furniture is the same. The bed is positively ancient. Honoria would burn it on sight. I don't like to think of what my great-uncle Fulsome may have gotten up to in here . . .

Aurelie never imagined she would actually get to see Crimson House one day. And she certainly never imagined that she would see Hapless lying in his room, completely motionless, pale against the sheets of the massive four-poster bed. Normally he was radiant, kissed by the sun, a healthy tinge to his cheeks. Now he looked . . . bloodless. Barely more alive than the marble insets on the windows and the fireplace mantel.

Aurelie, Iliana, and Quad had been forced to wait outside Hapless's bedroom while the physicians tended to him. If Hapless had been waiting there in the hallway with them, he probably could've told them some interesting fact about the elaborate pastoral scene that hung on the wall (one shepherd gazing dopily at another, the other shepherd gazing dopily at a sheep. It must've been painted by the same artist who did the painting in Princess Honoria's study—the sheep's expression was unnervingly sinister). But instead, they sat side by side on an elaborately carved wooden bench, entirely silent.

"This is miserable," Quad said eventually.

"I thought trolls didn't know misery," Iliana murmured.

"We know it," Quad replied gruffly. "We just didn't invent it." She paused. "There are many things we didn't invent that I still know of. Parasols. Riverberry tarts. Sarcasm."

Iliana stood and walked to the end of the hallway. It had a curved ceiling, and the walls were papered in midnight blue and gold. The floor was covered with a thick gold-patterned rug that muffled her footsteps.

"Closed-top carriages. Taxes. Conspiracy," Quad continued.

The door to Hapless's room suddenly swung open.

"It's the weapon," the physician told them, after describing Hapless's condition. "The Impossible knife. I'm afraid the damage inflicted by an enchanted blade is . . . unpredictable, and unfortunately . . . irreversible."

That was some hours ago. Hapless still lay unchanged, silent and motionless. Riders had been sent to the Capital. His family was on their way. The physician thought it was best not to move him.

Guards had been sent to search the campus as well, and Aurelie would later learn that Miss Ember and Professor Frison were found trapped in the basement of one of the school buildings. The professor was greatly weakened but still alive—kept so by Miss Ember.

But at the moment Aurelie sat unknowing in the stillness of Hapless's room, settled in a chair at his bedside. Quad stood by one of the tall windows, and Iliana sat slumped at Hapless's desk.

"Try it," Iliana said eventually, her voice hoarse.

"Try what?" Aurelie sounded no better.

"True love's kiss."

Aurelie looked over at her. Iliana's expression was entirely serious. It made Aurelie feel as if something in her chest might break open. For all Iliana's worldliness and *I know everything, Baker*, all the times she tossed her head and forged ahead and accomplished the unimaginable—she still didn't know. Or . . . she was naive enough to believe. It was enough to send a jolt through Aurelie's already shattered heart.

She swallowed. "There's no such thing."

"Of course there is."

Aurelie shook her head.

"How do you know?" asked Iliana.

"If it were real, no one would ever suffer the loss of anyone they loved, would they?" Aurelie looked back at Hapless, at the slight rise and fall of his chest. "If it were real, I would've tried already."

"Try it now, then."

"Iliana—"

"If you're invoking your name magic, then invoke it on him." She tried for a smile, but it ended up pathetically lopsided. "Darling, please. Please."

Aurelie looked over at Quad, who nodded too.

So Aurelie moved closer to the prince.

She thought of Hapless returning to school in the fall, to this very room, to start another school year, and she imagined herself doing the same. Not returning to this room, of course, but some small one, shared with another student maybe, lamps lit late into the night, poring over books, haunting the stacks in the Royal Library. She thought of walking with Hapless to class, and afterward, lunch by the bell tower, and it was springtime—why not—and the light would catch the planes of Hapless's face, golden again, and his lips would curve into a smile, about to break open with it, and she would kiss him and smile back and then kiss him again because she could and again when he moved forward to chase her mouth, and again and again and again—*You can stand under that roof if you'd like, but it won't keep rain off your head—*

She reached for his hand—it was cold—and spoke. "Hapless."

She looked at the curve of his knuckles, the smooth, rounded fingernails, the gaudy ring he wore, silver with a deep blue stone winking back at her in the candlelight.

When the time comes, speak his true name.

Her voice broke, and it was barely a whisper. "Dauntless." She pressed her lips to his knuckles.

And then the hand in Aurelie's grasp squeezed her fingers for just an instant. Hapless's lips parted, and his breath caught.

But then his hand went slack. The prince's eyes stayed shut.

"What was that?" Iliana said.

"That was not nothing," replied Quad. "I think it was very much something, in fact."

Fifty-One

It was indeed something.

It was Miss Ember who identified it. "The Stone of Circumspection," she breathed, examining the ring on Hapless's hand. He still lay motionless at that point, but the physicians had confirmed that he was healing, suddenly and rapidly.

The ring, combined with Aurelie's magic (Iliana was gleeful: *See, I told you, Baker! I knew it! I knew you had name magic!*) had broken the enchantment from the Impossible knife and jump-started Hapless's recovery.

The prince was going to survive.

The king, Princess Honoria, and the kingfather all arrived early the next morning, in record time from the Capital.

Aurelie, Quad, and Iliana were given rooms on the ground floor of Crimson House. Aurelie didn't see Hapless again once his family arrived, but the crown princess did visit her briefly. She clasped Aurelie's hand, head bowed, and dipped a small curtsy.

"Thank you," she said. "For what you did."

Aurelie barely understood what it was that she had done. For Hapless, and in the woods—so much of it was muddled.

It was Miss Ember who sat down with her to discuss it.

Their reunion had not been a tearful one. They were very much alike, Aurelie supposed, and while her emotions felt exceedingly close to the surface after everything that had happened, it just wasn't in her nature. They had simply embraced, and then Miss Ember held Aurelie at arm's length, assessing her.

"You've grown up," she said.

"I'm hardly taller," Aurelie replied, and a smile teased at Miss Ember's lips.

"There's more to growing up than height."

They sat together in the ground-floor study of Crimson House, surrounded by floor-to-ceiling bookshelves and a wall of windows that overlooked the back garden and let in the weak midmorning light of an overcast day.

"I never knew Sylvain Copperend," Miss Ember told Aurelie, clasping a cup of tea and a saucer. "But I knew Elias Allred."

Aurelie looked up from her own teacup. Miss Ember's expression was neutral, but there was sadness in her voice.

"I was born in the Capital, and we shared a magic tutor when we were young. He knew of my interest in seeking. I knew—I had heard—that he had disappeared in the Underwood. Some days ago, a man calling himself Sylvain Copperend came to see me, saying that he had new information about Elias's whereabouts and needed my help in seeking him. When I grew wary of him . . . well, he gave me no choice in the matter." Miss Ember looked away. "But he wasn't Copperend at all, was he? It was Elias. Hiding in plain sight. Enchanted to appear as his own mentor."

"I guess that's one way to accelerate the mastery process," Aurelie murmured.

One corner of Miss Ember's mouth lifted. "I wouldn't encourage it."

"What happened to the real Copperend?"

Miss Ember shook her head. "I can't say. It's thought he may still be in the Underwood."

"And Elias?" Aurelie swallowed. "After I broke the enchantment, he just . . . he disappeared—"

"I don't know," Miss Ember said. "I would hope that the palace plans to investigate further." It was quiet for a moment. Aurelie looked out at the garden, the branches of the ornamental trees bending slightly in the wind. It would rain later, a driving summer rain, and then the sun would break through the clouds. Though Aurelie didn't know it yet.

"You did the right thing," Miss Ember said eventually.

Aurelie was not thirteen anymore, sipping tea in Miss Ember's office after a magic lesson. Miss Ember was no longer her teacher—hadn't been for some time. And it wasn't as if Miss Ember was the utmost authority in absolutely everything; she wasn't granted the power to pardon.

But Aurelie felt it a little—she allowed herself to feel it. Relief.

"Thank you," Aurelie said. Miss Ember inclined her head.

It was quiet for another moment, until Aurelie couldn't hold it back any longer. "Why didn't you ever write?" She swallowed. "Not that . . . I mean, I know that you were under no obligation, of course, but I thought . . ." She felt foolish saying it out loud—childish, vulnerable—but she said it nonetheless. "I thought you might have wondered what happened to me."

"I did write." Miss Ember's expression was troubled. "I sent letters to you at the bakery." She shook her head. "I grew concerned after receiving no reply for some time. I entreated you to write back quickly, even just a note, so I would know whether you were settled, whether you were . . . happy. I even wrote of a plan to visit you, but then I received a letter from your mentor. She assured me that you were very well. That you were too busy in your training to reply, but . . . that you wished me well. I was relieved to hear that you were enjoying your apprenticeship." Miss Ember's voice was soft. "But now I fear that must not have been the case."

Aurelie felt a flood of emotions—anger toward Mrs. Basil was chiefly among them. But there was also grief and regret and somehow, even still, happiness. It felt like an impossible combination.

"No" was all Aurelie managed to reply in the moment.

A complicated mix of emotions played across Miss Ember's face as well. "I'm sorry," she said. "I should have persisted. I shouldn't have just accepted—"

Aurelie shook her head. "There's nothing to apologize for."

"I am sorry all the same."

Aurelie nodded. Took a breath. Looked out the window and waited for her gaze to clear before looking back in Miss Ember's direction. "My apprenticeship has ended now. It's over."

"I'm very glad to hear it."

Aurelie managed a small smile. "So am I."

Fifty-Two

Several days later, Aurelie stood on one of Crimson House's verandas, looking out over the manicured lawn. A door swung open behind her.

And there stood the prince. He was still pale, with deep shadows under his eyes, but he smiled brightly nonetheless.

"Hello," he said.

He was here. Alive. Whole. Existing. Aurelie could've said any of the myriad things she was thinking, put words to the numerous warring emotions in her chest, but instead, all that came out was "You're up."

"I am." He crossed to where she stood at the balustrade. "I'm told my recovery is progressing remarkably well. Dr. Veil says it's unprecedented. He wants to publish a paper on me." He paused. "I was also told . . . That is to say, I heard that you . . . assisted."

Aurelie didn't speak.

"Maybe you could be a co-author on the paper," Hapless said, and Aurelie couldn't help but smile.

"How do you feel?"

"Good. Sore. But . . . alive. Thanks to you."

"I can't take credit," she said. "I didn't even know what I was doing."

"But you did it all the same."

It was quiet. Hapless rested his hands on the balustrade. Light winked off the blue stone of his ring.

"The Stone of Circumspection," Aurelie said.

"Yes."

"It breaks enchantments."

"Combined with the proper words," he said. "Apparently."

"Where did you find it?"

"In a cave, off Lantern Bay. It was sort of a . . . second quest. That I undertook. A solo one. Except Steward was there."

"So not quite solo."

"Not quite." Hapless looked sheepish. "But I wanted . . ." He took a breath. "I just. Wanted you to know. That . . . it wasn't an enchantment. What happened between us. And I thought with the stone . . . you could be certain." He looked down at it. "Except I couldn't get it to work, and Professor Frison didn't think it was the real stone—it's meant to be 'as dark as midnight,' but this is clearly more of an indigo—"

"Oh, clearly."

He looked up at her. "I feel like . . . like I was meant to find it. And you were meant to use it."

Aurelie found she couldn't reply.

"It was completely worth falling from that rock face trying to grab it. Sprained my wrist and tore the sleeve of my best silk shirt, you know."

Aurelie smiled. "You're a hazard."

"I'm a delight," he replied, all mock offense and irrepressible smile, eyes alight with mischief and something like—something that was maybe—

If love stared me in the face, I wouldn't know what it looked like.

Maybe it looked a little like that. *Maybe this is how people are meant to fit together.*

"Hapless?"

"Yes?"

Aurelie looked at him and wanted to say . . . something. She wasn't quite sure what, but she had a suspicion. And the things that had happened had changed her, but not completely, not to the core. Maybe nothing could change you entirely. Maybe she would always doubt, or maybe she would always be a little afraid. Maybe Hapless would be all right with that—of that, she felt more certain than anything.

So she didn't say anything at all. If she couldn't say it, she could show it. She reached out with one hand and lightly touched the prince's face, leaned in, and pressed a kiss to his lips.

It felt like magic, and Aurelie knew now that it was. It was its own kind of magic. The prince's lips were soft. His fingertips as they grazed against her cheek were soft. The look in his eyes when she pulled away was soft. Aurelie loved all of it.

A smile broke over Hapless's face. "Why did you do that?"

Aurelie smiled back. "You know why."

Fifty-Three

It wasn't until later that Aurelie and Hapless reunited with Iliana and Quad on the lawn outside Crimson House. Iliana was reclining in the grass, and Quad was looking out at the campus as they approached. When Iliana spotted them, Aurelie wondered if Iliana could tell what had occurred between her and Hapless. There was something of a knowing gleam in Iliana's eyes, but to Aurelie's relief, she didn't say anything to that point. Instead, she acknowledged them both with a nod.

"Prince," she said. "All mended?"

"Certainly better than before."

"Glad to hear it."

Quad gestured to Hapless. "Come here," she said. "Look at me."

Aurelie watched with amusement as Hapless moved closer.

"Lower," Quad said, and Hapless stooped a bit so he was eye to eye with Quad. "Are you looking?"

"I am."

"Are you paying attention?"

"On my honor."

Quad slapped him lightly across the face.

"Never do something like that again," she said. "Got it?"

He nodded dutifully and straightened up.

Quad threw her arms around his waist. Hapless grinned and hugged back.

"Thank you, Quad," he said, turning to Iliana when Quad broke away. "And, Iliana—"

"Please," she said. "Keep your heartfelt thanks to yourself."

"Thanks for what? You were nowhere to be seen when I was getting run through with a magic blade."

Iliana grinned. "Fair play."

Hapless smiled back. "You know that I'm truly grateful for everything you—"

"No, please, don't ruin it now with your sincerity."

There was a cough from behind them.

Aurelie turned and saw Lord Defiance. He was standing straight and tall, finely dressed, not a hair out of place.

The smile on Iliana's face faded, and she turned away. "You're still here, then?"

"You're still angry with me?" Defiance replied. "Even though I could've died?"

"I'm angry with you precisely because you could've died," Iliana said. "And because you *lied* to us—"

"I didn't."

"You made a stupid decision without even *consulting*—"

"It was my job to protect the prince, no matter what—"

"For the record, I didn't ask you to," Hapless said.

"—with orders straight from the king," Defiance continued.

"I don't care what orders came from where," Iliana said, jumping to her feet and advancing on him.

"And I certainly wasn't going to let anything happen to you lot, either. Imagine the lashing I'd get from Mother if I let something happen to you and the lashing I'd get from you if I let something happen to those two." He waved a hand toward Aurelie and Quad.

"*Imprisoning us* was a strange way to protect us," Iliana said.

"It seemed pretty effective!"

"Until you got *yourself* captured instead!" Iliana smacked him on the arm. "You could've died! Don't swoop in and try to protect everyone if you can't even protect yourself!"

"That's . . ." Defiance let out a breath. "Fair. Probably. That's probably fair."

Iliana looked at him for a moment, and then she deflated as well. "Your enchantment on the door didn't even hold," she said.

"It only broke because Allred enchanted me," Defiance said.

"I didn't even know you *had* magic."

Defiance shrugged. "Didn't exactly see a reason to put it about."

Iliana threw her hands in the air. "You're infuriating."

"Now you know precisely what it's like to know you," Defiance replied.

"Are all mortal siblings like this?" Quad asked.

"I wouldn't know," Aurelie said. "I don't have any."

"I have two," Hapless said sagely. "And I'd say yes, more or less."

Fifty-Four

When Hapless returned to his rooms in Crimson House that afternoon, he found Gallant seated at his desk, poring over a pile of papers.

Hapless's family had been buzzing around Crimson House for days now. Honoria kept trying to feed him. His father kept laying a hand on his forehead as if he had caught a fever rather than a knife to the ribs.

And Gallant had hovered nearby, silent and grave, throughout Hapless's recovery. Hovering didn't suit Gallant—he was so much more suited to striding in and assessing.

He looked up as Hapless entered the room.

"Any news from the Capital?" Hapless asked.

"Nothing of importance," Gallant replied, looking back down at the papers on the desk. After a moment's silence, he stood.

"Hapless—" he began, at the same time Hapless said, "I've just been—"

"Pardon," Gallant said. "You first."

"No, nothing, just. I was with Aurelie just now, and . . . I'd like the two of you to meet."

Gallant nodded. "I'd like that."

"Were you going to—"

"I was completely in the wrong," Gallant said.

Hapless blinked.

"With the business in the Underwood. I thought I was thinking of the good of everyone, but I should never—I should have *never* put you in that position, never have used you in that way . . ." Gallant's mouth twisted. He looked away. "I hope one day you can forgive me."

Hapless felt supremely uncomfortable. He had never seen Gallant like this. It was so out of character, it was as if one of Honoria's dogs had reared up on its hind legs and began delivering a sermon on proper hygiene.

"I will never put you in harm's way again," Gallant said. "I will never act without your knowledge or permission. I will never involve you in things you want no part in. I will never underestimate you like that. I know you're smart, and strong, and brave—more so than me, infinitely more so, Hapless—"

"All right," Hapless said. "I don't . . . This is not . . ."

"I just had to say it."

"Because I almost died?"

"Because I was a supreme ass," Gallant said. "And then you almost died."

"The two things weren't exactly related."

"But you may have died thinking I was a supreme ass."

"I may still yet."

Gallant's lips twitched now, his eyes shining. "I'm sorry," he said.

Hapless nodded. "I know. Thank you."

Fifty-Five

What am I meant to do with a royal commendation?" asked Quad, as she, Iliana, and Aurelie watched several grooms prepare carriages for the royal family's return to the Capital. Aurelie was somewhat more interested in the sandwich she was currently making her way through, but they were admittedly very fine carriages—the newest and latest models. The prince's family did nothing inconspicuously, it seemed.

"Wear it proudly, I suppose," Iliana replied. "That's what my mother would say, anyway."

"Will it match my outfit?"

"Heavens, you sound like Hapless."

They were all receiving commendations, to be awarded in a ceremony at the palace in a week's time. *For brave service to the royal family*, the king had said.

Aurelie hadn't found him as imposing as she'd expected. They had met only once, and he seemed serious, to be sure, but there was a shadow of Hapless in the way he smiled. Not as full-out, not as limitless, but disarming nonetheless.

"I'm very grateful that my brother made your acquaintance," King Gallant had told Aurelie.

Hapless had coughed. "I don't know if I would exactly call us *acquaintances*."

Aurelie could feel her face burning.

The king had smiled then. "I'm grateful no matter what."

And now they were set to return to the Capital together. Before she knew it, Aurelie found herself in one of those lushly appointed carriages with Hapless and Princess Honoria. Iliana and Quad chose to ride ahead on horseback. "To take in the fine weather," Iliana had claimed, but Aurelie suspected she didn't want to be cooped up with the princess, who spent a large part of the morning talking about the new preparations for her wedding. (Nothing had gone forward after Hapless's disappearance. *Will we have to repeat the lovers' ball?* Hapless asked, and the princess's eyes gleamed. *Yes, and I know exactly what I'll do differently this time.*)

It hardly registered with Aurelie when they were passing through her village, and it was with a sudden jolt that she realized they had slowed in front of Basil's.

"We just need to make a quick stop," Hapless said with feigned innocence.

A crowd gathered on the street, people jostling to get a look at the carriage. Hapless handed Honoria down and then reached for Aurelie's hand to help her out.

"What are we doing here?" she asked.

"I owed you a visit," he replied simply.

"Mrs. Basil is going to go mad."

Hapless squeezed her hand and grinned. "That's precisely what I'm hoping for."

When they entered the bakery, Jonas was standing behind the counter, his expression completely awestruck. There was flour all over his apron, and his hair was as artfully mussed as ever. His eyes widened at the sight of—

"Aurelie?"

"Hello," she said sheepishly, and then turned to Hapless and Princess Honoria. "This is Jonas, the journeyman here at Basil's. Jonas, this is . . ." The notion of such an introduction felt absurd, but it was happening nonetheless. "Princess Honoria and Prince Hapless."

"Hello, Jonas," Hapless said. "You're taller than I imagined."

"Thank you?" Jonas replied. "I mean, thank you, Your Highness. Could I . . . Would you . . . That is to say, would you like any . . ." He waved a hand toward the case.

Honoria looked at Hapless conspiratorially. "I do love a riverberry tart."

"Then a riverberry tart you'll have!" Hapless declared.

Jonas hurried to get one, and Honoria bit into it on the spot, flecks of powdered sugar raining down onto the front of her dress. She didn't seem to care, shutting her eyes and letting out a hearty *mmmmm.*

It was then that Mrs. Basil appeared.

"Jonas—" she began with a harsh tone, but then she took in the sight of Hapless and Honoria standing in the bakery and the crowd that had formed outside the windows, peering in. "Jonas!" she repeated, alarmed. "There's—that's—" In an instant, Mrs. Basil shifted from stricken to a practiced simper. "Your Highnesses," she said, as if she had been expecting them all along. "What an incredible honor. A delight. Truly a—"

Her eyes landed on Aurelie and immediately narrowed. She stepped out from behind the counter. "Please excuse me. I'm terribly sorry, I need to have a word with my . . . *former* apprentice. She has no right to be here."

Mrs. Basil advanced toward Aurelie, but Hapless stepped in her way.

"Aurelie is traveling with us to the Capital," he said, "where she'll receive a royal commendation for service to our family."

The emotions that crossed Mrs. Basil's face at that moment—Aurelie wished she could capture the sight of it forever.

"How . . . lovely," Mrs. Basil choked out.

"Yes, and I've stopped by for my mail," Aurelie said.

Mrs. Basil blinked. "Your . . ."

"My letters. I was told that I received some from my teacher. I've come to claim them."

Honoria looked between Aurelie and Mrs. Basil for a moment and then said carefully, "Of course, you must deliver anything received on Aurelie's behalf. After all, it would be unlawful to withhold—or even worse, to *destroy*—another's personal correspondence." Her voice was crisp. "I *shudder* to think of the consequences."

Aurelie didn't think she would ever feel so fond of a second member of the royal family, but she felt a powerful surge of affection for the princess.

"I will . . ." Mrs. Basil swallowed. "I will cast a look around. There may be . . . something, somewhere . . ."

She retreated from the room, while Honoria, looking entirely unbothered, took another large bite of riverberry tart. Hapless shot Aurelie a wide smile.

"Here." Mrs. Basil returned and thrust a small packet of letters at Aurelie. "They must have been misplaced."

"How remarkable of you to find them so quickly, then," Hapless said, and Aurelie wanted to kiss him square on the lips.

Honoria finished the last bite of her tart and then said, "Who prepared the riverberry tarts?"

Mrs. Basil seemed to recover a bit of composure. "Why, I did, Your Highness."

Honoria's eyes glinted. "I should very much like to observe you making a batch, to see a true expert at work."

"Well." Mrs. Basil smoothed the front of her dress. "They were . . . prepared in *part* by my journeyman. But the recipe is my own."

"I should like to see this recipe."

"Jonas, bring me my recipe."

Jonas hesitated.

"Jonas. Bring my recipe forth."

"I cannot."

"And why is that?"

He set his jaw. "Because it's not your recipe."

For an instant, shock and rage flashed across Mrs. Basil's face. But it quickly smoothed. "My journeyman forgets himself," she said. "All recipes developed under my roof are my recipes. That is how it works until you yourself have achieved mastery. Have you achieved mastery, Jonas?"

"No."

"There you have it," Mrs. Basil said.

"Have you sat mastery yet?" Honoria asked Jonas.

"Tried and failed," Mrs. Basil replied quickly.

"He was never even allowed to try," Aurelie amended.

Mrs. Basil glared at her but could say nothing. Could do nothing to Aurelie now. An incredible feeling of lightness bubbled up in Aurelie at the realization of it. It felt like swallowing sunshine.

"Then you shall sit mastery now, Jonas," Honoria said briskly. "We'll need to sample a dozen preparations, which I see here in this very case, and I will start with another riverberry tart."

Jonas's smile, rare but effervescent, blazed across his face.

Fifty-Six

W here are we going?" Aurelie asked, not for the first time, but closer to the sixth or seventh. She couldn't help it. Iliana was being *enigmatic* in that particular way of hers that was equal parts annoying and intriguing.

"I told you, it's a *surprise*," Iliana replied. "Do I need to review the principles of a surprise for you?"

They had been back at the palace for some time now, and Aurelie still hadn't quite adjusted to the splendor of it all. But the staircase they were currently descending was much more ordinary than any of the others she had encountered thus far during their stay. It led beneath the palace, its stone walls growing damper on either side. Torches sprang to life at periodic intervals.

"No," Aurelie said. "And you actually telling me where we're going would be the true surprise."

"Ha ha."

"Have I told you that you're looking particularly *lovely* today?"

"I don't appreciate that in the slightest."

They reached a passageway lined with a series of doors. Iliana strode down it, stopping about halfway in front of one that was identical to all the others. She removed a key from one of her many pockets and stuck it in the lock.

"You'll need to place your hand on the door as well," Iliana said.

"Why?"

"Can't you just trust me, Baker? After all this time?"

"No," Aurelie said, but she pressed her palm to the door nonetheless, and Iliana turned the key.

When the door swung open, it revealed a small room lined with shelves. Upon each shelf was a row of wooden chests. Iliana stepped in and opened one—it was filled to the brim with gold coins. She opened another, which held a mass of silver pieces, and a third, filled with copper.

"You can check each of them if you'd like," Iliana said, gesturing to the other chests, "but I assure you, it's all here."

"What is this?"

"The bounty for Elias Allred," Iliana said.

Aurelie shook her head. The amount of money—the sight of it—the *thought* of it!—was incomprehensible. "I . . . This is . . ."

"All yours. You found him, after all."

Aurelie looked at the chest of gold and then back at Iliana, standing there. Not leaning casually against the door-frame, inspecting her nails, but simply standing, hands at her sides, eyes forward, expression serious.

"The bounty was issued by the palace," Iliana said, "when Elias went missing."

"But . . . he's still missing. He disappeared. He . . . died, maybe—"

"No one knows that."

"But I didn't find him, not really—"

"Good grief, Baker, you're the only person I know who'd quibble about a windfall."

"But I can't—"

"You absolutely can and you will."

"What will I do with all this?"

Iliana shrugged. "Whatever you want."

Aurelie felt it . . . uncertainty. Excitement. Disbelief. Something else, hard to define. A lightness, growing. Hard to qualify. Impossibly good.

Fifty-Seven

Whatever you want.

Aurelie sat in the garden outside the palace with the others. Quad was trying to show Hapless some defensive magic. All Hapless had succeeded in doing was making several bushels of heartfruit rain down from a nearby tree.

"Are you trying to feed your attackers?" Quad asked. "Does that seem defensive to you?"

"Depends. Maybe they're allergic to heartfruit."

Quad let out a deep sigh.

Aurelie sat on the grass with Iliana sprawled out next to her. Iliana had a novel in her hands titled *The Innkeeper's Daughter: The Second.*

"There's a sequel?" Aurelie had exclaimed when Iliana produced it from her coat.

"Of course there's a sequel. Everyone wants to know what happened with Isadora and her paramour. Not to mention all that business with her brother."

But Iliana had set the book aside to follow Hapless and Quad's progress sometime around when the second batch of heartfruit fell.

"Have you heard from your Miss Ember?" Iliana asked as she and Aurelie watched Hapless brush leaves out of his hair.

"I had a letter from her today," Aurelie replied. Miss Ember was settling in at the university. She had received her own royal commendation for saving Professor Frison's life and would be taking over his post in his retirement.

I hope to see you on campus, Miss Ember had written. *I would be honored to continue overseeing your study of magic.*

Aurelie kept the letter in the pocket of her apron. (She had found it difficult to stop wearing it—force of habit, and it was useful in its own right. Pockets, after all.) It was tucked next to a note from Hapless that she had received just that morning, which had been signed *Yours, H.*

She couldn't bring herself to sign *Yours, A,* but she did write, *Fondly, Aurelie,* and she suspected that Hapless liked it just as much. He had started using the word *fondly* much more in conversation, at the very least. He even at one point mused, "*Fondly* would make a very nice Court name, wouldn't it?" to which Aurelie replied, "Pardon?" and Hapless, growing rather red, said, "Just thinking aloud."

Aurelie also had a letter from Jonas, who had left Basil's Bakery upon earning his mastery and was to receive sponsorship from Princess Honoria to open his very own bakery. *With no employees, Basil's has been forced to temporarily shut its doors,* Jonas wrote. *I don't know if and when Mrs. Basil plans to reopen, but it is of little concern to us now. And what a blessing that is!*

Aurelie wholeheartedly agreed.

Iliana looked over at her. "Do you think you'll go to school, then?" she asked. "To study magic?"

Aurelie wasn't sure yet. What *whatever you want* meant to her. She could indeed go to school, or travel the Kingdom, or do something else—anything else. There were so many options, all of them appealing, all of it overwhelming, to even have options in the first place.

"Maybe," Aurelie said. It was the most she could commit to at the moment, and even that was exciting. "Maybe I'll start hunting bounties full-time instead."

"I thought this was it for you. Remember what you said? *It's over as soon as it happens?*"

"What is?"

"Uh, 'all this,' as I recall. This thing where I call on you and you drop everything and risk everything . . . Sound familiar?"

"Perhaps."

"But maybe risking everything pays off? At least occasionally?"

"I'll cede nothing to you on that point. You're far too smug."

Iliana smiled. "How do you feel, then, Baker? Right now? Right at this moment?"

"Happy," Aurelie replied, and it was the truth.

Acknowledgments

Thank you, thank you, thank you to my amazing editor, Reka Simonsen, and to the excellent people at Atheneum for bringing this story to life. Additional thanks to Kate Forrester for the beautiful cover illustration.

Many thanks to Bridget Smith, for our sixth book and first fantasy (!); to my family and friends, for their kindness, love, and support; and to everyone who has read one of my books over the years—I truly, truly appreciate it! Thank you to librarians, teachers, booksellers, bloggers, and book extraordinaires from all the various online spaces for all that you do to enthusiastically champion books.

About the Author

Emma Mills is the author of five contemporary YA novels, including *Foolish Hearts* and *First & Then*, and is thrilled to make her fantasy debut with *Something Close to Magic*. When she is not writing, Emma can be found editing scientific manuscripts, tending to her large collection of succulents, and deep diving into various fandoms. Emma lives in St. Louis with her dog, Teddy, who is best described as a big personality in a tiny package. You can find Emma on Twitter and Instagram (@elmify) or at emmamillsbooks.com.